DIRTY WICKED PRINCE

COURT LEGACY: BOOK ONE

EDEN O'NEILL

TABLE OF CONTENTS

CHAPTER ONE

Sloane

The screams hit the moment I braked at the stop light. A woman on the sidewalk just ran past my car.

A hooded dude sprinted behind her.

He chased her. He was big and broad, and I had a moment of: what the fuck?

I watched the pair in shock, an actual emergency taking place in front of my eyes. The light changed, but I pulled over and left my car. The man had chased her around the corner, and in a panic, I rounded my dad's old Chevelle to the back.

I popped the trunk, hoping my dad's baseball bat was still in there. The screams continued down the block, and I wrestled around until I found the bat.

And something else.

My father had a legit air horn back here, one of those with the funnel and everything. I wished I'd been surprised.

"Stop it!" the woman screamed, running backwards. "What do you want?"

My gaze shot forward, and I left my trunk. I left *my car*

and all sense included. To make myself appear more intimidating, I pulled my long hair in, then tugged my hood up. I raced down the street in an act of bravery I most certainly didn't have after that.

The woman's screams led me on.

I found the pair pretty quick, the woman on the ground and the guy above her trying to get her up. It was easily a guy. He was huge, large back and even longer limbs.

"Get up, you little bitch," he growled at her, tugging her. His voice was distorted and weird like he had some kind of scrambler on it. She kicked at him from the ground with her tennis shoes, and he cursed. "Fucking cunt. If you don't get up and make this easy, I swear to God—"

"Eh, motherfucker!"

Dude whipped around.

He wore a skull mask.

Like a full, evil skeleton mask and the hoodie and all-black attire made him even more intimidating. I had no idea what age he was, couldn't tell since he was dressed head to toe in black. He could have easily been older or even around my age, eighteen. "What the fuck—"

I raised my bat, ready to knock this guy's goddamn head off. "Want to test me? I'll knock your fucking nuts off. No fucks given." I gripped the bat with a confidence I most certainly didn't have, and maybe the guy saw that, because he merely tilted his head like I was crazy. He started to stride in my direction, but then I raised the air horn. I shook my head. "Don't take another fucking step."

I started to squeeze the button, but he shook his head.

"Fucking crazy-ass," his weird voice growled before doing a little jog backwards. He raised his hands, washing them of me apparently. He sprinted down the block around the corner, and I could breathe again.

I dropped the bat, my adrenaline pulsating. The woman

sat on her side, rubbing her hip, and I ran over to her. "You okay?"

She seemed like it, rolling to her front. She was older than me, middle-aged and with exceedingly red hair. She had gathered it up in a messy bun, and with all that Lycra she wore, something told me this woman had been out for a run tonight.

"Fine. I'm okay," she huffed, brushing her legs off. She sat upright. "Could have been worse. Would have been if you hadn't have come."

I supposed it'd been a good thing I'd been driving past. I placed my hands on my legs. "Can you get up? Do you need help?"

I could call someone, but when I offered, she passed that off. She did, on the other hand, allow me to help her up.

She brushed herself off. "I'm not parked far from here. Little miscreant thought he could rob me blind. Though, I told him I had no money. I don't carry any when I go out jogging."

Sometimes that unfortunately didn't matter and did make me kind of scared. I'd just moved here myself and would like to leave my house if I felt like it without getting friggin' assaulted.

"This a common thing around here?" I asked her, the woman getting herself together. "Being robbed? I have to say that wasn't on the brochure when I came to town."

Not that I'd gotten one, or really anything. My brother, Bru, and I had just gotten here a couple days ago, and we'd come with very little to our name. We really didn't have anything. Never had.

The woman gazed up at me after what I said, her expression curious. "Oh, did you just move?"

Nodding, I acknowledged that. "Yeah, my brother, Bru, and I start school on Monday."

"Which school?"

"Windsor Preparatory Academy?" I stated, her eyes flashing for some reason. "Why?"

After she got herself straightened up, she stood tall before me. She placed a hand on her chest. "I'm actually the head-master," she said, then gave me her hand. "Elaine Mayberry. Though, I suppose on Monday you'll be calling me Principal Mayberry or Dr. Mayberry. My students call me either or."

Well, this was a small world. I shook her hand. "Please tell me school's a little less rough than casually striding down the streets of Maywood Heights."

Really, I thought this would be a sleeper town, not much going on.

I compared it to bigger. Bru and I came from Chicago, so needless to say a city of less than two hundred thousand and surrounded by cornfields would be completely different for us.

Principal Mayberry didn't say anything at first, but she did smile at me. She placed her other hand on top of mine. "Mind your Ps and Qs and you should be okay." She eyed my bat on the ground behind me. "And something tells me you'll be all right everywhere outside of the academic sense anyway."

I had no idea what that meant, but I guess I had no reason not to trust her. She was my principal. I asked if she needed a ride to her car or anything, but again, she passed me off.

"Oh, and I didn't get your name," she said, popping one of her AirPods into her ear. This woman was brave. Appar-ently, she was about to finish her run despite what had just happened to her.

"Noa Sloane," I said, shaking her hand. "Though my friends call me Sloane."

Literally no one called me Noa, so best to get that going now.

Principal Mayberry smiled. "Nice to meet you, Ms.

Sloane," she returned, jogging backward. "I guess I'll see you on Monday. And thanks again for saving my life."

I saluted her off, which made her nod, and after getting myself together, I got my ass back to my car. I actually left it with the doors open and everything. Had I done that in Chicago, there wouldn't have been a car left to return to.

Maybe Maywood Heights wasn't as dangerous as I thought.

CHAPTER
TWO

Sloane

The drive back home didn't take long despite the fact my brother and I lived out in the boonies. Trailer parks most definitely used to be the norm for us, so pulling my father's busted Chevelle up to gates that required a key code entry was different, to say the least.

I tapped in the code I had written on the back of my hand, still trying to not be freaked out by that. Wrought-iron gates opened to me like I was royalty, and I simply shook my head, taking the paved path up to the garage. When the sun was up, a wide overlook of the city could be seen from my brother's and my new house. We were stationed up on a hill and literally lived out in the middle of nowhere. I hadn't complained because what was there to complain about?

We lived like royalty.

The house on the hill sparkled, all glass walls and modern like something out of a design catalog. The home was all hard angles and polished uppitiness, definitely not my style or Bru's. In this case, we hadn't had a choice. This was our digs.

This was home.

I kept trying to associate that term with myself, home and this town, but I kept having a hell of a time. I'd lived in several "homes" over the years, never having stayed at any of them longer than it took the time to unpack. My brother and I were always on the move, so there hadn't been a point.

My hand worked the steering wheel as I advanced toward the garage. It was motion-activated to my ride, so I hadn't even had to touch anything before pulling in.

That was another mind fuck I had to push out of my mind, and I got myself and my groceries out of the car. The new digs definitely had all the modern amenities, but what it hadn't had was actual food that two teenagers could eat without gagging. The fridge had been stocked with nothing but cardboard and health food when we'd arrived, and I supposed I'd have to have a talk with our guardian about it.

Then again, I obviously took care of things tonight, and I found my brother right where I left him.

"You get the milk?" he asked from his place on the couch, a flat screen about the size of the wall sat in front of him. My brother, Bruno, was playing a game system that hadn't even been released yet, video games included, and I'd been given an entire room for my art stuff. Really, it was completely over the top, but again, I hadn't complained. It would be both ungrateful and rude to the person who'd provided it.

I tossed my seventeen-year-old brother the half gallon I got him, cookies too, and he caught both with an ease like he actually played sports. He'd always been built to do such things. He'd just never had the opportunity. My father stressed relying on books and school to get us by.

He had *stressed.*

Like a savage, Bru ripped off the lid of the milk, then proceeded to down the half gallon right in front of me. We looked absolutely nothing alike. My brother couldn't hold a tan for anything, and I was naturally golden. Besides our heights being similar (crazy since I was a chick), I couldn't pass for this kid's sister any more than he could pass for my brother. My hair was even darker than his chestnut brown.

And I had manners.

"Use a fucking cup," I growled, heading to the kitchen. I dropped the bags of groceries off, then managed to find a drinking glass amongst the many pearl white cabinets. Those cabinets had been filled as well, crystal dishes Bru would make sure to take out with his butterfingers. I returned with the glass, but by then, he'd already drunk the thing down to half. I sneered. "You're a pig."

"And you took forever." He had a milk mustache when he brought the carton away. He wiped his upper lip clean. "Weren't you just going down the street?"

"Just down the street" was like five miles from our house on the hill. I knocked his head forward, and he didn't fight because he knew, despite being *slightly* bigger than me, I could handle my own. I had in the past. I shrugged. "Ran into a little trouble. Took me a second to get back."

That was putting it lightly considering I had to stop a near assault, and when I plopped on the sofa lounge, the look of concern on my kid brother's face was evident.

"What kind?" He put down his controller and everything. Apparently, this conversation was legit serious. The controller hadn't left his hands since he started playing two days ago. "You weren't fighting, were you?"

Despite what my brother may think, I didn't fight just to fucking fight. I fought when people messed with me, completely different. I rolled my eyes. "I wasn't fighting. But I did have to stop an assault."

"What the fuck?"

"Wasn't me. Relax." I tossed a pillow at him. "Some woman was running and this tool thought he could handle her." I reached for one of his cookies. "I used dad's bat. Took care of it."

Leaning back, I popped my leg up on the couch arm. Despite my reassurances, though, my brother didn't seem any more at ease.

He worked the controller in his hands. "Okay. Well, I'm glad you're okay," he said lounging back. He shrugged before playing his game again. "But maybe we should call Callum."

"Call him about what?" Callum was our guardian, a family friend that got us this place. He was a businessman, and Bru and I had never met him before circumstances occurred to bring him into our life. Circumstances surrounding our father.

We hadn't even known he had a will.

But our dad had, which I supposed matched his paranoia. He had always seemed to be *on* all the time, anxious. He'd had a hard time keeping a job because of it, and we'd moved so many places. He had struggled a lot with his mental health before he'd died over the summer.

Like Bru knew I was thinking about him, what brought us here and our situation, my brother left me to my silence for a second. He still continued to play his video game but looked over at me more often than not.

"Maybe we should call him about security or something," Bru said, shocking me. "He did say to call him if we needed anything."

My father's friend had been gracious to say the least. It'd been him to suggest us coming to Maywood Heights. He'd relocated us and everything.

"It'll be great for a fresh start," he'd said to us, the first time we'd met him at our dad's funeral. Our father had died in a factory fire at his last job, a job he'd managed to hold on to for almost a year. Things had been getting better toward the end there. Bru and I had actually been able to settle down at a school. Stay for more than one term.

But then the fire.

Bru and I had struggled a lot with our father. We loved

him, but my brother and I, i.e. me, had to be the parent a lot when our dad had hard times. He'd dealt a lot with depression too as well as anxiety, and most days I'd had to make sure he'd leave bed to *get* to his job. Not to mention my brother and I off to school.

I shook my head at the thoughts, those times severely hard. I'd had to step up from a really early age. Bru and I— most of the time—were *just* Bru and I with everything going on with our dad. Our mom had died when we were really little.

"What the fuck would we need security for?" I rolled my eyes. "It's not like we're the president's kids."

"Might as well be at that rich-ass school we're about to go to," he said, laughing. He wasn't lying. I had looked at the brochures for the place, and it was pretty crazy. My brother and I had only gone to public schools coming up, so a place that looked more like a college campus than a high school in the brochure would certainly be different. Bru chuckled. "I'm just saying. Might as well. If we ask Callum, he'll get us security." He threw out a hand. "Wouldn't put it past those other kids on campus to have the same. 'Staff' and shit."

He air quoted, and I laughed.

"We don't need to be milking this arrangement any more than we already have," I said. Callum had been more than generous to us. Besides a place to live and a new school, he was covering all our essentials. Food. Clothing. *Everything.* It'd been more than lavish and more than we could ever have deserved. We'd literally come to this town with nothing. Our dad most certainly hadn't been rich, and outside of a little savings and the Chevelle, he'd basically left us with nothing.

My brother and I would definitely have been out on the streets right now had Callum not come along with that will my father had created before his death. Or worse, in the system. Bru still was not yet eighteen and that, most certainly, would have been his reality. I had nothing either to take care of us with.

I tossed a pillow at my brother. "And you *are* milking things for all they're worth."

He'd put his grubby little hands on anything Callum had put in front of him. Hadn't blinked an eye after finding out our new guardian was rich. All his video games and his closet full of designer labels told that.

Bru popped a big shoulder. "I'm just trying to move forward." His gaze slid in my direction. "I don't know. Maybe be normal instead of slumming it for once? If Callum's offering it, I'm going to take it."

And why not, right? Play pretend? I eased forward. "You do know this isn't our money, right?" This was *Callum's* money. Not ours and never would be. We hadn't been well off before Dad died. Not by a long shot.

Bru knew that too, his jaw working. He'd had to sacrifice the nicer things in life just like me. We'd both worked jobs just to help Dad out when he'd been in between jobs. Bru huffed. "You're not going to make me feel bad for moving on. Callum's giving us an opportunity to live a normal life. Why not take it?"

"Newsflash, kid." I stole his controller, and he raised his hands. I frowned. "This isn't a normal life. It's a privileged life and one that's on borrowed time."

Callum's commitment to us was only as long as he was our guardian, or I guess Bru's. At seventeen, Callum was his legal guardian, and I only didn't fight my dad's will on that because I had nothing. I couldn't take care of my brother.

At least, not like *this* and all the stuff we had now.

Fact of the matter was, we were both still kids. Even with me being eighteen.

Bru ripped his controller away. "It may be borrowed time." He leaned back, playing his game again. "But you're not going to guilt me for not being the poor kid for once." His jaw clenched. "We're already going to be the new kids at school *again*." He shook his head. "Well, at least I'll have this."

I chewed the inside of my cheek, watching him play. I'd checked his ass for less, but I couldn't find it in me to do it this time. We had always been poor. We had always been different. We were always the new kids at the new school with a father who had a hard time providing for us. He'd actually only let us work jobs because we all had to in order to survive. Dad had been really anxious, didn't like us going too far. Bru and I never even brought friends over. Mostly, because we moved so much due to Dad's job situation and could never actually make any.

The pair of us had always been different like Bru said, and apparently, he was done being different.

I stood. "Don't play video games too late."

He smirked. "Yes, Mother."

I threw a pillow at him again before heading up to my room. I got any pick in this glass house, but before I went to bed, I did one more thing. We had academy uniforms in our closet to wear at our new school, and I decided to stay up and iron them. I spent extra care on Bru's.

I wanted him to have the best day.

CHAPTER
THREE

Sloane

On Monday morning, I was rocked awake.

My younger brother had a death wish.

Bru had his toothbrush in his mouth, half his academy uniform on with his shirt open. We probably had at least an hour before we had to be at school, but he was always on top of his shit when it came to academics.

That'd really been all we had coming up, school and not much else. I supposed it'd been the one thing we could rely on since we moved so much.

Groaning, I tugged the comforter over my head. I'd just gotten to sleep. I'd stayed up studying the academy's campus map after I ironed our uniforms, so I knew where the fuck I was going today. "Fuck off."

I loved my brother, but I didn't love him enough to lose sleep.

He ripped the comforter off my head, and I nearly decked his butt.

"What?" I growled, and he tugged me up. Really, I'd

forgotten when he'd passed me in height and then some. He had the beefy exterior of a linebacker, not one of the complete nerd he was. He was at the top of his class at pretty much every school we'd attended.

"You gotta see this shit." He drew back *my* curtains. He waggled his eyebrows. "We got a delivery outside."

Clamping down on his toothbrush, he grinned, and I ambled over, sleep in my eyes.

I nearly croaked.

Downstairs were two dudes with one of those trucks that (where I came from) usually took away cars.

Not delivered luxury vehicles.

But that was what these two guys were doing, one lowering a lime-green Audi off the truck while the other waved it down.

"What the fuck?" I pulled a veil of dark hair out of my eyes, shoving Bru away to figure out what was up with this.

I padded down winding vertebrae stairs, and my brother stayed hot on my trail.

I threw open the door, then walked with bare feet all the way up to these dudes. "What's this, and how did you guys get in here?"

I mean, we had a *coded* entry at the gate, and this wasn't normal. Fuck if Bru cared considering the way he waltzed right up to this ride.

"Sloane, this shit is fucking awesome." Jaw dropped, he pushed his fingers into his hair. "Holy shit."

"Don't get too attached," I gritted, standing in front of the dude who was waving this shit down. Upon seeing me, he held up a clipboard.

"The order is for this residence," he said, then flipped over a page. "To the Sloane children. Noa Sloane and Bruno Sloane."

"It's just Sloane and Bru," I corrected, and Bru's gaze shot over just the same.

"Dude can call me Nancy if we get to keep this." He started to touch the car, but then hesitated. "This is seriously ours?"

"Sent from a Callum Montgomery," the man said, smiling a little. "He gave us access to the gate."

Well, hearing this my brother basically lost his mind. He laughed, *manically* like some crazed kid in a candy store.

"Holy shit. Holy shit. Holy shit." He danced in front of the candied paint job, then even more when the guy who lowered the car gave him the keys. "Holy shit, Sloane."

This was more than generous, too fucking much. Turning, I raised a hand to the guy. "There has to be a mistake."

We had the Chevelle. We didn't need this.

"No mistake, sweetheart," he said, and I let him have that one because, well, he delivered a damn car, and I could get over the demeaningly submissive way he acknowledged me. He lowered his clipboard. "We were told to deliver this one by seven o'clock today." He lifted a second set of keys to me. "Consider it delivered."

This really had to be a mistake. I stared at the keys. "We have a car. We don't need this."

"I just deliver the cars, girlie." One more of those and this guy would see a fist, but I resisted the temptation. He dropped the keys in my hand since I hadn't taken them. "You want to protest delivery, I suggest you take it up with this Callum Montgomery."

He waved his cohort on, and together, the two got back in their truck. Bru and I were left standing there. Well, I was standing there.

Bru was currently in the fucking car.

He turned the wheel like he was about to take it for a test drive down the speedway. I waved him out. "Come on. I'm putting this thing in the garage."

"Why?"

I eyed him like it was obvious, waiting until he physically

got his ass out of the car so I could get inside. Once he did, I started it up. "Because we have a car, and we don't need this."

I accepted this house. Even took the education from Callum because of, well, Bru. We didn't have anything, and I did want him to have a good life.

This car was just too much though.

Bru's jaw dropped. "You're fucking crazy, right?" he stated, but did let me back the thing into the garage beside the Chevelle. The old beater looked laughable beside the luxury vehicle, but that was only in comparison. Dad had taken really good care of the muscle car. Powder blue, it had a sleek finish. There wasn't even a crack to the paint, and Dad had just gotten new tires put on it. This car was actually one of the only things he did keep up on, making sure we always had wheels.

I supposed that was because he knew he couldn't hold a job for anything, and after I parked, I got out.

"Sloane, you're not serious."

"But I am," I said, then took his keys too.

He growled. "Callum gave this to us."

"And we don't need it. We have a car."

"Okay, *you* have a car. But what about me? How am I supposed to get around?"

"I'll take you anywhere you want to go." I leaned back against the Audi. "And you can borrow the Chevelle as long as I'm not using it."

Clearly, I wasn't joking about this, nor was I moving on the issue. I was still his big sister.

I was still in charge.

"I can't fucking believe you." He pouted like a little kid, not the seventeen-year-old he was.

He ground out something about this whole thing being a joke on his way back inside, but I didn't care. He could pout all he wanted. We had a car, and this Audi wasn't it.

Gratefully, my brother and I got to avoid each other during our morning routine. The house was big enough, and we had our separate bathrooms so that made avoiding speaking to each other that much easier.

I didn't go out of my way to avoid him, but he did. He stomped around like a giant child all morning, which only proved my point that he didn't need such a nice car. He'd probably total the thing in less than a week.

We drove in silence most of the way to school, my phone prompting us directions on the drive. Callum had gotten us phone plans as well, so that meant we actually got something that wasn't two to three generations back.

I never minded that. My smart phone got the job done. Bru was playing on his when he got a call.

He looked at me. "It's Callum."

I wasn't surprised. I mean, he was Bru's guardian, and it was our first day of school. The other students were already a few weeks in, but it was the first day for us being new.

I prompted Bru to put Callum on speaker, and he rolled his eyes at me.

"He called me," he said, answering, and I almost knocked him across the head. He dodged it. "Hey, Callum. What's up?"

"Just wanted to wish you both a good first day at school," I heard Callum say despite not being on speaker. He was muffled, but I still heard him. "Did you children get the vehicle I had sent over this morning?"

Bru shot me a look that could have killed me where I sat, and I started to say something, but he spoke first.

"Yeah, Sloane almost had it sent back," he said, and I growled, ripping his phone away. He sneered. "Hey—"

I put his phone on speaker, then connected it to the phone stand on my dad's dash. "Hey, Callum."

"Good morning, Sloane." One thing about Callum Mont-gomery was that he sounded as much like a businessman as he came across in person. In the handful of times I'd seen him, he dressed in nothing short of a suit and never once stumbled over a syllable in conversation. He was also older, well into his sixties and carried a polish about him that definitely made me question how my father was ever in the same circle as this man. Let alone close enough to make him our guardian.

As it seemed my father must have had another life before Bru and me. I suspected this anyway because on the few memories I did have of my mother (she died when Bru and I were really young), my dad had been happy. He'd been *at ease*.

Though maybe this was the mere perception of a child. I didn't know, but what I did know, was that this Callum Montgomery was not only well versed but well off. I looked into him a bit, and he had businesses all over the world, a self-made entrepreneur, I guess.

Currently, he was on the other side of the world conducting business dealings, but had come back to not only settle my dad's affairs, but take care of his kids. Callum had literally taken care of everything after our father died, funeral included, and though I'd been grateful, we really didn't know the guy.

I supposed it was just one more thing my dad kept to himself in the virtual lockdown that was his head. He kept a lot to himself, his own personal vault.

"Good morning," I returned through the line. "We did get the car, and it was very generous."

"Of course. Of course, but was there an issue?" His voice was inquisitive. "Your brother said you were trying to send it back."

Bru eyed me from his seat, and I rolled my eyes.

"I just told the men I believed the delivery was a mistake. You see, we already have a car. My dad's Chevelle."

He remembered that, was there at the will reading when

it'd been given to us as well as all my dad's personal assets. Dad hadn't had much, but he'd had the Chevelle, and my brother and I had used it to drive down here from Chicago.

"I definitely see where the confusion would come from," he said, but sounded busy in the background. He probably was. "But there is no mistake. I know you have the Chevelle, but there are two of you. I figured you take one and your brother the other."

Bru raised his hand like that was obvious.

I eyed him. "Yes, but it was very generous." The Chevelle was worth like a few grand max. I shook my head. "It's just too much. I'm grateful, but yeah, it's a lot."

"I see," he said. "But then again, I don't. It's my job as your guardian to take care of you and your brother, and it's an honor doing so. Your father was a great friend to me, and with his passing, I simply want both you kids to be as comfortable as you can possibly be."

I looked away after he said that, studying the road. He'd said something similar at the funeral.

"I want you kids to ask if you ever need anything. It's the least I can do. You've both had such tragedy," he'd said.

I could imagine he felt sorry for us, two clearly poor kids in comparison to him. I shook my head. "Yeah, but I don't want you to think we expect any of this."

And technically, he wasn't my guardian just Bru's.

I felt some kind of way taking things from him because of that. Like all this stuff had a counter, and I didn't want to owe him anything. He never made it seem like we did, but still.

"I understand if you don't want to accept the car, but I hope you will," he continued. "You and your brother have both had a lot of changes. A new school. A new town and life entirely. Having two vehicles will help with that transition."

"I agree," Bru stated, putting in his two cents. He faced the phone. "I really appreciate it, Callum. Sloane does too."

"I do," I said, and I didn't want it to come across that I didn't. "I'm sorry if I came across any other way."

"You didn't, and like I said, I understand," he returned. "I really hope you'll accept the gift, but if you don't want it, I get that too. If you'd like a different vehicle, you can let me know that as well. I'll have anything arranged for you."

Now, I felt bad. "You really don't have to do that."

"Really, it would be my pleasure. You know, you and I had an agreement. I may be technically your brother's guardian, but that's just on paper. You call the shots always, Sloane."

He'd said that during the will reading, that the custody thing was just on paper and Bru and I were free to do what we wished. Even still, he wanted to be there for us and had plans to come out to Maywood Heights often to check on us. He was supposed to after he concluded his latest business endeavor. I guess he was building an airport in New Delhi or something. Wild. Even still, he found a way to fit us and our unusual situation into his life. I was grateful for that.

Traffic started to pick up as my phone stated the school was a couple miles away, and Callum mentioned our class schedules after hearing that.

"I've got all of that arranged for you," he said. "And, Bru, I got you into all the accelerated classes, but the school assures me if it's too much, you simply need to speak up and they'll make accommodations for you. Tutors or anything you need. Sloane, I also got you into a few art classes. I hope they're advanced enough for you."

I wasn't a prodigy or anything, and certainly not a wiz kid like Bru, but I did enjoy art. All kinds.

The fact Callum had listened to our interests in the short time we knew him meant a lot, and I thanked him again for the gesture. By the end, both him and Bru convinced me to accept the car. I supposed it made sense for us to have two. Callum even urged us to try out for any sports or join clubs we were interested in despite the school year already in full swing. Classes may have only been in session a short while, but I could imagine all those extracurriculars had already started.

It seemed Callum had arranged that too. Before we wrapped the call, he said we'd just have to speak to the head-master, and she could arrange for us a meeting with any coaches or club heads.

I left out the fact I'd already met Principal Mayberry, but had a feeling for once in my life, things might be going a nice way. I was at a new school, but I'd already met the principal. I was in a new town, but Bru and I had someone in our corner who was willing to help us have an easier time in the transition.

"I'll be checking in," Callum said at the end of the call. "You both have a great day."

"You too, Callum," Bru and I both returned. Callum also said before he left, that he was working on coming out to visit us soon. Apparently, he moved us to Maywood Heights because he lived here for a time way back when. He'd even gone to the academy.

And holy fuck, this school.

The old brick building divided up into several quads defi-nitely put the brochures to shame. There was both a north and south campus, and a stadium-sized football field with multiple practice fields to accompany it.

Bru and I passed them all, the soccer pitch and baseball field too. The school also had a rowing team, and Bru and I cruised by a lake filled with rowers with long limbs and extended reaches.

"We're not in Kansas anymore, Dorothy." Bru whistled, our Chevelle passing about a gazillion students rocking the Windsor Preparatory Academy's navy and orange crest. I heard some kind of gorilla was the school's mascot, and I saw enough King Kongs on the way to student parking to prove

that true. Known as simply "The King," the big honking ape
was everywhere. People had it stamped on their backpacks
and clothes. It also adorned flags hanging around the
campus, and its life-sized form stood robust as multiple
sculptures decorating well-trimmed grass.

I adjusted my necktie after I found a parking spot. I ended
up sliding between two luxury vehicles worth easily more
than my life, and suddenly, I wished we would have driven
Callum's gift. If anything, just to fit in.

I got out of the Chevelle once the car was off, as did my
brother. Our bags were in the trunk, and I sent Bru to get
them.

"Eh, bitch? You're in my fucking spot."

I jerked around. A, I wanted to see who in the fuck called
me *bitch*, and B, I needed to tell whoever off for claiming
spots like an idiot.

I saw a beast.

Well, not an actual beast but close enough.

Bastard hung out of another expensive ride, a cobalt-blue
Hummer truck with black interior. On the hood, an animal
symbol stamped into the paint, a wolf scrolled in cool silver,
and by the size of this guy, he could leap over the design in a
single bound. He had himself angled out of the car, getting to
his feet.

Yeah, he was big.

His stance easily leveled him well above his truck. He
slammed the door, dark and shaggy hair breezing in the
wind. It was also wet like the lazy ass couldn't dry his hair
before coming to school.

Not to mention dress properly.

His tie hung loose around his neck, his dress shirt open
and his ribbed tank on full display. Yeah, this guy was definitely a lazy ass. He slammed a hand on the hood of his car.
"*Move*, bitch. I said this spot is mine."

Male laughter sounded from not far away, two dudes in

particular. One was about the size of a Mack truck and was also quite pretty with dangly piercings in his ears and his dark hair slicked about in a messy fashion. He had his head turned toward an ultra-blond dude. Not like beach bottle blond, no.

The guy looked like he walked off the set of *Game of Thrones* without his dragons. Cuffing the sleeves of his uniform jacket, he wasn't trying to hide the fact he found all this funny with the big dude. They had one other member of their male harem, and this particular dude wasn't laughing at all.

He was smoking.

Thick white smoke curled richly from between his full lips. He licked one when he removed his joint, and tendrils of natural-blond hair breezed lazily over his eyes. He was completely devil-may-care from his military boots to the fact he had his jacket sleeves bunched up. I'd read the Windsor Prep handbook and both were against it.

Not that he cared.

Extremely good-looking, he had a chiseled jaw that just may well be sharp enough to cut polished crystal, his jawline clean shaven as he straddled the line between boy and man. His body told one thing, but his face another. He filled out his academy jacket to the point where it bulged around his big shoulders and thick arms, and his pants basically painted on his muscular thighs.

He stared at me with that boyish gaze, but the man beneath lingered there hot in the wings. Like the guy was just waiting to be tag-teamed in.

Like he was waiting to pounce.

He did neither. His beast of a friend was basically yelling at me in front of him. Blondie and his other two crew had already parked, convening between two Audis. A third Audi was there too and that let me know the three had probably traveled in a unit.

Beast boy, on the other hand, had obviously showed up late and, apparently, had jokes for me calling me out of my name. I crossed my arms in front of him, the guy still standing next to his hood. I tilted my head. "I don't see your name on it."

Dark eyes flared from beneath shaggy hair. He directed a finger toward me. "Use your fucking eyes, little girl."

Um, no this bitch did not?

I was by no means *little*. I possibly might be considered shorter compared to his behemoth ass, but not little by any means. At five foot ten, I was lanky as hell, but clearly, this guy was just trying to place me beneath him.

It wouldn't work, but I did decide to entertain the asshole when I turned around. Funny enough, I did spot a sign. It said "Student of the Month," and I spotted it the moment Bru came around with our bags. Clearly missing my heated exchange, my brother handed me mine. I wasn't surprised he missed it, I suppose. Bru had the trunk up when beast boy was yelling at me.

"What's going on?" Bru asked, now seeing the big guy staring me down across the fool's ride. Bru's eyes twitched, going back and forth between me and the large boy, but I waved my brother off. I could handle this.

"What exactly did you do to achieve such an accomplishment?" I asked beast boy, goading him. I leaned back against my car. "Blow your history teacher?"

This set fire off in his eyes, and Bru grabbed me.

"What the fuck are you doing?" my brother gritted, as the beast of a man bounded around his car.

He got up in my face.

"*Move* your goddamn car," he growled at me, like an actual beast. It seemed that the wolf on his hood was fitting, and the only reason he didn't get too close to me was Bru.

My brother jerked me back, trying to keep me out of a clearly brewing fight, and I'd be lying if I said my brother hadn't done something similar before. He often played the middleman when people started shit with me at our other schools. Bru pushed me back. "Stop it."

"I'd listen to him, girlie." Beast sneered and he nearly got a backhand for that one. This guy definitely had a limited vocabulary. Especially when it came to women.

I started to go in for round two with this guy, but at this point, his friend called him back.

Blondie.

He'd called him by the name "Wolf," and I nearly laughed my ass off. The fact beast boy actually went about town with such a name just about sent me into hysterics. Either he was arrogant enough to go by it, or his parents were assholes.

Maybe a little bit of both.

I kept that last thought to myself, not really wanting to get in a fight on my first day. But mostly for Bru.

Beast boy listened to his friend, falling back and Blondie seemed more consumed with finishing his smoke than getting in the fight himself. He jerked his chin toward Wolf, an obvious gesture of retreat and that definitely told me something about their ranks. Beast boy wasn't in charge.

Blondie was.

Blondie stared at me through narrowed eyes, so obviously trying to figure me out. He flicked his joint butt, then put it out with his boot before tapping the chest of the other two guys with him. All three boys grabbed their bags off the cars, and in their distraction, my keys were taken from me.

"I'll move the car," Bru growled at me, and I did feel bad. I hadn't meant to embarrass him or anything, but someone needed to stand up for us. We couldn't go around letting people think they could take advantage of us because we were new or unfamiliar.

Even still, I gave my brother his way, and after shooting me a look that could kill, Wolf got back into his ride. He waited for Bru to clear our Chevelle before peeling into the spot and nearly clipping both cars surrounding his Hummer. After that, Wolf slammed the door, heading over to his three waiting friends.

"Yo, bitch?"

Wolf jerked around, actually answering to what I'd called him. This had his friends in tears. Well, everyone but Blondie.

The big blond guy merely stared on, seemingly fascinated by the exchange. I pointed to him, this guy clearly Wolf's handler. "Better go back to daddy."

A feral growl boomed from Wolf's lips, and he shot in my direction so fast I thought he might get a hold of me. Bru came between us, though, and Blondie, once again, called Wolf away.

"Let's go," Blondie called, almost lazy about it. He started to walk away whether Wolf was coming or not.

Biting back a curse, Wolf trailed after him. He caught up quick, but one of the guys lingered back.

The platinum blond who appeared like he belonged in *Game of Thrones* stared at me, his own curiosity to his gaze as he stared.

"Wells?"

But Blondie called him back too, clearly in charge here. Who he'd called Wells caught up, and my brother shouldered me.

"I can't believe you," he said, leaving my ass, and I sighed. He didn't wait for me, getting the hell out of Dodge.

I guess we're off to a great start.

CHAPTER
FOUR

Sloane

Moments later, my younger brother and I sat in the headmaster's office. Well, the lobby that led to her office. We were told to wait so she could hand us our welcome packets and answer any questions we might have about attending the academy. This task was apparently something the headmaster did personally, and I was happy it was her since I'd actually already met her.

I looked forward to seeing Principal Mayberry again, but I had to say, the wait had been awkward as hell. Bru was still mad at me, obviously. He pretty much steamed beside me, and I'd already apologized.

Twice.

I really hadn't meant to go off the handle. I never did, but it just happened. We moved a lot, and people tended to bully us because of that.

"I just don't get why you can't keep your mouth shut for once," he huffed, folding his arms. His head touched the back of the wall in his chair. "You're going to get me fucking killed. You're going to make shit a nightmare once again."

It was because I stood up for us that life at all these schools we went to *weren't* nightmares. I crossed my legs, my heel bouncing. "You're being melodramatic."

"I'm not."

I started to give a retort, to check him. I was the older sibling. I was in charge and needed to take care of him.

So why did I feel socked in the gut when I looked at him?

He sat there completely locked up, looking at everything but me in the wide office. I think he really had wanted a fresh start here, to be normal. I dropped my leg and turned to him. "I'm sorry." I really was. I shook my head. "We have to draw first blood. Otherwise, *our blood* will be the ones that coat these pretty walls."

It was the simple "get them first before they got us" mentality, and I didn't understand why he didn't *get* that.

"You're so goddamn negative," he said, facing me. "Maybe if we came at people right, they won't handle us."

"You don't know that."

"You never gave us a chance to try. Always flying off the handle." He leaned back. "It's like you're doing everything you can to be the opposite of Dad."

Our dad who hadn't fought. Our dad who had stood back. He used to get so mad when he'd gotten calls about me. His stance had been to stay out of things first and definitely not my approach.

I cuffed my arms. "I'm really sorry, Bruno."

"Say you're sorry by staying out of shit," he said, then we both sat up when the secretary said the headmaster was ready for us. Bru and I stood, grabbing our bags, but before we could go anywhere, we were met in the lobby by a familiar face.

"Noa Sloane," Principal Mayberry said, certainly different today when she stood in the center of the Windsor Prep crest donning the cherrywood panels. She wore pressed pants and a white blouse, her hair pinned back like a disciplinarian. She pointed at me. "I mean, Sloane. I haven't forgotten that."

And I appreciated that, smiling when I took her hand. "Good to see you again."

"And you," she said, studying me. I was different today too, I supposed. I mean, I wore a fucking pleated skirt, and that didn't happen. I even rocked the heels with dark knee-highs, wanting to really put an effort into this. My navy jacket lined with orange trim was ironed and crisp, and though I didn't pin my hair back like the headmaster, I'd braided it down. Currently, my dark hair sat at my butt, and though I'd have to avoid sitting on it all day, it was a far cry better than my normal messy bun.

Bru had even worked mousse into his chestnut-brown locks, trying to empress too, and the fact the headmaster and I knew each other clearly threw him for a loop.

I think the headmaster picked up on that after she introduced herself to him because after, she waved a hand in my direction.

"Met your sister last night," she said, Bru's eyes twitching wide. "She saved me from a thug. The guy tried to rob me blind."

Bru's brown eyes expanded. Not two seconds ago he'd gotten onto me for being the first to jump into battle, but at this, he smiled.

I supposed the circumstances had been different.

"She's good for that," he said, with a smile in my direction. He pocketed his hands. "She's always taken care of me."

And I had, but somewhere along the way, I think I had forgotten that he'd gotten older. That he probably could take care of himself.

If you let him.

"She is very brave," Principal Mayberry said, then waved her secretary over. The headmaster's digs were quite frankly ridiculous just like the rest of this place. The administration building was lined with dark oak in the interior, the building wide and all brick on the outside. A handsome garden led up to the whole thing, and we were only on the main point of the campus.

Bru and I watched as the secretary handed Principal Mayberry two packets. The headmaster gave us each one.

"Your welcome packets," she informed, smiling. "They have your schedules, maps, and everything else you need. All that's left now is, I suppose, the tour." The woman angled around to her secretary, who had returned to her desk. "Diane, I'll be back in an hour. I'm going to escort these students around campus, then to their first classes."

Floored, I simply stared at here. "You're giving us a tour?"

The woman was already putting her suit jacket on, the Windsor Prep crest on her chest. "Of course, I am," she said, passing me a smile. "It's the least I can do. You saved my life after all."

She waved us out, and I exchanged a glance with Bru. It seemed maybe I was doing well at starting to get some of those brownie points back.

I guess that was a start.

Principal Mayberry had a golf cart set up outside the administration building for our tour with another staff member driving it.

That was how big this fucking campus was.

She directed the driver, and he took us where she wanted, which was as much of the campus as she could show us in an hour. She mentioned she had another meeting to attend after, but in the meantime, proceeded to show us all she could before class. Bru and I got to skip first period, which was apparently typically homeroom anyway.

With classes in session, we stayed on pathways usually filled with walking students but were currently clear for our tour. She pointed out the academy's greenhouse, as well as the various sport pitches and buildings reserved for classes. Apparently, each year held classes in their own buildings, so the juniors, where Bru's classes would be held, were separate from mine since I was a senior.

I wasn't sure about how good I felt about being separated from him, but he was a big boy I guess and could take care of himself. I needed to start giving him a chance to start doing that, and I supposed the distance was good for both of us. We dropped him off at his building first, where he was to be handed off to another student. The student hadn't arrived yet, but Principal Mayberry said he would be there soon. He'd be Bru's guide for as long as he needed him, a junior like himself.

"His name is Wells Ambrose," she said, smiling at Bru from the cart. "He'll be around to help you with anything you need, but if you ever need anything else, please feel free to stop by my office anytime."

Principal Mayberry was super accommodating, and I really was confident Bru would be okay. I left him via the cart with a wave, one he gave back as he waited for his guide.

He'll be fine, and you will too.

I hoped we would. I wasn't one of those people to say life constantly kicked me in the ass, but my brother and I held our fair share of traumas. I mean, we were orphans at seventeen and eighteen.

I supposed others had it worse, and I tried to remind myself of that as the tour concluded and Principal Mayberry dropped me off at the buildings reserved for senior classes. I thought she'd leave me to wait for my guide like Bru, but she physically escorted me inside to the first class.

Again, she said it was the least she could do.

I really appreciated that. This transition would be hard enough, and it'd be nice to have someone in my brother's and my corner. I shook her hand outside of the class, and while I did, I noticed a set of eyes on us.

He passed us.

The blond guy from outside, the boss dog.

Daddy himself.

He was sans Wolf and his other friends at the present, and where his gaze had casually passed over me before, it didn't now.

If anything, it blazed.

Seriously, his expression cut in my direction, but through further observation, I noticed it more so laid on Principal Mayberry beside me.

Noticing my attention had shifted, Principal Mayberry shifted hers in the same direction. And I noticed she stood taller in front of the guy. Like he was the headmaster and she was the student. I found that weird as fuck, and she didn't look at me again until the boy passed and turned a corner down the hallway. I had no idea where he was going, but I still felt that heated gaze well after he'd disappeared around the corner.

"So your guide will meet you inside once next period starts," she said, but I noticed her attention still at that corner. This possibly could be in my head, though. I mean, he was just a boy, a student. Even still, she obviously noticed the look. She pressed a hand down her jacket before facing me. "Her name is Bow Reed. She'll help you."

"Thank you."

"Of course, and if you need anything…"

She didn't finish, instead nodding before heading in the opposite direction of the boy. Again, that felt weird, but I'd had a rather exciting morning, so I passed it off. Instead, I headed inside the classroom, and since second period classes hadn't started yet, the room was empty.

Not for long. The bell rang, and seconds later, the room's activity started.

I took a seat, watching as the room filled up and students milled about in their academy uniforms. Many of the girls had designer handbags, labels I'd only seen knockoffs for where I came from.

The culture here was most certainly different.

I waited, feeling awkward. I wondered if I'd need to tell the teacher I was the new kid so my guide could find me. I stood, starting to do that.

"Holy crap, you're tall."

I directed a look down, way down to what looked like a little girl, but then again, I was tall. The girl had dark hair, wavy and long, and so much fire red in her cheeks one would have thought she ran all the way here.

Maybe she did.

She shot a hand out. "Are you Noa Sloane? If so, I'm your guide. Hi. My name's Bow. Well, Rainbow, but most people call me Bow. My whole name's Rainbow Reed, but you can call me Bow like everyone else."

She said that in one breath if one could imagine.

I took her hand, and she shook mine so hard I questioned her size.

She grinned. "Wow, you are tall. How tall?"

"Five ten," I said, eyeing her. She wasn't tall. Maybe five foot. *Maybe.* I studied her sparkling broach where normally an academy tie sat. The thing looked real, like an actual ruby.

Well, she has money.

I supposed like the rest of them. I took in the heeled Mary Janes on her feet. She wore knee-highs like me, but along with her height, the shoe choice made her seriously look like a little kid. I frowned. "You sure you're a senior?"

"Oh, no." She giggled so spritely she gained the attention of the others who'd filtered in. She tucked hair behind her ear. "I'm a sophomore, but I'm advanced for my age. I rock at math, hence why I'm in a senior algebra class with you."

I looked behind the girl, wondering if the enchanted forest animals would catch up behind her. She was literally adorable, rosy cheeks and everything. They went along quite well with the ruby studs in her ears.

They matched the expensive-ass-looking broach.

As it appeared, she'd come by herself to this class, no animals in tow. She proceeded to wave to the teacher ahead, informing him of my presence in this class, and that I was the new kid.

The man seemed unconcerned but did make me introduce myself to the class. Our teacher was Mr. Green, and he informed me to take a seat at the front with Bow.

Once seated, the little one continued to *assist* me by taking my bag. She even tried to hang it on the back of my chair like my mother.

"I got it," I said, the girl moving a mile a minute. She spoke just as quick, a full smile on her face. I watched in fascination as she told me she'd be with me for the next two weeks and was here for anything I needed.

She'd again, said it all in one breath.

"Of course, let me know if you ever need anything," she ended with. "I'll be outside of all your classes. I have many in the same building already."

This girl was obviously smart like Bru if she was taking senior-level classes. She kept talking, seriously *happy*. I mean, there was nothing wrong with that, but she was going so fast I wasn't quite sure I could keep up.

She giggled after the last thing she said. Like all that happy just had to seep out somewhere. She pointed at me. "So Noa, that's a really cool name."

"Sloane," I said. "No one calls me Noa."

"Sloane because that's your last name," she said, obviously putting that together. "That's so cool. Mine's Reed, I could never go by that."

She laughed again, loud enough where someone actually jumped in their seat. By the way Mr. Green lifted his eyes, something told me this might be a normal occurrence with this girl.

She grinned at me. "Can't wait to show you around campus. This place is awesome. You're going to love it. Like I said, I'll be escorting you to all your classes, so you won't have to worry about getting lost or anything."

She said this right before Mr. Green started senior algebra. A girl named Rainbow Reed would be my personal stalker for the upcoming days. A girl who spoke a mile a minute, and with her speed, seriously made me question if she had rabbit DNA.

Life at Windsor Prep was most certainly going to be interesting.

CHAPTER FIVE

Dorian

"You sure that's her?"

Wells dropped a calf, working his shoulders after what I said. He stepped forward, resting an arm on my shoulder.

"Positive," he said, eyeing the girl across the football field. He frowned. "Definitely her. I'm her brother Bru's guide around school. He mentioned she was his sister." He tipped a chin in the girl's direction. "Saw her leaving on a cart on my way over to meet her bro. I assumed, going to her next class." His eyes narrowed. "She was with Mayberry."

I'd seen her in the hallway with the headmaster before.

That made two strikes against this chick, then.

I dropped my own calf, studying the girl who apparently liked to get in the way. I'd admit. That shit with her and Wolf this morning had been funny.

I certainly wasn't laughing about shit now.

Of course, like this morning, neither was Wolf. Currently, my buddy helped Thatcher stretch on the track surrounding the field. We'd all managed to get the same gym class despite Wells and Thatch being juniors.

Then again, we did get whatever the fuck we wanted around here.

We did because we were legacy, owned this place, and Little Miss Getting-in-the-Way over there was about to figure that out. Wolf helped Thatch up after helping him stretch, a feat in itself since his ass was so big. A lineman for the academy's football team, the dude had definitely earned his spot.

"Didn't recognize her at first," Wells continued. He was platinum blond and actually got ladies (and dudes) with that shit. I guess that'd been the reason he'd done it his freshman year. It got him the attention he wanted. The guy was a manwhore, just like the rest of us. Wells tilted his head. "She had a hood up that night, but I'm sure it's her. She drove right past me on that cart. Got a good look."

Pretty much all the fucking guys around here were, and she'd gotten more than one look stepping out onto the field in her booty shorts. Long, basically black hair pulled up into a high ponytail, her complexion like an Egyptian fucking princess. Add that to the full ass cheeks pretty much hanging out of her shorts, and she had all dudes of the straight orientation looking at her. Even Wells, who was more into dudes than chicks.

Wells eyed her appreciatively, doing one better and even whistling. The girl was a walking Kardashian without all the plastic surgery, and the fact she'd stood toe to toe with Wolf told me something about her. People didn't fuck with Wolf.

People didn't fuck with any of us.

Thatcher chuckled after what Wells said. Patting his chest, Thatcher eased between us. Thatch grinned at Wells. "I bet you didn't recognize her," he said, passing his own appreciative gaze in that direction. Anyone with eyes could see the girl was a smoke show. The fact she stood out like a goddamn giraffe with her height only helped. Thatcher laughed. "Too busy checking out that ass."

"Like you fucking weren't." Wells shoved him. "Anyway, it should have been your big ass out there that night doing the heavy labor. You chose to stay in the fucking van."

Thatcher frowned. "Last I checked, I won the toss-up, which meant *I* was driver and *you* were supposed to be the bitch wrangler." He muffled Wells's white-blond hair. "Not my fault whittle guy couldn't handle his job."

The two proceeded to punch on each other like a pack of kids, which made Wolf growl and me roll my goddamn eyes.

"This is what happens when you let kids handle shit," Wolf surmised, and Thatch blazed at him.

"Fuck you and your ancient ass," Thatcher shot back. He shoved Wolf. "You're all of nine months older than me."

Which was enough to make Wolf and myself superior to him, as far as we were concerned. Wells too since he was a junior. We all may be best friends, but we could and did use whatever we could against each other. I think that came with the territory of us being buddies. We'd known each other since birth. Our parents were all friends before that.

"I'm just saying. Y'all's asses had one thing to do that fucking night." Wolf growled, sounding like an actual wolf. He'd gained the term on the football field, but it stayed long off. Not only did the fucker look like a wolf, he acted like one too. "You fucked shit up, and now, we all have to deal with it."

Thatcher rolled his eyes. "It was Wells who ran like a little bitch ass that night." Chuckling, he tossed an arm over Wells's shoulder. "What did she have again?"

Wells shoved him off. "A bat, and hell yeah, I ran. Bitch had a fucking air horn."

"She apparently still likes to make noise," I said, recalling this morning in clear detail, and with the words, my buddies silenced. They weren't looking at the big picture here.

They knew that.

I assumed *they saw* that all over my face, and even Wolf went silent.

He didn't do that for many.

"What did you find out about her?" I asked him, telling Wolf to look into the new girl. Wells had texted me about her the moment he'd realized she was the girl he'd allowed to escape that night. The one who'd gotten in the way.

The one who fucked everything up.

She was the one who made *noise,* so naturally I needed everything that could possibly be found out about her. Normally, Thatcher would do such a job. His father, my god dad Knight, put the Windsor Prep's online security system in. Because of this, Thatcher knew the firewalls like the back of his hand. He was good like that, a tech genius like his dad.

The new girl was still too new, though. Her files wouldn't be uploaded into the system yet.

That left Wolf.

His mom used to be headmaster of the school back in the day. This was before the guys and I came to school here, but we'd known one day the headmaster's keys might one day be put to good use. Wolf had made dupes of everything before his mom returned the keys, and that came in handy during times like today.

When information was needed.

I'd sent Wolf along to records today to get the girl's hard file, study it a bit, then bring the information back. He'd texted he got the info before gym.

He eyed the new girl across the field, the girl ambling around like she didn't know what to fucking do. Her gym class played volleyball, but despite her height, she was just standing around like she had no idea what was going on.

Wolf sneered, as if at the audacity.

"She's trash," he said, that familiar bite in his voice returned from before. She'd danced with the devil getting in his face this morning. I'd give her that. He grunted. "She and her brother have been in about a million different schools in the last few years. Came here from Chicago. Inner city. She's nothing and nobody."

"What's she doing here?"

He eyed me. "Her father died," he said, surprising me. "A factory fire at his job according to her file. Didn't find much more about that and don't know anything about her mom. It just lists her as deceased in the record."

So she and her brother were orphans. Interesting.

I questioned if her dad had been someone for them both to be here amongst us, the elite, but Wolf just said the girl was trash and had nothing.

"It seems to be just her and her brother," Wolf continued. "Some guy named Callum Montgomery footed their tuition bill. I assume that's their guardian."

I stiffened a beat at the name. I knew a Callum, but the name Montgomery didn't ring a bell.

"Don't know too much about him either," Wolf informed. "Doesn't even fucking live here."

"Where does he live?"

"All the fuck over." Wolf picked up a football off the field, gripping it. "I did a little search on my phone between classes. He's a billionaire, but I couldn't find much besides his company name: Montgomery Holdings. Couldn't even find a picture of him. Seems he's got other people being the face of his company for him. Might be a hermit or something. Probably enrolled the new girl and her bro here for the academy's rep." Wolf eyed Thatcher. "Bow's also been assigned the new girl's guide. Says so in her file."

"The fuck?" Thatch questioned, then lifted his eyes. "Leave it to my sister. She's such a kiss-ass."

She just liked to be involved and was smart, like Wolf in that light if he let people know. There were times it was exposed like his Student of the Month shit. He couldn't always hide his smarts behind a bad attitude and a growl.

Opening my hands, I had him toss me the football. "What's her name?"

"Noa Sloane," Wolf stated, aggressive about it. She'd obviously already made a new best friend with him.

I squeezed the ball.

Noa Sloane, huh?

"I need to know more," I said to my friends, and the girl better hope I liked what I found.

Sloane

Blondie and his friends sure garnered a lot of attention.

It helped they liked to dick around shirtless.

Four golden bodies tossed a football back and forth, both long and short passes. When they actually collided (muscled bodies slamming against each other in a sweat-ridden array), the girls out here basically lost their shits.

Some of the boys did too.

The guys weren't being casual about literally playing football when the other gym classes were forced to do other things. My class had to play volleyball (which I sucked at) and the others were either jogging the track or doing something else in a group.

The four Adonises seemed to be exempt, though, fooling around and occasionally laughing. The group appeared to be quite acquainted with each other.

Not like I noticed.

At least, I tried not to notice, brushing myself off after face-planting to hit back a serve. Despite my height, I epically sucked at sports, something Bru liked to remind me of since he was actually good at them. Never played them, but when he did, he was good. He might have actually tried out for something had my father not been against it.

He'd been against a lot of things.

He had kept a short leash on us, not wanting us to go out really. If he didn't leave the house, he didn't want us to either, and I had resented him a lot because of that when it'd all been going down. I had pushed back a lot, something I wished I hadn't done so much now.

Losing a parent definitely put things into perspective. I missed my dad, flaws and all. He loved us. He was just troubled.

A tall girl on the other side of the net drew back to serve, I squatted down to actually maybe hit the thing back. She hit it over, a player on my side hitting it back. The opposite side returned it, but when it was my turn, I missed and the volleyball flew over my ponytail.

Did I mention I sucked at sports?

"I got it," I called, jogging over to get the thing. I picked it up.

"Watch out!"

I jerked my head around when one of my teammates told me to, the football flying at my face. It would have hit me full on.

Had not a hand shot out.

Lengthy fingers gripped the football, tucking it into a set of firm abs. I followed them up to ebony-dark eyes.

Holy shit, this guy was beautiful.

Of course, I noticed it in the parking lot. Golden body, huge hands.

Thick thighs.

Solid muscle weaved all the way through him, even that jawline he had for days. It clenched as he made eye contact with me, and without missing a beat, he drew back one of those big biceps and tossed the football to his friends. They all went for it, but the asshole who'd bugged me this morning caught it.

The guy merely reached out a hand to, his long mane drawn up and out of his eyes aside from some obviously pesky tendrils. Dude had hair like mine, wispy and long. Though, obviously mine was longer. He even had dark hair like me, more tan than his friends.

"Good catch," I breathed, but not to the asshole over there. Blondie still stood in front of me, maybe a foot away.

I could taste him.

Arctic gum breezed coolly over my face, a stark contrast to the sweat and boy smell that chased it. The guy was flush all over from his broad shoulders to his boyish features. Color crushed the harsh definition of his angular cheekbones, and his blond hair was slightly around his face like Brad Pitt in his *Meet Joe Black* days.

Blondie pulled his fingers through his hair, an action he'd clearly done a million times judging by the way it tamed back. His hair didn't return to his eyes, stayed in place. He jerked his chin at me. "Why the fuck are you at my school?"

The fuck?

I twitched, like seriously took a double take here. I told the guy he'd had a nice throw and he came at me like this?

I was honestly gobsmacked, and in my stupor, his friends jogged over.

One by one, the male parade surrounded him, and Jesus, these boys were big. Blondie himself took up a ton of surface area, but the guy with dark hair and piercings behind him even managed to have him on that. The guy had exactly two piercings, a dangling cross in one ear and a stud in the other. The shortest was the platinum blond, but he was by no means small. He could definitely handle his own with the thick, corded muscle lining biceps and forearms.

And then, there was Wolf.

Seeing him this close, he towered over these guys, the

asshole smirking at me when he got there. Upon his buddies' arrival, Blondie reached into his pocket, giving Wolf what was clearly a wad of cash. I saw easily a few hundred-dollar bills in that stack.

Rich kids.

I saw exchanges like that all the time when the upper elite managed to mosey over to my neck of the woods back home. Rich kids had to buy their blow from somewhere, but I saw none of those exchanges here.

"I guess you win, Wolf," Blondie said to him and didn't look happy about it.

I frowned. "What?"

Chuckling, Wolf tucked the cash in his pocket before dropping an arm on his blond buddy's shoulder. Wolf jerked his chin at me. "I bet him you were as much of a bimbo as you looked."

"And idiot me bet in your favor." Blondie eyed me. "So, I'm going to try this again. Slower this time for you." He leaned in. "Why in the *fuck* are you at my school?"

These guys weren't serious, right? With this shit?

My lack of answer *again* had Wolf laughing, but this time, I wasn't gobsmacked.

This time, I was pissed.

"Excuse me, bitch. Was someone talking to you?" I shot in Wolf's direction, which effectively cut off his laughter. He shot forward off the bro line and put his finger so close to my face I debated breaking it off and feeding it to him.

"You little cunt," he said, laughing with it, and started to get closer had not a whistle blown across the field.

Two gym teachers formed a beeline right for us. One of them I recognized as mine and the other could have been theirs had they actually participated in class. Something told me these guys just did whatever the fuck they wanted.

"Mr. Mallick, is there a problem here?" the one who wasn't my teacher asked, and Wolf whipped in his direction so fast I questioned if the dude gave himself whiplash. Wolf opened his mouth, no doubt to shoot off something.

But then, Blondie raised his hand.

He'd done it in front of his friend, but he stared at the teacher.

The teacher stopped in his stride. Like actually legit stopped and mine did too beside him.

One of the men wet their lips. "Mr. Prinze, is there a problem?"

Hesitance backed the words, a caution like the teacher was speaking to an animal.

Or a dark prince.

With Blondie's last name that seemed fitting.

Mr. Prinze lowered his hand and both of the teachers swallowed hard. They really seemed to be intimated by the guy. What the fuck?

The platinum blond, Wells I remembered, hooked an arm around the dark prince. "Dude, I don't feel like hearing it from my dad today."

"Right, bro." The colossal-sized guy with the piercings shrugged his shoulders, casual about it. "You know my pops. Dude's crazy. You know I don't mind backing you boys up, but only if shit's worth it."

The guy jutted a chin in my direction and, apparently, today's match wasn't worth a brawl with whoever his father was.

The others seemed to share the same sentiment, even Wolf who raised his hands.

"Whatever," Wolf said, backing off, and once Blondie did too, the teachers visibly relaxed. The four boys ventured back, but it was Blondie who pointed at me.

"See you around, Noa Sloane," he said, obviously having gathered enough intel about me to know my name. With a smirk, he proceeded to toss the ball back and forth with his boys.

"Ms. Sloane, back to volleyball with the others," my
teacher said. Suddenly, his balls had been restored. He left
with the other teacher without a response from me. Eventually, I did make it back over to my class, but it was hard to
play with the watchful eyes clearly behind me.

It lasted the rest of class.

CHAPTER
SIX

Sloane

The next few days, I attempted to avoid the dark prince and his boys. This was made gratefully easier since we managed not to share any classes. Even that gym class we hadn't shared. Our classes had just both happened to be outside that day.

That fucking day.

It'd been truly fucked up and nothing I'd ever experienced. Bru and I had gone to the absolute worst schools, but even the guys and girls with attitudes there didn't fuck with the teachers. They'd rather not come to school than deal with any disciplinarians.

But these boys...

They were in a different breed, clearly. Especially that dark prince. I hadn't made any friends yet at Windsor Prep, so unfortunately, I hadn't been able to get any information about him or any of them. I needed to know what I was dealing with here.

I needed to know exactly who I'd pissed off.

Bru and I were still at odds, so besides passing each other in the halls or around the house over the next few days, no information was being gotten there. That was of course if he had any information himself.

I was aware his new guide was named Wells, but I wasn't exactly sure if that was the same Wells from the dark prince's friend group. In any sense, the odds of my brother telling me anything about the guys I'd pissed off were slim. He'd want me to stay out of trouble.

Bru and I shared a lunch period, but talking to him about anything there was a dead end too. Right from the jump, he started taking his lunches into the computer lab, claiming it was easier to study with the quiet. He was trying to catch up after we'd enrolled late, and respecting that, I started eating lunches by myself. I usually slept or drew through them. I had an art class both before and after, so lunchtime proved to be good for something.

"Oh, Sloane. Hey!"

As well as avoiding the little rabbit.

This was the nickname I'd given Rainbow Reed, aka the little rabbit, since she both walked and talked a mile a minute. She and her pep fortunately only had the one class with me, but she was still acting as my personal stalker everywhere else. She met me both before and after each one of my classes, hot on my heels the whole way. When I wasn't trying to get to my classes super quick and avoid any unnecessary confrontations, I was attempting to dodge her and had managed it a time or two.

She talked my *ear* off.

I guess one could call me a bit of a loner. An introvert, I kept to myself and liked it that way. Bow Reed was making me *not* be an introvert and times like lunch were usually pretty easy to avoid her. For starters, the lunchroom was broken up into two sections, not to mention the outdoor courtyard. I'd never gotten that far, but I knew about it.

Needless to say, blending into the sea of many faces had been easy, but today, the little rabbit found me in the lunch line.

I actually chose to eat lunch today, in the lunch line at Windsor Preparatory Academy like a bougie salad bar at a restaurant. These people had actual menus, options divided up by what part of the world you wanted to eat at for the day. This afternoon, I chose Chinese, and Bow caught me at the fried rice.

"I missed you after your gym class," she said, her long hair in a tight braid today. She really was a lovely girl. She just... hovered. I didn't do hover. At least, not well. She grinned up at me, placing her tray on the line. "Did you see me?"

I actually hadn't and missed everyone at gym today since I'd hidden in the library through the period. Gym had been scheduled outside this morning, and I wasn't trying to take the risk that a certain boys club was out there too.

"Sorry," I said. "Must have, uh... must have missed you."

She waved me off, still grinning. "That's okay. Found you now."

"Yeah," I stated, then eyed her. "You know, I probably don't need you anymore. I'm sure you have other things to do. People to escort?"

She appeared very accomplished, and since she'd told me about her life story on any given day, I actually knew a lot about her. She mentioned her work as student guide was to help with her college applications, as well as one of the many things that'd look good when she went for student body president when it was time.

"Oh, don't worry about that." She grabbed some egg rolls. "Escorting you has been fun. Besides, we still have a few days together yet."

I forced a smile, hoping I and my introvert could endure it. I really was an awkward fuck.

Even still, I started to tell her I was probably just going to take this and go eat in the art room or something. It was usually empty before my next class, and I could use the quiet.

But then, I spotted the pack of hungry wolves.

Or rather one "wolf" and three others who were equally vicious. The dark prince and his buddies ate in the courtyard outside the cafeteria. I assumed this was a pretty popular place to eat considering all the traffic that flooded out there, but since *I* never ate out there for that particular reason, I had never bothered looking to see who ate in the area.

Had I, I would have spotted my Windsor Prep tormentors again, and of course, they were popular. Their table was a cluster fuck of ladies and dudes—mostly ladies. Wolf himself had two under his arms at their picnic table, and the big guy with the piercings had a girl actually feeding him.

I rolled my eyes at that, able to see them over the a la carte line through the window. Their attention (gratefully) wasn't focused in my direction, otherwise Blondie might have had something to say. He was definitely there too but seemed to be more occupied by his phone than the chaos around him. A chick had *her* arm around him, massaging his big body with her little hands.

Mr. Prinze barely acknowledged it, actually yawning at one point. Whoever this girl was, she was boring him, and when another girl joined, slinging an arm around his waist, that confirmed this activity was just another day for this guy. He was as arrogant and privileged as he came across, *clearly.*

Bow caught me staring above the line and popped up on her Mary Jane heels. "What are you looking at?"

It took but a moment for her to see despite her being shorter. There was enough action over there for her to easily see the popular kids having their good time. Wells, the platinum blond, was there too, but while the other guys sat in the center of their ladies like the god of their harems, he kept his attention on just one person. He actually didn't sit with the other guys, lounging against a tree with another boy. He had his arm around the guy, laughing with him.

Wells bit his mouth, full-on making out with this dude in the courtyard, and that showed me his privilege too. There were teachers everywhere out there, *well* within sight of his make-out session, but the guy clearly didn't care.

The elite indeed.

"Oh." Bow's cheeks colored as she returned her heels to the floor. She clearly spotted Wells and no doubt the others too. She shrugged. "That's just my brother and his friends."

I just about stumbled. "Who's your brother?"

If she said Blondie, I seriously was about to lose it. There was no way in hell something as bright and sprightly as this little rabbit was related to something as dark and brooding as the dark prince. I didn't believe it. Refused.

She pointed over the pass. "The one with the dark hair, earrings?" she stated, laughing. "Can't really miss him."

She was right about that. That guy was huge and, currently, was taking selfies of himself (by himself) like he was the shit.

"Oh, the pretty one." I rolled my eyes, and the little rabbit snorted. Like full-on snorted at the pass.

Her cheeks colored again as she covered her mouth. "You're really brave. I'm pretty sure no one around here has ever referred to Thatcher Reed as *pretty*. At least, audibly." Laughing, she lifted her eyes. "But if it's not the truth. He spends more time in the mirror in the morning than I do."

I had a laugh at that.

"Yeah. Brave." Either that or stupid depending on how one looked at it. Those fuckers over there were scary as hell, and I managed to call them out like my first fucking day. I jutted my chin in their direction. "I'm assuming they're the popular clique?"

If that wasn't already obvious, and after getting our trays filled, Bow and I took seats at an inside table. There was no way I was going to eat outside. Not after what had happened at the beginning of the week.

Bow opened her carton of milk. "Legacy isn't popular. Popularity is Legacy," she stated, the reference lost on me. She blinked. "You've been here a full week, and you don't know anything about them?"

I'd managed not to, shrugging.

She did the same. "I'd just stay out of their way. Since they are Legacy, that basically means they are the *it* around here. My brother and his friends are the Nile and everyone else is just the lakes and streams that run off it."

"What's legacy?"

She cuffed her arms. "In a nutshell, Legacy are the direct descendants of the last generation who roamed these halls from Maywood Heights's most prestigious families. They basically shaped this town, and it's been a while since Windsor Prep has actually had any blood relatives from one of those families. My brother and his friends are direct descendants."

"Which makes you Legacy too, then?"

Her cheeks flashed in red color. "I guess, but I'm not really active in the Court or anything. I'm in the Court on paper, but…"

When I obviously didn't know what she was talking about, she laughed. She laced her fingers. "The Court is a small society of those in the upper echelon of the town. It's like a club for the elite. Basically, the really rich families of the city." Her eyes lifted toward the heavens. "I'm only in it because it helps with college applications and stuff. The Court also does a lot of active work in the community since our dads, some of the Legacy fathers, started reform a few years ago. The Court used to only let boys in if you can imagine."

I definitely could with the way those Legacy boys were out there flaunting who they were. It'd looked like a circus at their table. "Who are they all? The Legacy guys? I know you said your brother."

Bow speared her salad. "My brother's Thatcher." Angling around, she directed her fork toward the view outside. "And by the tree with that girl is Wells Ambrose."

My eyes twitched wide. The platinum blond did have a girl *now*. He'd been making out with a guy before, but this time, he had his arm slung around a brunette.

She kissed his neck while he lazily ate a cheese stick, and after shaking her head, Bow pointed back over to the guys' table.

"Ares Mallick," she said, referring to Wolf. "Though most people call him Wolf. Don't call him that to his face, though. That's only reserved for my brother and his friends. It's a football thing. They're all football players."

And why wasn't I surprised? A classic cliche of elitist power. I folded my fingers together. "And Blondie?"

He was still out there on his phone, no actual lunch in front of him. In fact, he'd *just* put his phone down and started looking around. Like he was looking for someone.

"Dorian Prinze," Bow said. "Basically their leader and most certainly the last person you want to get in the way of. Really, any of them. It's been a long time since this school has seen a Reed, Mallick, Ambrose, or a Prinze. My brother and his friends definitely play it up. They pretty much run things around here, and anyone else should probably just back up. I heard before my brother and his friends got here, being in the Court was the *it* thing." She faced outside. "But now, it's Legacy. Court kids are just their minions. You know they're Court by their rings. These."

She put out her hand, the school's mascot on it. At least, it appeared to be that. The chrome ring below her knuckle had a growling gorilla in the midst of a bite.

How symbolic.

I'd taken Bow's hand to get a closer look but let go when I

noticed the dark prince rise from his table. He greeted a new arrival, one of those bro combination hug handshakes. He let go of the guy with a snap, and I realized who the guy was when he drew back.

What the fuck?

"Sloane?"

I got up, ignoring Bow.

It was like I was on autopilot.

It was like I was ignoring *everything* she said about confronting Legacy because I was storming right out into the courtyard.

And into the belly of the beast.

A circle of popular girls and boys milled about, and I forced my way through them to find my brother.

My brother who just shook the hand of a dark prince.

His lunch tray in hand, Bru literally was about to sit between Dorian and Bow's brother, Thatcher. The two boys were moving to make room for my brother and everything.

In the distraction of that, I grabbed my brother's arm, and before he or anyone else could say anything about that, I dragged him back into the cafeteria.

"Sloane, what the fuck?" Bru jerked his arm from me. He'd actually been about to sit with them. *What the fuck?* His eyes blazed. "What do you think you're doing?"

"What the fuck do you think you're doing?" I shot back. "You're sitting with those assholes?"

Or had he forgotten one of them called me *bitch* only days ago?

Bru's attention was on anything but me, completely red in the face while he stared outside. Dorian hadn't followed us, but he was definitely watching.

They all were.

Thatcher, Ares. Even Wells had gotten up to see what was going on inside the cafeteria. He'd slung his arms around his buddies, the four of them speaking amongst each other.

I whipped Bru around to face me.

"Have you lost your mind?" I blazed. "You do remember what they called me, right?"

"Oh, yeah. I remember," he said, making me twitch. He actually got in my face. "I also remember you didn't help the situation."

"So is that what this is?" I raised and dropped my hands. "Revenge because I embarrassed you?"

He shook his head, cutting around me. I reached to grab him again, but he was too quick this time. He backed up. "Not everything is about you, Sloane. Actually, none of this shit is."

"What are you talking about?"

He forced fingers into his hair. "Those guys are on the football team. They approached me about going out for it. I was messing around tossing footballs one day in gym class. Word got back to them, I guess. They think I'd be a good fit and said they'd speak to Coach about me if I was interested in playing."

Wait. What?

"Callum said we should look into clubs and stuff, so this is me trying to do that." He raised and dropped his hands. "Do something fucking normal and make some friends."

At this point, we'd gained the attention of those in the cafeteria as well, and even from my table, Bow was staring at us. She stopped eating her food, looking on like everyone else, but I didn't fucking care. I folded my arms. "You don't even like football."

"What would you know about what I fucking like?" Bracing his arms, he angled close to my face. "You're too busy being like dad. Suffocating and shit."

He'd spoken the words in a whisper, making me swallow.

With a sigh, he rubbed a hand behind his neck and obviously realized what he said.

He went on anyway.

"Just back off of this," he said, leaving me with little more than that. I started to go after him, but stopped.

Dorian.

He stared my direction through the glass, and though Bru had returned to him, Dorian's attention was on me. He winked, *right at me*, then waved a hand in my direction.

Motherfucker.

This wasn't some kind of scouting or friendship he was genuinely brewing with my brother.

This was something else entirely.

The dark prince was making a statement.

I heard it in bounds.

CHAPTER
SEVEN

Dorian - age 10

I couldn't find Charlie, but he was really good at this game.

I hunkered down behind one of my mom's flower pots. I watched for my best friend Ares but hoped I wouldn't have to tag him. He was really good at laser tag too, like Charlie, but he got really aggressive about it and sore when he lost. He wasn't the one anyone wanted to find them.

I stayed quiet.

I couldn't hear anything, but everyone was so good at this game. Even Wells and Thatcher despite them being smaller. They bugged the crap out of Ares and me until we let them play this time. I wouldn't mind it, but Ares got crazy sometimes. Last thing we needed was someone getting hurt and all our moms and dads yelling at us. Last time we'd played hard together, Wells had skinned his knee and Thatcher had tackled Ares because he'd been the one to do it. I just wanted to play a game, not get our parents screaming.

A shuffle sounded directly behind me.

I stiffened behind the pot, my finger hugging the trigger of

my laser gun. I eased out for a look, but a hand slammed
against my mouth and, next thing I knew, someone was
joining me behind the pot.

Charlie.

He placed his finger to his lips, telling me to keep quiet.
He had dark hair, real dark like my mom, and in their kid
pictures, they looked exactly the same. He waved at me to
come with him.

I went.

I followed close behind, trusting him for some reason
despite us not being on teams. I always trusted Charlie.

I was right to.

He pushed me out of the way, as Ares launched at us. I
didn't know how Ares could see with all those brown curls
surrounding his face, but he always managed.

"Take that, suckers!" Ares called, shooting at both Charlie
and me with a quick finger.

Charlie was quicker.

Holding me back, Charlie used his height to shoot a direct
shot right at Ares's laser tag vest. The lights on Ares's vest
went off like crazy, and Ares started groaning as he ripped it
off and tossed it to the floor.

"No fair," Ares gritted, his face changing in color. He
pouted. "Charlie, you're like way bigger than the rest
of us."

With a chuckle, Charlie stood tall. He was taller than us
since he was twelve and we were ten. Charlie pointed at him.
"Didn't stop you from taking out Wells and Thatcher so
quick."

I'd seen it too. Ares had gone for them first despite them
being weaker, and Thatcher had been so angry he'd said a
curse word and left the game.

Wells hadn't been far behind.

We were all best friends, but Wells and Thatcher were
close like Ares and I were. I think that was mostly because of

our ages. Ares and I were ten, and Thatcher and Wells were nine.

Charlie was all our buddies, though. Especially mine. He was my mom's brother despite him only being a couple years older than me.

The other guys always joked about that, about Charlie being my uncle when uncles were supposed to be really big. Charlie always got on them real quick about that, though, and he was like a big brother to all of us.

I mean, he was Batman.

Tackling Ares, Charlie told him to go find Thatcher and Wells and apologize. Ares grumbled about it, but he eventually left. Charlie stayed behind with me, and after he showed me a couple moves with the laser gun, we decided to go to the kitchen and get a drink.

"I bet Mom made lemonade," I said to him.

She always did when Charlie came over, knowing it was his favorite. He didn't come by a lot since he and his parents, my grandparents, traveled all the time.

Grandpa Lindquist, my mom's dad, married Charlie's mother, my grandma Helen, before I was born, but Grandma Helen wasn't my biological grandma. My blood-related grandma died before I was born.

Grandpa Lindquist was really fun. He took Charlie and Grandma Helen all over the world, and Grandpa always brought stuff back for me. Because they did travel a lot, it was always extra special when Charlie came by. Usually, it'd be for a few days or something while Grandma and Grandpa went on weekend trips. Charlie had been here since Friday, and we'd had a blast all weekend with Thatcher, Wells, and Ares.

Charlie chased me down the hall and together we ran into the kitchen, laughing. It took us a second to realize we weren't alone.

And that my dad was here.

Dad shouldn't be here. He worked in business and was always busy.

He wasn't alone.

He held my mom. Her face was red. My great-aunt Celeste was there too.

My stomach twisted.

Great-Aunt Celeste held Mom's hand, rubbing it. Dad ran his hand down Mom's back, and when Mom faced Charlie and me, her eyes were all red.

Like she'd been crying.

I started to go toward her—why was she crying?—but Charlie held me back.

He had my shoulders.

"Hold on, Robin," Charlie said to me. I was the Robin to his Batman always.

Charlie's words came out whispered, though, and when I looked up at him, his eyes were wide. Like he'd seen a ghost or was scared or something. Charlie rubbed my shoulders. "What's going on?"

My parents said nothing. Great-Aunt Celeste said nothing.

But then my mom moved.

My dad allowed her to, her steps so quiet when she came over to me. She placed a hand on Charlie's face, smiling at him, but it looked weird.

My stomach clenched again.

She squeezed Charlie's face before going down to me. She took my hand. "Love, I need you to go with your dad for a little bit," she said, gazing back at him. "Your great-aunt and I need to talk to Charlie."

Charlie's eyes expanded, his face white like an actual ghost.

I faced Mom. "Why, Mom?"

"Honey, I just need you to go. Just for a little while, okay?" She placed a hand on my face and, suddenly, my dad was in front of me.

Dad placed out his hand.

I took it, but I didn't want to go. I couldn't leave Batman.

"Batman?" I said to Charlie, but all he did was blink. He said nothing. He couldn't.

My mom and great-aunt were too busy leading him out of the room.

Dad took me outside, just the pair of us, and I didn't understand. He also told me he'd had my god dad Ramses come by to pick up Ares. He was Ares's pop, and Ramses also took Thatcher and Wells home. Dad said they had to leave because we all had to talk about something here.

My palms sweated in the garden built by my dad's mom. She'd planted all the flowers in our backyard by hand. My dad grew up here, and I'd heard him say once that the garden was the only reason he kept the house.

I never understood why he'd ever want to get rid of it. Our house was really nice and big. The garden planted by my grandma only made it better.

Dad had his hands in his pockets, walking beside me. "Do you remember the story I told you, son?" he asked, causing me to look up at him. Most people said I looked just like him, but he always said I had my mom's eyes. I didn't know if I liked that because my mom was a girl, but Dad said it was a good thing. He said it all the time actually. His lips thinned. "The story about your grandmother. My mom?"

He told me a lot of stories about her. Like how beautiful she was.

She had to be if she planted all these flowers. I twisted my hands. "Which one, Dad?"

He stopped in front of a willow tree, a koi pond circling it. He faced me. "How she's always here in this place, and even though we can't see her, she's always there. Her and your aunt Grace."

My aunt Grace was his sister. They had both died before I was born.

I nodded. "Yes."

Dad took a seat with me on a concrete bench, and my stomach got all queasy again. I didn't know why we were out here, or why they'd all separated Batman and me.

"There was an accident, Dorian," Dad said to me, his voice rough and weird sounding. It sounded like Mom a little bit inside. He folded his hands. "An accident involving Grandpa Lindquist and Grandma Helen."

"What kind of accident?" My voice was quiet, and I wondered if my dad heard it.

But then, he looked at me full on. He always looked me in the eye. Like he could see me when sometimes adults didn't always do that. My teachers always made me feel little or invisible, but Dad never did. He placed a hand on my shoulder. "It was while they were away. A traffic collision late last night."

"Well, are they okay?" My voice sounded funny now, and I turned back toward the house. I wished I had X-ray vision, or some kind of cool tech like Batman. I wanted to see in the house and *find* Batman.

Dad squeezed my shoulder, and I stared up at him. He shook his head. "They didn't make it, son."

His voice was quiet now, but I didn't understand. Didn't make it? "Dad?"

He brought his arm around me, cupping my arm. He squeezed. "Do you understand what I've told you, Dorian? What this means?"

I gazed away, the wispy tails of the koi moving around in the pond. I nodded. "Grandma and Grandpa are gone." I stared up at him. "They're not coming back."

I wouldn't get to see them again, and I already didn't get to see them a lot.

My chest hurt, my stomach like someone punched me again and again. I didn't realize I was crying until I had my dad's shirt clenched in my fists, and I sobbed in his chest.

He let me stay there, holding me while he rubbed my back. He held me so tight, my dad's hugs always solid and strong. They always came when I needed them.

And when he gave them, he didn't let go.

"What about Charlie?" I heard myself say. Again, I didn't know how Dad heard me. I sniffed into my dad's shirt. "What will happen to Charlie?"

"He'll live with us now, son," Dad said, hugging me so tight. "He'll live with us, and he's going to need us. He's going to need family."

I couldn't hear his words after a while, not over my own tears. I didn't like crying in front of my dad. He never cried, and neither did Charlie. They were both Batman.

I needed to be Batman.

CHAPTER
EIGHT
TWO MONTHS LATER

Dorian - age 10

Charlie's room was quiet again that night.

It was like he didn't exist.

He never left his room, and the house staff brought him all his meals.

Mom and Dad were worried. Especially Mom. I knew because she let Thatcher, Wells, and Ares stay over again tonight.

It was a school night.

The guys came over all the time these days. Sometimes when I just wanted to be by myself too. I heard our dads talking and saying it was best we were all together now. Our parents were all friends, and the last couple months had been bad.

Mom had just stopped crying.

She always did it at night. Before my dad came home from work, she'd be in their room, and her crying made me want to cry again too.

I didn't. I tried to be strong every time, but I couldn't help

it during the funeral. There'd been two caskets, one for
Grandpa and one for Grandma. Dad said they weren't inside
it. He'd also said Grandpa had wanted something where they
turned his and Grandma Helen's body into ash, and Ares got
real gory when he explained it to Thatcher and Wells. He
hadn't told them when I'd been around. He'd whispered that
one night after they thought I'd fallen asleep during one of
our sleepovers.

I heard it.

We always invited Charlie to play video games with us,
but he never came, no matter how many times I knocked.
Dad told me one day Charlie just needed some time.

I gave him that until tonight.

I couldn't help it, passing by his door after getting some
milk from the kitchen. My buddies were asleep in my room,
but Batman was all alone in his. Mom and Dad put him down
the hall from me, his own room.

I started to knock, but decided not to since he never
answered. I opened the door, and the light from my flashlight
bled inside.

He sat on the bed.

He had his arms wrapped around his legs, and my chest
hurt seeing him. I missed him so much. "Batman?"

He turned to me real slow. Like he was a robot, and the
cogs needed oil. His legs lowered when I came in the room,
and when I sat on his bed, his lips lifted a little.

"Hey, Robin," he said, his smile put on. It was like he was
trying to do it for me. "You still up?"

I nodded, turning my flashlight off. I looked at him.
"You?"

He laughed for some reason after I said that, a really small
laugh. It made my chest hurt again. He tilted his head at me.
"Want me to tuck you in?"

He had in the times he'd come over when I'd been sick or
something. And though I didn't feel good tonight, real sad

too, it felt weird him doing that for me. I gripped the flash-light. "Want me to tuck you in?"

He smiled again. "Last I checked, I'm *your* uncle, Robin."

But he wasn't my uncle, not really. It had never felt that way, not to Thatcher, Wells, or Ares either. Charlie had always been our brother.

Wells, Thatcher, and Ares were my brothers too. If I could be brothers with my best friends, then that made what Charlie and I had even stronger.

I jerked the sheets until he moved enough to get under them.

"I'm tucking you in," I said, making him smile, and I didn't stop until I got him snug in there. I made sure it was real tight like when Mom did it, but not too tight like Dad. I wanted him to actually breathe.

Charlie watched me the whole time, another one of those sad smiles on his face. Dad said he might have those for a long time.

I'd wait as long as they took to fade.

I caught myself doing them too, but I never did in front of Batman. He needed to see I was strong.

After I got him in, I sat beside him. He looked at me. "Now, what?"

I shrugged. "Now, you sleep."

I waved a hand over his face like it was magic, making him laugh again. He shook his head. "Thanks, Batman."

My eyes twitched wide. I frowned. "But you're Batman, Charlie."

Charlie wriggled out of the tight tuck of the bedding, taking my hand with a small grin.

"Tonight, you're Batman," he said, my insides whirling. I never got to be Batman. I was never big enough. Charlie made a fist, putting it out to me.

I tapped it.

I started to get up but stopped. "Charlie?"

He opened his eyes, having already closed them. "Yeah?"

I played with the flashlight. "We're brothers now," I said, nodding. "I know not technically but..." I shrugged. "We're brothers now. We're brothers."

I wanted him to hear that, to *know* that. We always would be brothers, and brothers protected each other.

Charlie put his fist up again, tapping mine. "For life, Batman," he said. "For life."

CHAPTER
NINE

Dorian - present

I didn't sleep last night.

I kept seeing Charlie's face.

It whirled in my memory like a goddamn wound, and I ended up in my sweats. I jogged around the neighborhood until I tired my goddamn legs out, then ended up in the basement gym after that.

Chestnut, our family Labrador, stared at me like I was fucking crazy, but I didn't stop curling weights until I couldn't feel my arms. I even lifted like a fucking idiot, spotter be damned. Working out helped me not think so much, and I needed not to fucking think. I sweated through my top until I had to take it off, and by the time I thoroughly wiped myself out, I had time to sleep for about an hour before my alarm went off.

I hit it without missing a beat.

A quick shower, then I was downstairs, academy uniform on and making smoothies for Mom and me. She liked hers completely green, but I still needed some kind of fruit in mine to make it tolerable. Going vegan my freshman year had been a son of a bitch, but after I researched on all the ways going meat-free could enhance my playing ability, I decided to give it a shot.

Needless to say, my plant-based mother had been thrilled, but I didn't give a fuck about saving the animals or some shit. I just wanted my body in top form, and eating this way, my body got stronger and faster on the field. I'd been quarterback since junior year and ran circles around my teammates. Lifted more too.

Mom was late.

She used to be up before me, but today, the coffeemaker once again said she'd stayed in her room long past her usual time. Mom made her own hours. She worked for the city, but they didn't give a shit when she showed up.

She came into the room frazzled.

Her hair was still wet too when she breezed into the kitchen, purse on her arm and looking like she was trying to go a million different ways. She was dictating a laundry list of tasks she obviously had to do for the day into her phone, but even when she was all over the place like this, she still managed to look lovely. I knew because if my dad was here, I'd catch them doing things that made me want to burn my eyes out on any given day.

It was sick catching them sneaking around like a couple of teenagers. Even with their room being on the other side of the house, it wasn't enough to not hear *things*. I had to go to the basement if I wanted to drown that shit out.

"Dorian, love, did you happen to make an extra—"

I handed her the smoothie I'd made. "Green like you like it."

She took a sip, and the euphoria in her brown eyes told me I'd done a good job. It was just about the only thing I got from her, her eyes. My mom had hair nearly raven black, real dark like Chestnut's fur, but her skin was fair, and she couldn't hold a tan to save her life. We went to the beach enough, and she burned just stepping out of the car. She draped an arm around me. "You're a godsend, honey. Thank you."

"No problem." It really wasn't. "You got your car keys and your date book?"

She wrestled around in her bag for a minute. She raised a finger. "Yes, but I don't have—"

I handed her cell phone to her. The one she'd apparently lost in the five seconds she'd been in the kitchen.

Upon taking it, she eyed me. "Who's the parent in this situation?"

I shrugged and didn't fight her when she brought me into a hug.

Nor did I let go.

My mom hugged me all the time. This was not unusual. But what was unusual was how she didn't seem to want to let go these days. Like there was something there behind it while she attempted to meld herself into me.

I held her back, letting her stay as long as she needed to before letting go.

She kissed my cheek before squeezing it. "Have a good day, my love."

"You too, Mom." She gave me another quick kiss, then she was on her way. But I didn't move until I heard her Mercedes pull out of the garage and she made it out of the driveway. She tended to forget things lately, come back.

She didn't today.

I was right on her heels after that, finishing getting ready and all that. I strapped my bag on. Keys and smoothie in hand, I started for the garage too, but someone called my name down the hall. I assumed it was Ronald our butler, but when I doubled back and caught my dad in his office, my eyes flashed.

My father was behind his desk, working through papers

on it. He waved me inside. "Come in, son. Just need two seconds from you."

This was *unusual.* Dad was usually at work by now, and Mom had never mentioned him being here. Maybe she hadn't known. She'd been running late too.

Pocketing my keys, I angled into the room, closing the door. "Yeah, Dad?"

He waved me to come deeper inside, and I took a sip of my smoothie while I waited for him to get off a call. He had his headset on, something I hadn't noticed when I'd first seen him. Apparently, he was doing a little work from home before going into the office. My dad had many businesses, but I supposed what he and the Prinze name were known for was Prinze Financial. Our family name was tied to ninety percent of the banks in town.

My father paced behind his desk, shooting off commands. I heard the name Cliff a time or two, which let me know he was talking to his personal finance guy.

My finger tapped the pendulum on his desk while he spoke, and that used to piss him off when I'd been a kid. I broke the thing more times than I could count.

"Thank you, Heathcliff," he said. "I'll see you at the office."

My gaze jerked up, as he told me to take a seat. I took my bag off.

He ruffled through some papers. "Just got off the phone with Cliff," he said, flashing his green eyes at me. "Was just going over the household budgets. Credit card statements too."

Well, fuck that wasn't good. I laced my fingers on his desk. "I'm sorry if I've been spending too much…"

"You know, I don't care how much money you spend, Dorian." He propped his hands on his hips, his pants pleated and crisp. "I work hard so you can spend it." His eyes narrowed. "Within reason."

I nodded, relieved a little. But then, he tossed a statement toward me.

He pointed at it. "He's alerted me to the fact that there's been a lot of transactions upstate." His eyes narrowed further, deeper creases in his eyes. My dad was in his forties, but he barely looked thirty. It was only the harsh lines around his eyes that gave him away. Mom had the opposite problem. The lines around her mouth were because she smiled so much. Dad's were nonexistent. It wasn't that he didn't smile. He just didn't do it often and probably even less than before I came around.

Hence the soft lines.

I took the credit card statement, swallowing as I read it. It didn't take a scientist to know that the credit card in question was mine.

Or that these transactions were mine.

"Lots of gas stations upstate, son, and fast-food joints. I'm assuming since you stopped at some point to eat."

I eased my head up. "Uh, yeah. Yes."

"Yes." His eyes narrowed harder, a confusion that I didn't blame. It wasn't just that I went upstate. It was the towns and cities I was passing through. It was the path.

It was the destination.

All that passed over my father's green eyes as they stared at me, suddenly wild where they hadn't been before. Out of all of us lately, he'd been the one keeping his shit together the most, always good for that. My father was an unmovable force.

But something like this would move him.

"Why in God's name," he stated, but then his fingers folded over his face. This was an action he often took to calm himself. People who shot off at the cuff disappointed him. Most especially when it came to himself. My dad liked control. He faced me. "What's the meaning of these trips?"

I had one shot at this. My father could smell a lie a mile

way and always had. I didn't get away with shit as a kid. I wet my lips. "Football."

"Football?" His eyes flashed. He directed a finger toward the statement. "You've been going upstate for football."

"Yes, sir." I nodded, hoping it didn't give me away too much. I opened my hands. "Football. Camps and stuff."

The lines around his eyes deepened. "I know your schedule, son. I know." He paused, then lifted his head. "I *knew* your coach."

Knew my coach.

A heavy breath escaped him, as he faced out of the window of our large home. All brick, we basically lived in an enchanted castle, and my dad had grown up here, him and his sister.

Now, he was the only Prinze to remain from that life long ago. Obviously, I was around and our extended family, but the other Prinzes who had lived in this house were long gone. We didn't speak about my grandfather, his father.

The man was a curse in this house.

I'd found this out later in life, sitting here before my father now.

"Your schedule doesn't have any trips upstate, Dorian." Dad would know since he *loathed* football. He and his friends, my god dads Knight, Jaxen, Ramses, and LJ had all played lacrosse when they'd been in school. My dad had learned to endure football for me. Dad lifted his head. "Dorian."

"The trips weren't with the team," I said quickly. "Ares, the other guys, and I signed up for our own day trips and scrimmage weekends. You know how we like to perfect our game."

He knew how *I* liked to perfect my game. I didn't do anything in my life half-assed. I worked hard, getting that from my dad.

Dad stared at me then, real long and hard. He wet his lips.

"I do." The words arrived on a breath, as his hand rose. "Lord knows you eat all that cardboard with your mother."

Dad was a meat eater through and through. I nodded. "Yeah."

My father's visible relief at what I said was evident. He believed me. He did when he shouldn't have, and that told me something. It said that he *wanted* to believe me, and that when it came to an alternative, well, there wasn't one. I was going upstate for football.

That was why I went.

I could imagine this was something his brain could compute, and I was grateful for that. He faced me. "I'm assuming the trips are done, then?"

This wasn't a negotiation, not the way he said it. I bobbed my head once in acknowledgment.

"You don't go upstate," he finalized, then sat in his chair. "You don't, Dorian. And if you need to, you talk to me first."

My stomach twisted up, adrenaline raised to hell. "Yes, sir."

He sat back. "You can go now. Have a good day at school."

I didn't give him a chance to question me more. I just grabbed my smoothie, my school bag, and got out of there. I went to close his door and noticed his hand rubbing his brow. He was tense, but I noted something else.

He'd believed a lie when he never *ever* did.

CHAPTER
TEN

Dorian

I arrived on time to school, but didn't get out of my car right away. I texted the guys I'd be in later, then parked in a random spot in the lot.

I lit up a joint.

I just needed a moment to fucking think, and I did that for a while. After taking the seconds I needed, I eventually parked my car with the rest of the guys, then hit the halls of the school. First period was most people's homerooms, but usually the guys and I just dicked around. Really, we did whatever the fuck we wanted to do, but today, Wells said he needed to talk to us. When we all needed to meet, we met in the computer lab only the tech kids had access to. Thatch was one of those since he was a tech boy genius. He had keys to the lab, then made us dupes.

The lab was basically Legacy's personal fucking room, a place where we brought chicks and smoked weed. We usually didn't fuck girls together in there, but there'd been a time or two where things had gotten crazy.

I didn't go out of my way to see my buddies' dicks no matter how close we were, though. So if I needed the space, I usually texted ahead. The other guys didn't give a shit, but there were plenty of places to take girls on campus where we didn't have to smell each other's fucking cum.

Today, we were just meeting to talk and shit. We'd, um, acquired all the other tech kids' keys so only Legacy had access to the place now.

I unlocked my way in, and Wells passed me a bag of food from Jax's Burgers. His dad owned several burger joints around town, and Wells knew I liked the tots from there since they were vegan. I usually only ate the shit when I wasn't training, but I'd had a hell of a morning and texted him to get me some since he always stopped. Anything he got at his dad's franchises was free, so why the fuck not.

I devoured the tots after barely bumping Wells's fist for the grub, throwing myself in a swivel chair. Wells and Thatcher already sat around a computer screen, playing video games, and Wolf sat beside them with an empty wrapper. No doubt from those egg sandwiches he liked to eat in the morning. He crumpled it, tossing it at me. "You all right?"

The others swiveled in my direction, and I hoped to fuck my face wasn't telling shit. I didn't need any of them on my back either, their suspicions and shit. Especially Wolf. He also hadn't known I'd been going upstate. None of them did.

They wouldn't agree.

None of my buddies would, but Wolf? He'd kick my fucking ass. It'd be World War III in this motherfucker if my best friend found out what I'd been doing behind his back. Behind *everyone*'s backs. I shrugged. "Just got a late start."

"You don't get late starts." Wolf frowned, then looked at the other guys. "*We* get late starts."

"You do." Thatcher slapped Wolf's chest, and Wolf brought him under his arm. This worked for all of the two seconds it took for Thatcher to strong-arm him back. Wolf may have the height, but Thatcher Reed was a fucking tank. Thatch threw him off him. "I'll kill you. I swear to shit."

"Haven't yet, kiddo," Wolf chuckled, and I smiled. I enjoyed easy times like this where we could just sit around. No drama or women. We'd been having a lot of drama.

"I got bad news," Wells rolled in, sitting back and crossing his legs. He lifted a hand. "We can't get a van for a while."

"What the fuck?" I shot forward. "Why?"

Wells popped his big shoulders. "My dad's piece-of-shit employees have been stealing stuff off them recently." Wells frowned. "Because of that, Dad's monitoring his delivery vans. They're completely locked up, and I'm not sure when I can get another."

Wells had been able to get a van from one of his dad's restaurants, and without it, that made shit real fucking difficult.

It made a lot of things difficult.

We'd had a window the other night, a short one, and we'd had the van then. I huffed. "When are you thinking something will open up?"

"Hard to say." Wells opened his hands. "I'm sorry, man."

Thatcher fell into silence too beside him, both of them looking guilty. Had they done things right, we wouldn't need to get a van for a second time.

Shit would have been done.

But I'd be lying if I said I had no fault in what had happened. Wolf and I had been at the drop-off location, preparing shit.

I should have been there.

This was *my* responsibility, my cross to bear.

My burden to settle.

The rest of these guys had just been there with me. They had a stake in this too but not like me. Thatcher tapped his knees. "This sucks, D. This is our fucking fault."

He gestured to Wells, my other buddy nodding. Wolf waved them off.

"It's not about whose fault it is," Wolf said. "It's about what we're going to do about it."

Wells shook his head. "I'm going to keep watch, and I'll let you know the moment I hear something."

"We can't mess this up again," I told them. "We're not going to."

I had my dad on my back now. We were running out of time, and there were no do-overs. No time to muck shit up.

"And there's something else," Thatcher said. Reaching back, he got something off the computer table. "Noa Sloane's records and everything finally got put into the computer system. Her schedule too."

I didn't know what the fuck that had to do with anything. Noa Sloane had obviously been a pain in my ass. She'd gotten in the way that fucking night with Mayberry, which was why I'd brought her brother into our circle. I wanted him close to fuck with her.

But now…

I saw it right in front of me, my eyes blazing at the schedule Thatcher gave me. He nodded.

"She's student assisting for Principal Mayberry during the headmaster's free period," he said. "Which means the one hour we might have had access to the bitch, new girl is going to be in there with her."

"You're fucking kidding." Wolf ripped the schedule away. He scanned the page, his eyes darkening. He tossed it. "Can that little shit *not* get in the way for once?"

The answer seemed no in this case.

We didn't have a lot of time to get to Principal Mayberry, but one of those was the period the bitch used to do coke. The woman had a chronic drug habit, and catching her in a moment of vulnerability was our next chance to do what we needed to do.

We could get her then, *make her pay* then. Since we'd missed our first window on the street that night, the head-master's free period was a second option. The layout of the office made it easy to get to her through the janitor's access. The Windsor Prep's campus was laced with secret hallways the janitorial staff used to get somewhere quickly.

My buddies and I had memorized it all, knew the academy like the back of our hands. If we wanted to get someone out of the place without anyone noticing, we could.

The other night an opportunity had snuck up on us when Principal Mayberry had chosen to take a late run. She had Reed Security Systems in her home, so we knew where she was at all times. Thatcher could hack into the security feed, but his father's security system was too good. *The feed* and knowing her location was all we had. We couldn't override any of the systems, and Principal Mayberry didn't normally leave her house. Locked up like Fort Knox.

Something told me what had happened last year had something to do with that.

The woman was a paranoid coke whore since she'd returned to town, her life clearly fucked.

But we could do more.

We *would* do more. I rubbed my jaw, staring at the schedule on the floor. Up until this point, Noa Sloane had just been a fucking nuisance.

But now, she was in the way.

CHAPTER
ELEVEN

Sloane

Yeah, sports and me?

Really fucking sucked.

I was last on pool day. In fact, I sucked at laps so bad my gym teacher left me in the pool to finish after everyone concluded theirs. Apparently, this place was full of Olympic swimmers.

That shouldn't have surprised me.

I'd looked into the Court after Bow had told me about it. The affiliation had bred celebrities in the past, CEOs and even presidents.

I'd poked into Legacy too, and the Legacy boys were apparently the snot-nosed kids of some of the big dogs in that Court group back in the day. Because of that, Dorian Prinze, Ares "Wolf" Mallick, Thatcher Reed, and Wells Ambrose walked around this place like they were the shit.

Bow appeared to be immune to the toxicity of her brother and his friends, cheery and personable. She always stopped to say hi to folks when she walked me around school, but there was always a hesitance from others when interacting with her. Something told me a little fear might have to do with that, her brother and his friends hovering over her like a goddamn Legacy cloud of privilege and clout.

That fucker Dorian Prinze drew first blood.

My brother was actually *hanging out* with those tools, and I couldn't do anything about it. He was eating lunch with them, walking with them and their Court group in the halls, and I'd definitely noticed. If he was going out for the football team, I suppose he would need to be around them.

But that didn't mean I had to like it.

I kept an eye on Bru and *them* every time I saw their pack at lunch, but any other time, their interactions were out of my hands. My brother had his own life, and I had to have my own as well. Even if that did mean I spent most nights in my art studio or doing homework to stay busy.

I should use the time to practice swimming.

Our place had an indoor pool, but hell if I'd used it.

Struggling in the academy's pool now, I had to pause in the middle of a stroke just to catch my breath. I still had two laps before I could get out and shower like the other girls.

Better get this shit over with.

I glided through the water, grateful I actually had been taught to swim. When Bru and I were kids, Dad had taken us to the lake sometimes. That'd been when Mom was still around, but those memories were pretty fuzzy.

I missed my mom, what I remembered of her. But mostly, I missed her because my dad had been so different. He had taken us to places like the lake and played sports with us, sports with Bru. I remembered not ever being in the house most days.

I always suspected my mom's death may have had something to do with how withdrawn he had gotten. I'd been really little at the time, but a noticeable change had occurred in the house after my mom had died. She'd been killed while

Bru and I were at school, a home break-in when my dad had been at work. Dad kept the news clipping of her obituary, and I caught him reading it all the time.

Well, he used to.

Now, it was in a box with the rest of who my parents were. Not much. IDs and other things. It was all just a box of fucked-up memories, and I never looked at it.

With a final stroke, I got to the end of the pool, panting as I thought about my father and all those memories far away. I started to get out when a howl sounded throughout the aquatic area. Like an actual howl.

A fucking animal.

Ares Mallick twirled a bat, spiked with nails poking out of the end. He had a lit joint in his mouth, grinning as he waltzed across the wet tiles fully clothed.

I shrank back, going deeper into the water. He chuckled, then howled again.

The others surrounded me.

Thatcher Reed and Wells Ambrose, large boys in their academy uniforms. They didn't have bats, but they covered the exits to get out of the pool.

"All alone, *little* girl?" Ares stated, his eyes dancing wild. He flicked his joint butt into the pool water. "How unfortunate for you."

"I agree."

On the bleachers sat a boy, one I hadn't noticed on the stadium seating used for swim meets. Dorian Prinze was all alone, but he took up so much of the bleachers one would have thought they were miniature. They labored and screeched with his weight when he came down them, and he had a bat too. It wasn't spiked, but he still *had a bat*.

What the fuck?

I didn't know what this was, watching as Dorian twirled his bat as well. He pointed toward Wells and Thatcher at the various exits. "Get her out of there."

The two boys stripped.

Not completely, but they were definitely getting *naked*. Down to their boxers, they tossed their clothes, golden bodies stretching and flexing. Wells tossed me a wink before he did a side flip into the pool, and Thatcher jumped in his end cannonball-style. They came up with a snap of wet hair and slick muscles, proceeding to stroke out to me from various angles.

Freaking out, I splashed away from them, and from my closest exit, Wolf chuckled.

"Not so brave are you now, little," he said, winking. He pointed his bat toward Dorian. "Don't play with your food too much, Dorian."

Wolf muttered something about going to watch the door, chuckling the whole way, and all the while, their other bros homed in on me.

Wells got there first.

His long reach shot out, tugging me. I got an elbow out of the water and clipped him right in his steel pec. That shit fucking *hurt*, but it got the job done. Wells cursed, but I barely got around him before Thatcher bear-hugged me from behind.

"Such a pretty, pretty princess," he growled into my cheek, his tongue out and his earrings glistening from the pool lights. He actually *licked* my cheek like a fucking freak, and the feral noise he let out made my stomach curl. He grinned. "Mmm. Taste as good as you look. Like goddamn candy."

"Let me have a taste, bro," Wells crooned, getting closer. He seemed to have recovered from the job I did on his chest. His tongue came out too. "I like candy."

"Get the fuck off me!" I bucked, but big boy had a good hold. He locked his big beefy arms around me, and he wasn't letting go. I jabbed back. "Stop."

"Ooh, there's some spice in there, though." Thatcher had

his arms locked tight across my breasts, but that didn't stop him from feeling up my arms. "Is that cinnamon, princess?"

"Oh, I really, *really* like cinnamon," Wells stated, his eyes crazy and wild.

Was he getting *off* on this?

They both sounded as if they were. Wells stroked closer. "Don't be selfish, bro. Share."

"There's enough of her for both of us." Thatcher's arms unlocked enough to come down to my hips. He drew me back, his dick *hard* and right up against my ass. He pressed his face into my neck. "I'll take the back."

I kicked, screaming, and a thundering *twack* hit from somewhere in the pool room.

Like wood hitting metal.

Wells and Thatcher whipped around, me with them. Dorian pulled his bat off one of the pool's handrails.

"I said *out* of the pool." He almost sounded bored. His bat touched his brawny shoulder, his boys redirecting their attention to fulfilling a command.

"Stop it! Let me go!" I bucked, both boys with their hands on me and no escape. I was also a sucky-ass swimmer, so they got me with ease to the pool's handrails.

To Dorian.

The dark prince shot a hand out, grabbing me with his big mitts. He pressed me up against his big chest, academy uniform be damned.

He smelled so good, *raw* like heated flesh and scented boy. His breath was also minty, his eyes surging ebony coals.

He forgot about his friends. He forgot about everything when he strong-armed me and forced me back to one of the pool room's walls. He still had his bat in his hand, something he used to hook behind my neck and bring me closer to him.

I was hugged between two thick arms, his friends behind him. Thatcher and Wells had a fascination in their eyes. Like two boys wanting to play.

Wanting to play with you.

I had a dark thought in that moment, wondering if these boys would do something to me I didn't want done.

Would Dorian let them?

He scanned my eyes like he not only would but would ringlead that shit.

And that heat in his eyes didn't leave.

I'd seen this look before on him, like that day he'd spotted Principal Mayberry and me in the hallway together.

Like he hated. Like he hated *me*.

Pure.

All-consuming.

Hate.

He appeared as if he despised me, which made no fucking sense.

I didn't know this boy.

Even still, his dark gaze shifted across me, the bat digging into my neck so bad I thought he'd snap it in two. He had my hands pinned against his chest, trapped between my breasts and his hard pecs.

That was how hard he squeezed me.

This wasn't a lover's hug. This was how an enemy broke another into submission. I wriggled, but he only tightened the hold.

"Go to Wolf," he breathed over my mouth, hot while at the same time being cool. He still tasted like mint, but no gum. He turned toward his friends. "Leave."

Thatcher tsked. Like actually tsked like a goddamn loon. He was a little boy not getting his candy. He frowned. "D—"

"I'll kick every inch of your ass," he shot. "Leave *now*. Go to Wolf." He faced me again, his friends gathering their clothes, then ambling out of view in the distance. Dorian grinned. "Now what are we gonna do?"

I shot my head forward, but I'd give it to him.

He was quick.

He had the reflexes of an athlete, easily dodging the head-butt, but the attempt pissed him off. He chuckled manically as he grabbed my hands in one fist, then used his bat to spread my legs apart.

"Stop it. Stop it!"

He pressed the bat right between my legs. He smiled. "You're in my way, little fighter."

"What are you talking about?"

He inched up closer, and the air seeped from my lips. "And I don't like it when things are in my way."

I had no idea what he was talking about.

His bat didn't stop.

He moved slow with it, and my thighs trembled around it. My legs hugged the wood, and I swallowed hard. "Why are you doing this?"

He didn't stop, and I gasped when he was mere inches away from my pussy.

I throbbed. He was too *close*, and my teeth clacked when his hard body pressed against me. I'd dampened his dress shirt, the white material clinging to his hard chest. He noticed me staring at it and chuckled. "You like what you see?" he asked, his bat tap, tap, tapping between my quivering thighs. "Let's see how you like this."

My hips arched when he grazed my pussy, and I shot my head forward again.

He dodged it only too easily, angling his head away. The flick and sway of all that blond across his eyes only made him too sexy, and I hated myself for the thought.

I hated I wet my lips.

I hated I *drenched* over his bat like some psychopath, trembling as much from fear as something else I didn't like.

My nails bit into my secured fists as he rubbed that bat into my sex, his name falling breathily from my mouth.

He noticed.

He noticed a lot of things as he played. He smirked. "You

like this," he said, a statement. He eyed me, that lovely face so beautiful and wicked. "How much do you like it?"

He rubbed me again, rubbed me faster, harder. I shoved at him, but eventually I slacked, my teeth biting my lips. My nipples beaded bullet hard. I actually tried to rub them against him, but couldn't with how he held my arms.

"Dorian…"

That was when he stopped, full-on *stopped*. He pulled the bat from between my legs, leaving my thighs quaking beneath me. He hooked an arm above my head, his face washed of his wicked grins. His gaze smoldered. "You're to leave my school. I want you *out*."

I scanned his eyes, disoriented.

Unable to freaking breathe.

I still felt his bat between my legs, the rapid heat. "What?"

He chuckled like I'd said something funny, twirling the bat before touching it beside my head. "You're making a lot of noise for me. *Getting in my way*. You're to leave my school." He tipped my chin with the bat. "You don't want the alternative."

I didn't know what the fuck he was talking about, making noise for him? What the fuck?

He didn't say, but he did let go. My back hit the wall with the release, my wrists red and prickling from where his digits had pinched into me.

"You don't own this school." That was the only thing I could come up with. He didn't own this school.

He looked at me like he did.

He *smiled* at me as if it were so, a dark smile, a foreboding smile. He pointed that bat at me. "You either don't exist in this school or I make it so." He lifted his hand. "Your choice."

He touched the bat to his shoulder, waltzing out of the pool room. I touched my head back to the wall, looking up.

What the fuck just happened?

CHAPTER
TWELVE

Sloane

By the end of the school day, I'd been given a new name: Vapor. It was written on my locker when I went to get my things. Apparently, Dorian was literally trying to make it so I didn't exist. I was vapor. I was nothing.

The pranks started the next day.

It started out as little stuff, people throwing shit at me in class behind the teachers' backs. I got wads of paper tossed at me. Spitballs.

Amateur stuff.

I'd gotten more ridicule than that over the years with all the schools I'd been to. But by the end of the week, they upped their game.

People stopped acknowledging me, like literally looked the other way as if I didn't exist. When I did overhear people whispering, they used the word "Vapor" or "that girl." I'd literally become Voldemort, or the girl who should not be named, overnight.

And the pranks didn't stop.

I never saw people doing shit, but they somehow did it. I found sanitary napkins stuffed in my lockers. Like enough for them to fall out in an avalanche and make everyone laugh. Of course, when I looked at said laughing folks, they didn't look directly at me. I was still *Vapor* or *that girl*. I was apparently the idiot who'd pissed off the Legacy boys, and they were getting people to do shit in their honor.

I just didn't understand what I'd done.

I mean, I got that I'd talked back to Wolf. I had called him a bitch a time or two, but none of that had resulted in the hate that I'd gotten seemingly overnight from the dark prince. He'd come at me hot with little to no explanation.

And they still hung out with Bru.

He'd started his football stuff, and he now left before I woke up and returned long after I'd gotten home from school. He was at football practice. At least, that was what I'd had to sleuth about the house to discover. I found his football schedule on the fridge and gear in random places. He mostly kept it in the garage, but I still saw it.

My brother suddenly had this other life I wasn't a part of, and whenever I did catch him (aka tried to say hi to him), he barely looked at me. I was sure he'd heard about the whole "vapor" thing.

Not that he did anything about it.

I hadn't expected my little brother to fight my battles for me, but I assumed, unlike the rest of the school, he'd at least have my back. I knew we felt different about things that had occurred that first day at school. He was under the belief I'd gotten myself into this mess, but all this abuse from his "friends" was a new level.

Those dicks even had someone mutilate my gym stuff.

I'd literally caught some chick with a Court ring dunking my clothes in the girls' locker room toilets while her friends watched. I yelled at them, but they divided like scared little bitches, and when I went to tell my gym teacher about it, the man hadn't even looked at me. He just told me to get a new set from the extras before class.

And *he* hadn't used my name either.

Dorian Prinze and the other Legacy boys certainly had clout around here, and their latest prank came in my English class.

My bag was buzzing.

Like it was buzzing to the point where the teacher had to stop class and see what was going on. Everyone looked around but they homed in on my stuff when the sound was so obviously coming from my direction.

I made the mistake of opening my book bag publicly.

A million and a half dildos buzzed around in there, and the teacher asked me to leave class to take care of it. I dumped the whole thing in the trash, then went to my locker instead, too embarrassed and frustrated to go back to class. I thought the dildo nightmare was over.

But then I opened my locker.

More fell out, a never-ending sea of pleasure wands at my feet and right when the bell happened to ring. The hallway filled with students as I did all I could to stuff them all back into my locker.

Laughter ensued around me, mocking me, and this whole thing was getting completely ridiculous.

He's taking things too far.

I wasn't going anywhere, but I also wasn't submitting to the likes of this shit either. I'd been bullied before, and these Legacy guys weren't breaking me.

Dorian Prinze wasn't going to break me.

I slammed my locker, then stormed the halls.

I found Dorian at his locker with the rest of the Legacy spawn, laughing with all their women and, in Wells's case, a guy and a girl. It seemed he was pretty open with his tastes.

He saw me first when I charged up, mentioning something about "Pretty, pretty princess." Ares shot him a look, and Wells cleared his throat.

"Afternoon, Vapor," Wells corrected, the latter apparently being my official name, and Dorian barely looked up from his conversation.

A conversation he was having with my brother.

I recognized a Windsor Prep playbook when I saw it. Bru left his own copy around the house enough for me to see.

Currently, he was nose deep in it with the dark prince. I'd heard Dorian was actually the quarterback, the arrogant fuck.

I shoved him. Like legit, lost my mind and shoved Dorian in the middle of the hallway. The colossal man boy barely moved, a smirk to his ridiculously perfect pouty lips, but all activity in the hallway stopped.

His boys stepped around him immediately. Even Wells who was more or less the laid-back one. He puffed up like I'd actually taken a piece of candy from him this time.

Seeing all this activity obviously blew Bru's mind. I hadn't told him about my near assault, so all this was pretty much coming out of left field for him. I had no particular reason not to tell him about everything, but maybe in the back of my mind, I feared if he'd even care. I mean, my brother cared about me. Of course, *he'd care* but he also had been pretty vocal that I'd been the one bringing all this negative shit into my life.

He believed these guys to be his friends.

Maybe that was me falling on the sword a little bit too. His life hadn't been ruined by all this shit, and I didn't want to have to be the killjoy.

It still sucked when my brother growled at me in their defense.

"Sloane. What. The. Fuck?" Bru questioned, but even though I was falling on the sword, I wasn't *not* going to stand up for myself. I didn't care who his little friends were.

I edged around him, sneering right at the dark prince. "This sophomoric shit needs to stop *now*."

I admit I was acting braver than I felt in that moment. I'd never been handled this much in school, and Dorian was, well, Dorian. He was all presence, all commanding and beautiful. Where he moved people followed, and I might have found that sexy had I not known about the piece of shit he was.

The one who stomped all over people beneath his designer military boots.

He was the only one who didn't dress by the school's code. Even Ares buttoned up and tucked in his shirt by the time first period started. Today, Dorian had on a wool sweater shoved up to his big arms, that chrome Court ring blinging on his hand. His had rubies for the eyes, something I'd never seen on anyone else's.

Dorian raised a hand, and his boys relaxed. The activity in the hallway also proceeded to move.

God, why do they all *listen* to this asshole?

Because he was one, completely.

"I don't know what you're talking about," he said, eyes dancing at me. Without missing a beat, he went right back to talking to Bru. He flipped that playbook right open, even doing a little dramatic dampening of his finger before turning the page.

I admit I didn't think.

I grabbed him. I literally grabbed his arm, and he must have put up with it because he actually moved his big honking body. I think he found it funny because he started chuckling along the way.

I left a jaw-slacked Bru. Dorian's buddies even blinked their eyes. Ares growled. No doubt from my audacity. Even still, they all let me go with Dorian, and I didn't stop dragging their leader until I got him around a corner from all other eyes. I didn't care about anyone else seeing us, but I wasn't my brother's favorite person right now and didn't want to create a scene.

When I let go, Dorian licked his lips, eyeing me.

"Glad you got that out of your system," he said. His hands shot out, and then, he was on me. Chest to chest.

Breath to breath.

Our heated breaths intermingled, and his wicked gaze gleamed on me like Hades in the Underworld. His smile was coy.

"Have you finally decided to submit, little fighter?" he asked me, his grin stretched. "I have to say, you could have just left town. Or maybe since your eyes like to fuck me so much you couldn't help but get one last touch. For the road?"

He grabbed my hand, placing it on his chest. Hard muscle formed solidly underneath my palm, and visions of him on that football field assaulted my already fogging brain. Him half naked tossing a football with his friends. He was golden and beautiful as he caught a football not a foot in front of my face. It was a power play that day what he'd done.

Just like this.

I shoved at him, and he got my hands.

"I'm assuming that's a no," he said, a pout to his full lips, and I jerked my hands away.

I growled, "I'm not leaving." He couldn't force me out of his school, and the pranks forced upon me by his minions wouldn't work. I sneered, "I don't care what you or your little Court groupies with those gorilla rings do."

He stared down at his, fisting it before smiling at me.

"Oh, I wouldn't say that." He crowded me, his big body enveloping me against the lockers. "That would be a mistake."

Pure venom seeped from his voice, but with him, he liked to put a sweetness behind it. Like a deadly viper toying with his kill.

I supposed he really did like to play with his food like Ares said.

His thumb touched my lip, and I hissed.

His smile stretched.

"Be careful, Noa Sloane." Reaching down, he squeezed my hip. I kneed at him and all he did was wrap a hand around the back of it. He jerked me forward, my mound brushing his length. He was hard, and he wasn't being shy about showing that. He even ground on me a little, his gleeful expression cruel and equally dangerous.

I pushed at his chest. "Stop."

He didn't. He leaned in, way too close. I could nearly taste him again.

My throat constricted. He had me right where he wanted me, completely locked beneath him, and it probably didn't matter who came down this hallway.

It probably didn't matter if I screamed.

The dark prince had too much power around here. He had too much everything.

"I am going to make you scream for me," he promised, that venomous smile in his voice now. "And it'll be too sweet to break you."

"Good luck with that," I bit at him, and he held me back by the throat.

His grip tightened. "The dildos were a gift," he said, actually admitting to them. Though odds were, he didn't do them himself. His eyes narrowed. "When I take you, it will be much, *much* harder."

"Eat shit," I hissed, but the flash of the thought tingled a tightness between my legs.

It was like he knew.

His thumb drew a soft line down my throat, one that hummed warmth in my core.

And slicked wetness.

I had to shift my thighs just to keep them from shaking. He eyed my lips.

"Do me a favor, huh?" he asked, tilting his head. "Stretch yourself real good for me? It'll make it so much easier for you later."

He let go. He was truly vile. The asshole actually chuckled to himself as he strode down the hallway. Like I'd just made this the best game for him.

I probably had.

The day continued to be the day from hell when school finally did wrap up, and I got to leave the hellhole that was Windsor Prep Academy. My car hadn't been where I had left it, and when I finally found it, my dad's Chevelle had been parked where Ares Mallick had claimed his spot was. My tires had been slashed, and the words "Student of the Month" had been written over and replaced on the sign.

It said *Legacy's Bitch* instead.

CHAPTER
THIRTEEN

Sloane

My gaze jerked up when the little rabbit cruised into the headmaster's office, always going a mile a minute.

Bow stilled upon seeing me.

"I was just getting the mail for some teachers," she said, her head bowed. "I help some of them out by getting it in between my classes."

She then proceeded to head over to the teachers' mailboxes, completely avoiding eye contact with me, and I shook my head. She too had been avoiding me since Legacy had started blackballing me. I had honestly expected it from everyone else.

Not her.

She'd always been the nice one, but even she had stopped talking to me.

She even sat with them all at lunch.

That first day I had simply thought I'd lost her. I'd still been trying to dodge her. She clung like glue when she was around, and my inner introvert screamed every time. There was nothing wrong with her, but I'd never been cool with people hovering over me.

I had gotten into the a la carte line that day honestly thinking I'd won, but then I spotted her already in the courtyard. She'd been tucked between her huge-ass brother and Dorian Prinze, and I knew exactly what was going on there.

They'd gotten to her too.

In front of me now, Bow swallowed, backing away. She'd gotten the mail and what other reason did she have to be in there with me. She said nothing as she left, and I dropped my sketchpad, heading into the hallway after her. I was student assistant for Principal Mayberry during this period. I had a free one and figured I'd fill it in the headmaster's office since she seemed cool enough.

The woman wouldn't miss me for a few moments. She literally never came out of her office when I was there. It was her free period too, and she said she preferred quiet time with no disturbances. Her secretary even left for the hour, so assisting the headmaster during this time was a match made in heaven for me. I did tend to be a lone wolf.

I tracked down Bow, hard to do since she walked so fast. She literally was like a ball of energy. Like because she was so small, she had to overcompensate. I ended up finding her at her locker, and when I did, I crossed my arms. "How's lunch with Legacy been?"

She'd been grabbing a book but stopped. She faced me. "Sloane…"

"You know, I guess I shouldn't be surprised," I said, shrugging. "You are Legacy after all, right?"

I'd crossed them, so why not her too?

Her face charged in color. "It's not like that."

"Well, what's it like, then?"

She lifted and dropped her hands. "I didn't want you to have any more trouble than you were obviously having," she said, surprising me. "And it's not like they gave me a choice. I didn't want to fight and make things worse for you."

So she'd given in? Perfect.

She closed her locker lightly. "And I'm not stupid, Sloane. I know you were dodging me between your classes." She gazed around. "That I was annoying you."

Well, fuck. I whipped my hair around, and she chewed her lip. I put a hand out. "I shouldn't have done that."

I was rethinking a lot of things now. A lot of things like, was all this labor I was putting myself through worth it? *Was going to this school* worth it? I'd had to call Callum for help getting me some new tires, and that had been really fun trying to lie my way through how that happened. I'd ended up telling him I'd hit a patch of ice.

In the middle of fall.

Since I knew Midwestern weather to be temperamental, I'd gotten away with it, but that hadn't stopped him from questioning me. He'd even asked if everything was okay, stating he could come visit Bru and me sooner. He was still traveling but could make arrangements.

I turned him down, passing the help off. I could take care of myself.

I could take care of this.

I cuffed my arms. "I'm sorry about that," I said to her, honest. "I did you bogus, and that's on me."

She nodded, but still gazed around the hallway. She was Legacy herself and still answered to these creeps. She started to leave, but I found myself going with her.

"I was actually wondering something, little rabbit—"

"Little rabbit?" she asked, turning.

I smiled a little. "Well, you do kind of run around here like your ass is on fire."

Her face lit up, all that cheery brightness returning. I was surprised to find I missed it, her pep and happy. She hugged her books. "Little rabbit? Like a nickname?"

She said that unbelievably cute, and I laughed. "Yeah, like a nickname."

Her grin widened. "I could be about that. Cool. Little rabbit."

She tested the term out, as if awed to hear such a thing. Surely, she and her friends had little things they called each other? I smiled. "I was wondering how well you're doing in our algebra class."

This was a leading question. I could assume how well she was doing. She was a *sophomore* in a senior-level math class.

She shrugged, being modest. "I do okay. Why?"

"I could use a tutor," I said. "I could be doing better."

I did all right in class and could do better. But I also knew she was the only link I had to these boys. If I wanted to strike, *find out something* I needed to know more about who they were and how they worked.

This way of thinking was completely cheap I knew, but they hadn't just gotten to me.

They'd gotten to Bru.

I didn't even get to see my brother anymore he was so busy. Dorian Prinze had taken away the only thing I had and soiled my name on top of it. Hell, Dorian had done worse than that to my name.

He'd completely removed it.

Upon my proposal, Bow gazed around again. Really, us having any kind of open conversation like this could get back to her brother and his friends, but I had to take the risk. Dorian had gotten to my brother.

And I had to do something.

"I don't know, Sloane," she said, and I deflated, frowning. It was probably a dumb idea anyway, and using Bow, even dumber. She had been nice to me after all.

I lifted a hand. "Sorry. I know you don't want to make waves."

"I don't." She chewed her lip again but surprised me

when she got out her phone. "What's your number? You can probably come by after school or something…"

"Come by?"

She nodded. "I could help you with some of our assignments. Today would be good. I have a student council meeting until three thirty, but after that, I'm free. Let me give you my address."

She was being serious.

This is what you need.

It did feel weird, though, giving her my number so she could text me her information.

"We can't just meet at my place?" I asked. Being in the belly of the beast would be a good thing. I could poke around, get some information, but getting caught at a Legacy house was more than a bad idea. I could probably just pick her brain about her brother and his friends. I didn't necessarily have to be at one of their houses.

Bow smiled, putting away her phone after texting me her address. "Thatcher won't be around until super late. He and the other guys have football practice until like six. Drives my mom crazy since he's always late for dinner."

Well then, this was perfect.

"Be there around four?" she stated, backing down the hallway, and I nodded. I just needed a little information. I had that, and she could go back to ignoring me, and I could go back to being Vapor. What I was about to do wasn't wrong at all.

And if I told myself that enough times, I may actually believe it.

CHAPTER
FOURTEEN

Sloane

Rainbow Reed didn't live off the beaten path like Bru and me.
Where we virtually had no neighbors on our little hilltop in
the sky, Bow was in the middle of the ritziest cul-de-sac I'd
ever seen in my entire life. I honestly questioned if I was in
California taking a tour of the stars' homes considering how
each house just seemed to get bigger as I passed.

And not just bigger.

Lush gardens and old brick homes donned with ivy and
regency elements filled my vision. She also lived in a gated
community. I had to be buzzed in after they made "a call" to
the Reed Manor to confirm I was an allowed visitor.

They had a manor.

This was a new level of wealth here, and I already questioned coming around. I wasn't particularly excited about
using Bow to dig up dirt on Dorian, but I'd do what I had
to do.

Like I said, he drew first blood.

I used those thoughts to take me up to Reed Manor. I was let in by another man at a wrought-iron gate. He directed me up to the main house, and I had to drive a little bit to get to the circle driveway. Bow lived in an aged brick home that had many staff grooming and trimming the hedges. They all waved at me in a friendly fashion upon passing, and I smiled, trying to look like I saw shit like this every day.

A man in bibs knocked at my door.

I jumped before rolling down the window of the Chevelle.

He smiled at me. "Noa Sloane, I presume?"

"Sloane," I said, eyeing the house behind him. This house was something else, flower boxes filled with light pink roses and even columns outside. Where Bru's and my place was more modern, this place had an ancient storybook look.

The man nodded. "I'm Henry, the Reeds' groundskeeper. I'm here to take your car to the garages if that's all right."

The man said *garages*.

Well, all right then.

I gave this Henry my keys, heading toward the main house with my purse and book bag. I did bring my textbooks because I planned to study. I was just going to casually ask Bow a couple questions about Dorian and the others.

This wasn't going to be some kind of CIA mission. Bow was a nice girl, and I wasn't trying to take advantage of her. Odds were, since her brother's friends weren't really *her friends*, she didn't know too much anyway.

"Sloane!"

Bow waved spritely at me down a shiny hallway. Her housekeeper Janet had let me in, and I wondered how many staff these people actually had.

"Hey," I said, eyeing the interior. Her house was *crazy*, an actual chandelier glistened the ceiling from above, and they had wall sconces with candles in them. Though, I supposed those could have been electric. "You got a nice place."

"Thanks. Want to get a snack before we study?"

She'd changed into shorts and a T-shirt, and I had too before coming over. I slipped off my sandals, then followed her to the kitchen, where several staff members were hard at work cooking stuff and wiping down counters. Several platters of cakes, cookies, and desserts lined the counters like a buffet, and my eyes twitched wide.

"You guys having a party?" I laughed, but then she picked up one of the platters. She handed it to me.

"I guess I did go a little overboard," she said, rolling her eyes. She chuckled. "I just didn't know what you liked."

I nearly choked on the macaroon I took a bite of. I hit my chest. "Sorry?"

She took the platter back, laughing again. Her face reddened as she looked at me. "Janet said it would probably be too much. That two teenage girls couldn't possibly eat it all. But like I said, I just didn't really know what you liked so…"

All this was for… us?

Staff continued to put food on the counter. People were *still* making food. I was asked what I'd like to drink too before another platter was forced in my face.

"We have watercress and tuna salad as options today, Miss Sloane," the staff member said to me, smiling. She directed the little sandwiches toward me. "But if you want something different, we can make another option for you. Miss Reed told us to be prepared to mix it up if you wanted something different."

Holy shit.

"Uh, these are fine." I took a tuna, feeling obligated. Bow had filled this whole kitchen up with food for our study session.

And now, I really felt like shit.

I took a bite and didn't fail to notice how excited it made her to see me try it. I waved the sandwich. "Really good."

"Great." Her fists balled. Like she almost wanted to punch

the air in victory. The way she acted it was like she never had
people over.

But then again, knowing who her brother was…

Sheer intimidation alone may keep people away, and since
Bow didn't play up all that Legacy shit, something told me
folks may not want to take the risk to get closer to her. She
certainly came with a lot of baggage.

It was either bow or break when it came to those boys and,
apparently, I was stupid enough to get caught up within their
crosshairs.

I finished the sandwich quick, then brushed my hands off
on my shorts. Bow's staff was ready with napkins too, but I
turned them down. Really, the service around here was boss
as fuck.

Bow said we could take whatever we wanted up to her
room with us to study, and after we both picked a couple
things, we took the journey through her large house. She gave
me a little tour on the way, pointing out the guest rooms and
her parents' room. They had their own wing, I guess, and
good for them. It was their house.

"Grandma's room," Bow said, breezing past that. "She's
not well, so we need to be quiet."

I nodded, not pushing her on that. We passed Thatcher's
room too, but I wasn't curious enough to try to make up an
excuse to poke around in there. I did need dirt, but with how
accommodating Bow was being, I was already feeling like
shit about my plan for today.

Instead, I let her take me to her room, which was decorated for a princess high in her castle. Her four-poster bed
was donned in golden silks, the oak floors polished and pris-
tine. She appeared to be a heavy reader and had one of those
bookshelves where a ladder was needed just to get to the top
of it. It wouldn't surprise me if she'd used it just that morning
since there was a nice little stack of reads by it. Besides that,

nothing was out of place, so she probably had just used it this morning.

"On a scale of one to ten. How ridiculous did I just embarrass myself downstairs?" She pressed her hands to her face. "Janet really told me we shouldn't have made that much food." Her leg shook, her hands balled. She really was worried. "I'm sorry. Mom and Dad always say I do too much. I can't help it. My ADHD makes me all over the place."

She laughed that off, like it didn't bother her so much but was a reality. I supposed that explained a couple things too. She really did go a mile a minute. I smiled at her. "It was cool."

"Really?" Her mouth parted. "I know it's a lot. I'm know I'm a lot." She chuckled. "I really didn't mean to be all up on you when we first met. I tend to do that. I know it can be annoying."

She chewed her lip after that last statement, and the nervous laughter that followed was more dry. I started to say something, but her door breezed open and a man the size of a building barreled inside. He wore a suit sans tie, his hair dark, and he looked so much like Thatcher my eyes twitched wide.

"Door stays open when boys are over," the man grunted, letting go of the doorknob. He took in the room. "Where's the boy?"

Bow and I glanced around, then she rolled her eyes.

"Dad, when have you ever known me to bring a boy over?" she asked. She placed a hand toward me. "It's just me and Sloane."

The man directed his gaze toward me. It was uncanny how much he looked like Thatcher. I supposed that made sense considering this was their dad, but Bow was so petite and little I wondered if she got anything from him. This guy was a semi. He frowned. "Sloane?" He eyed me. "Janet said some boy named Noa Sloane was here."

Bow chuckled. "Yeah, Dad. That's Noa Sloane. She's a friend from school. We're studying today."

He grunted in my direction. Though, I noticed there was a sizable sigh in his big body upon noticing I wasn't a boy. I raised a hand. "Happens all the time, Mr. Reed."

I mean, my parents gave me a traditional boy name, constant confusion a given whenever anyone met me.

He nodded. "I see. Well, nice to meet you, Noa."

"She goes by Sloane, Dad." Bow placed her big blue eyes upon her dad, and something told me she was a complete daddy's girl the way the large man tilted his head at her.

"Sloane, then," he said, then directed a hand toward Bow. His eyes crinkled softly at her. "Sorry about that, baby girl."

She merely laughed in response, but then, the man frowned.

He pointed. "Rules still stand about the boys, though," he said. He left the room on a laugh to himself, and Bow lifted her eyes again.

"Sorry about him," she said. "I'm honestly surprised he didn't bring my god dads up here with him if he thought I had a boy in here." She stopped when my eyes narrowed. She laughed. "Wells's and Dorian's dads. They're all around here someplace. Tonight's poker night for them. I'm sure they'll all eat whatever we don't."

She chuckled on the end there, and my jaw freaking dropped. I put my hand out. "Wait. The dads of Wells and…" I paused, frowning. "*Dorian* are your godfathers?"

She shrugged that off, casual about it. She nodded. "Mmhmm. They've all known each other since they were kids. Ares's dad too. Though, he's not my god dad. All our parents are good friends, though."

But god dad status? What the fuck? But then, Bow got up. She went to a pushpin board above her computer desk that had a bunch of photos and stuff on it. She plucked one, then gave it to me. "That's them. They all used to play lacrosse together at Windsor Prep."

I stared at the photo, five guys in total. If she hadn't told me these were the dads, I would have thought they were the kids. They were the spitting image of the boys who'd come to hurricane through my life since I arrived.

Bow pointed them out. "Wells's dad and Dorian's dad," she said, pointing to a guy with cropped hair, then a blond respectively. Her finger touched the biggest guy in the photo. "Thatcher's and my dad."

Definitely him, Thatcher's twin. Their dad stood next to the tallest guy, a lacrosse stick on his arm. Seriously, this tall guy had to be Ares's dad.

"Ares's dad, Ramses," Bow confirmed.

I scanned the photo of the five. There was a tall blond guy in the middle with long hair. "This guy?"

"Oh, that's LJ, my third and final god dad." She took the photo. "He doesn't have kids, but he's just as protective. I'm the only girl amongst the kids, so all my godfathers tend to hover."

My gaze circulated the photo, stopping on who she stated was Dorian's dad. As with the rest of the crew, he was Dorian's clone. He was the only one not smiling in the photo, though, and Dorian most certainly didn't mind flashing his dark grin. I think he did that on purpose, the expression simply simmering with cruel venom.

I wet my lips. "You said this is Dorian's dad?" I asked, and she nodded. "Did Dorian's mom go to Windsor Prep too?"

I asked casually, and again, she acknowledged that.

"Their names are Royal and December," she announced, and they certainly were regal names. Fitting, I supposed. She placed the photo down, and I watched when she picked up her book. She obviously wanted to get started on tonight's homework, but I certainly had more questions. If their families really were that close, she'd most definitely know a lot about the Prinzes.

And I wanted to know as much as possible.

CHAPTER
FIFTEEN

Dorian

"Good work today, man." I'd give credit where credit was due, taking Bruno Sloane's hand. I shook, then snapped it after practice. "Good hustle today."

The kid was actually pretty decent on the field. He kept up with us, and what had started as a way to get under his sister's skin, might actually turn out in Windsor Prep's favor. At least, when it came to football. The kid was fast, strong, and caught everything I threw at him.

He could stand a good chance at becoming quarterback next year after I left, and where Thatcher and Wells might disagree with that (they'd always been aiming for the spot), they may not mind. They were getting along with the kid too. I always saw them talking with him, in the hallways and at lunch and shit. The three's teamwork on the field was impeccable, and something told me I wasn't the only one who didn't completely hate the kid.

Even if I wanted to.

My hate was obviously reserved for his sister, but it was

harder to pass off to her brother, who actually took direction and did so humbly, respectfully. It was easy to want to treat him as an equal. He was a genuinely nice guy and did enjoy the game. Most people around here looked at me and the other Legacy guys as gods, completely enamored and were a bunch of follower fucks. Bru was more of a leader, though, which was rare with all this alpha shit running around on the field.

"Thanks, man," Bru said, and like stated, humble. It sucked I was trying to drive him out of this town, but he was a casualty. Noa Sloane was still in my fucking way, and we hadn't managed to break her yet. She was around, still in the way, and didn't seem any closer to leaving.

I apparently wasn't laboring hard enough, but in the meantime, we at least had a good player on the field. I slapped Bru's back in the locker room, letting him go. He left the locker room, but Wolf caught our exchange as he'd been coming out the showers. He had a towel cinched at his waist, the other drying all that crazy hair.

"Don't get too fucking attached," he grumbled, tossing the towel he'd been using for his hair. He opened his locker. "Kid has a target on his head."

He didn't need to fucking tell me that. I was the one who put the target on it. I smirked. "Just taking advantage of the fact that we have some decent fucking support on the field for once."

"Fuck you," Thatch stated, coming into the room. His hair wet, he had nothing on but a pair of jeans, and Wells flanked him. They both shouldered past me, obviously in their feelings about what I said, and I rolled my eyes.

They must have not been too sore about it, because they did tap my fist on their way out after they'd dressed. I told them not to be late tomorrow since they'd been dicking around before practice. This was something else Bruno Sloane didn't do, and I reminded them of that.

They both jostled me, and after they left, I tugged a shirt on. "They could learn a lot from the target. Bru was hustling his ass out there, unlike them."

"Maybe." Wolf stood. Fully dressed, he closed his locker. "But the guy's still a target." His eyes narrowed. "His sister is still the enemy."

We kept our enemies close, hence the connection to Bruno, but I didn't need him to remind me of the rules.

I fucking made them.

"Right, Wolf," I said, turning away. It was all I could do not to start some shit with him. Ares Mallick may be my best friend, but I had to check his ass more often than not. We were two guys filled with testosterone and malice, a deadly combination. Wolf had his own reasons for that, and though I respected him, I didn't put up with it. Nor did he put up with my bullshit. Honestly, between the two of us, we flew off the handle just to start shit, but I really didn't have time for it today.

He tapped my back since I didn't give him my fist, pretending to be busy getting my belt on. He left after that, and a sophomore player came in to get me after I was all alone.

"Hey, Prinze. Your mom is looking for you out by the field."

I didn't think I'd heard him right. Neither of my parents came to practice, but I nodded at him. I honestly expected to find a fuck buddy or something when I got out there, maybe someone using the excuse of my mom as a way to get me out of the locker room quicker.

Girls had attempted crazier things to get my attention, so imagine my surprise when my mom was standing out near the field. She was on the sidelines actually, still dressed for work in her heels and pantsuit. She was pacing the track surrounding the field when I jogged up to her.

"Mom." I went quick, *worried*. She didn't come to my practices. In fact, the last time I'd come upon her pacing like this, things had been bad.

Stuff had happened.

My family had experienced more tragedy than what should be humanly possible, most of which had occurred before I was even born. I'd heard stories, tales of murder and darkness and a chilling family legacy well before any breaths I'd breathed. I was experiencing the backlash of it now, but even with as numb as I started to get to bullshit occurring in my life, I hadn't been prepared to come outside and see my mom pacing rogue on the racetrack.

And with flushed cheeks.

She'd looked like she's seen a ghost, and I pulled her off to the side. "Mom, what's going—"

She wrestled around in her purse, moved things around like crazy. She seemed frazzled, panicked, and when she pulled out a bag holding a long skinny object, *I* fucking panicked. I didn't know why she was showing me this.

"This was delivered to my office," she said, holding it up. She waved it at me. "Why was this delivered to my office, Dorian Prinze?"

I eyed what she had in the bag with no words. I mean, I knew what the thing fucking was.

She shoved a note in my face.

"It came with this," she huffed, gazing around, and I read the note while she took the bag back.

"*Ask your son about this,*" the note said. "*Thought you should know.*"

No sooner had I read the note than she was shoving the bag back in my face. Inside was a long stick.

A pregnancy test with blue lines.

My mother was *basically on the football field* showing me a pregnancy test, and the note she apparently got to go with it. She shook it. "What is the meaning of this, Dorian?" she asked, her voice low. "Did you get a girl pregnant?"

The words came out whispered, thick and loaded with emotion. I had no idea what the fuck was going on, but whatever it was had nothing to do with me. I shook my head. "Mom—"

"Don't you lie to me, Dorian." She gazed around. No one was out here because practice was over. Everyone had gone home, the field cleared. She hugged her arms. "Dear God, are you making me a grandmother?"

My jaw dropped, fucking shocked to hell. "No, Mom. No—"

"Then what is this?" she whisper-shouted. "Why did someone have this delivered to my office *via carrier* instructing me to ask my eighteen-year-old son about it!"

Shaking, she shoved her hand in her hair, and I took the note from her, reading it again. This was a goddamn mistake. I hadn't gotten a girl fucking pregnant.

At least, I didn't think I had.

"Dorian—"

"I use protection, Mom," I gritted. I couldn't believe I was actually having this conversation with my mother—on the football field. I homed in. "Dad would fry my ass."

"*I* will fry your ass." My mom cursed all the time. She did because sometimes, I'd overhear her, but she always tried to act like she didn't around me.

This time she hadn't bothered.

"Dorian Prinze, if you've made me a grandmother, I'm going to ship your butt to boarding school so fast you won't even know what *girls are*." She directed a finger in my face. "Now, tell me the truth."

"I am, Mom," I said, kind of panicked now. "I didn't. I wouldn't. I'm responsible."

"Yeah, well, honey. Sometimes responsibility doesn't cut it." She gazed around, even though no one was there. "Sometimes good intentions aren't good enough. I know things have been hard. I know I haven't always had it together. I know you've been left to fend for yourself these past few months after…" She paused, her eyes shining. Like she was on the cusp of tears but fighting it. "After everything with Charlie."

My stomach clenched.

"I know that, more often than not lately, I've needed you and your father's help to keep things running smoothly, but…"

"You've been fine, Mom. I swear it." I looked around, hating to see her fucking cry. It was only worse because it was something I'd potentially done. I didn't make my mom cry. I only made her smile, a promise I made because she had been struggling. But it hadn't been a big deal. Dad and I filled in the gaps and would always be there for her. She'd do the same and always did. I faced her. "Mom, this is a mistake. Probably someone working up shit."

"Dorian…" Her faced scrunched up, and she covered her mouth. I assumed so I couldn't see her cry. She shook her head. "I need to go."

"Mom—"

"I said I need to go. We'll talk about this later with your father."

Shit, when Dad found out…

He really would fry my ass. My mom would have nothing left *to* fry.

Mom started walking away, but when I chased after, she told me we'd all talk about this tonight. We needed to have my father there so we could discuss things, her words.

What the fuck just happened?

I grabbed my legs after she left, scanning the grass.

"Maybe you shouldn't mess with people's lives so much."

I turned, righting. Noa Sloane sat in the middle of the bleachers.

She frowned. "Because it sucks, doesn't it? People *working shit up* in your life? Causing chaos?"

My words stated back to me, I saw red.

She waltzed down the bleachers in her little booty shorts, the confidence of a queen in her stride. She thought she'd gotten something over on me, paid *me* a lesson. She lifted her chin. "You fucked with my life, Prinze. You're *fucking* with my brother, and because you are, you're fucking with me." Her frowned deepened. "You've slashed my tires, had your friends manhandle me, and turned the entire school against me."

I'd given her an option to leave. I'd told her to do that, or I'd make her disappear. I'd given her an option. I'd been generous, gracious even.

She was going to wish she'd taken the fucking deal.

I'd shown her mercy before. She stumbled upon shit bigger than her that night she got in Wells's way. I'd given her the benefit of the doubt.

My mistake.

I ran at her. I could get across a football field in seconds, and there was no getting away once I gained momentum.

Noa fucking Sloane didn't have a chance.

She screamed when I grabbed her, but there was no one to hear her, all lifelines gone, and it was just us out here. Her chest collided with mine, and I took her with me into the bleachers, lodging her between them on the creaking metal.

"Get the fuck off me!" She kicked, clawed me. She scratched the shit out of my arms and neck, but I wasn't letting her go. She was *mine*, my ass to own.

My ass to take when I wanted.

I'd promised her she was going to scream for me, my cock instantly hard at the thought. This was probably some kind of real sick shit, pinning her outside where whoever wanted to look could fucking come along and look. All reasonable and logical thought evaded me. This girl had become my obsession in little more than a tango with me, a vice with her little shorts and bare midriff top. Her naked shoulder eased out of one of the sides, strikingly tan and luscious. She'd gone home first, obviously changing before coming back to witness what she'd believed would be my demise. She'd clearly set this shit up.

I grinned. "You get off making people hurt," I hissed. I jerked her to me. "Making my mother *fucking* cry."

"Dorian—"

Her slender body quivered beneath me, soft hips and an even softer ass. I got a handful beneath her booty shorts.

"Don't touch me," she ground out, but she had a poor poker face. Her eyes rolled back the instant my hand slipped beneath her cutoffs, breaths panting and belly trembling. She was reacting to me.

She liked what I was doing to her.

I was fucking steel beneath my jeans, the fact she was fighting me making me even harder.

"How bad do you want this cock inside you?" I asked, sounding manic to even myself. I didn't take girls like this, fighting me like this. What was the fucking point? I got a lay in under a minute with a text. I growled. "How much do you think about me when you're using those dildos?"

"Fuck you," she snapped, and I bit my teeth at her. It made her lips quiver, her body tremble.

"You're a bad liar, little fighter," I said, my finger tracing the line of her fly. I started to play with it, but I grabbed her hand instead. I made her touch me through my jeans, and she hissed again.

Hell, I fucking did too.

I took a chance. She could have easily snapped my dick off.

She didn't.

I forced myself into her palm, made her cup me until the tension eased out of her hand, and she was squeezing me back.

"Dorian," she warned, but still stroked me. "I—"

I kissed her, borderline fucking manic. We were playing a dangerous game here, one I wanted to win.

She kissed me back, melded beneath me when she not only rubbed my dick but forced her hips up to meet me. She was a greedy little thing, this little fighter.

"You want this cock in your mouth?" I grunted, and I didn't care if she wanted it or not. She was going to get it, take me. *I owned her.* I bit her lips apart. "Open your mouth."

She did, letting my tongue in, her taste exploding around me. It hazed my head until I couldn't see straight, and all I could taste was candy lip gloss. This girl was making too much noise fucking everywhere. Especially in my mind.

I unzipped my fly, taking myself out and guiding her up. She looked like an erotic vision waiting there to receive me. She may not have wanted this at the start, but the lust in her eyes told of something different now.

"Beg me for it." She was going to submit to me. She was going to *admit* I owned her. "Beg to suck my cock."

Her eyes hazed, charged with heavy need, and I nearly forced myself on her. I waited. She was going to take it because she wanted it, the *real* win here. I'd own her because she'd want me to own her.

Her lips parted. "I want it," she panted, blinking like she wasn't even sure if she knew where the words were coming from. She nodded. "I want to suck you. I want to taste you."

I blinked, shocked myself. In fact, my dick kicked against my hand, and I nearly rolled off her. I didn't know if I liked how readily I was reacting to her.

I angled forward instead.

She came up to meet me, on her elbows, and when I pushed the head past her full lips, I nearly blew my load.

Holy fuck.

I shifted, in my own fucking haze as this girl not only took me to the back of her throat but tongued my shaft on retreat. I growled, easing her hair out of her ponytail and coiling it tight around my fist.

"Open up for me," I gritted, trying to maintain a semblance of control. I felt like I was on the brink of losing it, literally about to spill into her mouth like I didn't jerk myself off at least three times a day. Most of the time, I didn't need assistance, a groupie bitch wanting a taste.

Noa Sloane wasn't a groupie bitch. Her perfect fucking lips around my cock sent me into ecstasy. Never-ending strands of silk hair clenched beneath my fist as I gripped her to hold on for the ride.

She moaned over me, holding my hips, and bobbing her head below. She was goading me to spill into her mouth, even more when she palmed and played with my balls. She knew what she was doing, releasing my shaft to slide one into her mouth.

Holy shit.

I gripped the bleachers, needing to push this chick off me. I was losing my goddamn head and didn't like it.

I came in seconds.

At least it felt like it, my roar into the bleachers as I pumped into her throat again and again. At one point, I believed I hurt her. Her eyes swam in tears, but even still, she continued to suck me off, suck me *down*. She drank my seed greedily, but before she could finish, I pulled her mouth away.

I kissed her again. I shouldn't have, so fucking dangerous, but the need to taste her mouth hit me like a goddamn train, and I lost it.

What the fuck?

I tasted myself on her, a lethal combination me and her. It made me think about her taste and if her pussy tasted as good as her mouth did.

I couldn't take the chance in knowing.

I just knew I'd lose my mind again, and this game we were playing *I* would lose.

Her eyes were closed when I came away, her chest trembling, her lips pinked and angrily bruised. She wanted more, and she wanted me to give it to her.

I didn't.

Instead, I tucked myself away, zipping up my fly.

"Not bad," I said, not missing the twitch in her eye. I stood. "I've had better."

A bald-faced fucking lie, but that didn't mean what I said sounded like it.

I didn't catch her response to my words in the end. I left. She had a terrible poker place, and I wasn't about to stick around.

I didn't need her seeing if mine was just as shitty.

CHAPTER
SIXTEEN

Dorian - age 16

Parties at Pembroke University were a bitch to get to, but they were worth it for a few hours out of town and a good time. Ares and I loaded up my Audi with a few girls, a six-pack, and some smoke. We'd even been feeling gracious this evening and brought Wells and Thatcher along for the more than two-hour drive. I supposed they were getting their corruption pretty early only being freshman this year, but the two shitheads were into way more foul shit than I'd been just last year. I came to Windsor Prep only *slightly* less corrupted, but once Ares and I realized what being Legacy of some of the elite families of Maywood Heights meant upon entering high school?

Yep, we'd been good as opportunists, and we took full advantage of that. The college party tonight had been one of those advantages. Graduates from Windsor Prep ruled Pembroke-U, most of the alums rolling through it. The four of us Legacy kids were greeted like gods to the party filled with more booze and women than any of us could ever consume.

Though, we sure tried.

We'd made Ares the designated driver, so he was only slightly less intoxicated than the rest of us. I'd lost him first, then Wells and Thatcher second to the party at a multilevel home in the upper westside hills. We had no idea whose house this was.

Who fucking cared?

The DJ played on the top level, indoor pool flashing with neon lights below and filled with half-naked *women*. Not girls. The fellas and I had ditched our female companions sometime between the car and the bar. There was much better ass to own here tonight. I'd already seen several posts on social media about what the girls we'd brought here were up to in our absence, though. Something told me they were getting just as much out of this party as we were. It'd been an honor to come with us tonight, a mutual exchange. They were getting their stories, and we were getting ours.

I was fucking *baked*.

I had a blond on my lap and a brunette under my right arm, our little party of three passing a joint around. They had the best bud at these parties, and I was coming away with more than one story tonight. I sat back and enjoyed it, one girl asking me if I wanted a drink while the other asked if I wanted to get out of there—with her friend. Both options sounded nice, but I had to take a leak.

I left them to make out with each other. Trying to find a fucking bathroom in this place was hard with all the weed smoke that filled it. I eventually found the bathroom line but wasn't trying to deal with that.

I ended up using a plant.

Not one of my finer displays, but I wasn't going to go outside like some barbarian. I did my business, then started to go back to the girls, but some sighing took more of my interest.

Heavy pants and excited moans from nearby shot my cock

up, and I wondered if it was a female party that needed a third. Ares and I had lost our virginities together, but not *together*. We'd been in the same house, different rooms screwing separate chicks.

I was wasted enough where participating in my first orgy didn't sound like a particularly bad idea. And if there were dudes, I didn't care, as long as they kept their hands (and parts) to themselves. I was a pussy killer only, but had no problem having other guys around. One of my best friends, Wells, was bi. Wasn't a thing.

I edged a look through the plant (not the one I'd pissed in) and spotted a couple on the other side.

A guy and a girl were there, and he had her pinned against the wall, luscious red hair gripped in his fist.

He jerked his conquest back by it, laughing as he forced kisses into her neck. His head was bowed so I couldn't see his face, and the girl had so much hair I wasn't seeing hers.

That was until he grabbed her neck.

A mouth smeared with red lipstick angled in my direction, a familiar face I had to take a double look at. I'd seen this girl, this *woman* before.

And this guy.

He'd let his hair grow out over the summer, but there was no mistaking the familiarity. The guy had the same face as my mother.

Because he was her brother.

My uncle Charlie was making out with the headmaster of our school, Principal Mayberry, and I was standing there high as hell thinking I was making that shit up. This wasn't possible. Charlie *was a senior* at my school. He was eighteen, but a student nonetheless.

"Make me come, baby," Principal Mayberry panted. My jaw dropped to the floor, as she reached behind Charlie and grabbed his ass. He shot his dick back into her from behind, nothing but their clothes keeping them apart.

Chuckling, Charlie kept her mouth away by the tight hold he had on her hair.

"So greedy," he growled into our principal's neck. He tongued and bit it so hard she cried out, and I wasn't imaging this shit. This was happening. My uncle was having an affair with my high school principal.

My *married* high school principal.

The woman's husband literally coached our football team, a team Charlie himself was on. He played too with Ares, Wells, Thatcher, and me.

I started to back away, not knowing what else to do, but then heard my name and stiffened.

"Where the fuck did his ass go?" I heard Ares call from somewhere, called *too close* from somewhere. He grunted. "He knows we gotta be back at a decent hour. It's a two-fucking-hour drive just to get back to town."

"Right. Dad's already blowing up my phone wondering where I'm at," Thatcher said, the voices even closer.

The shuffling in front of me stopped.

"Someone's coming," mumbled Principal Mayberry, freezing. The woman stiffened against the wall Charlie had her pinned to, but he kept her there. He didn't want her to move.

I supposed because he spotted me.

He stared at me, right in the eyes in that very moment, and the horror within his couldn't be denied. He'd been caught.

And I'd been the one to find him.

Currently, he had his side piece's (well, I guess *he* was the side piece in this scenario) head in the other direction. Like stated, he had her pinned down so she couldn't move, and I assumed so she couldn't make any noise. The voices of Thatcher, Ares, and Wells grew closer, and Charlie's head shot forward.

He heard them too.

Charlie and Principal Mayberry had maybe moments

before the other three guys knew as well. I mean, I was standing there, looking at something. It wouldn't take long for my best friends to move the same plant.

Charlie made eye contact with me again, a plea in them that told me all he wanted to say. He didn't have to say it.

I'd always have his back.

I pushed out of the plant, striding down the hallway a few feet before making myself known. "Fellas!"

I overinflated the hell out of the declaration, not that high but I made my buddies laugh, which did the job required. I spread my arms out, coming to them, and Ares faked me out with a sock to the gut. We'd been calling him Wolf on the field recently. Dude was a crazy good player and annihilated anything in front of him.

"You're trying to get us killed, kid. You know we gotta be home soon," Ares said, but pounded my fist with a grin. He dropped an arm around my shoulders. "Sorry to break you away from your pussy."

Had he done that, he knew I wouldn't be so lax about it. I rolled my eyes, the other two immediately asking about my activities like a couple of virgins. God knew they weren't, but these guys liked to fucking talk since the notches on their belts were so few and far between. They were still trying to establish themselves.

I draped my arms around the youngins before leading the whole group away, and when I gazed back, I saw no one coming out from behind the plant.

"Come on, guys. Let's go," I made sure to say nice and loud. The coast was clear for Charlie. I'd watch his back always.

Moments later, the boys and I found ourselves on the lawn with our chicks. It'd taken too long to find these girls, and had we been lesser guys we might have left them. We didn't, the girls stumbling-ass drunk on the way to the car. We had to hold them just to keep them on their feet.

"The fuck is this," came from behind us, and when I turned, I spotted Charlie. He came alone, stalking the lawn like a caveman.

His mere presence had the other guys stiffen. Charlie was the responsible one out of all of us. He may technically be my uncle, but he was like a brother to us. He *was* my brother. He'd lived with Mom, Dad, and me since I was ten years old, so yes, this guy was my brother.

And he looked pissed.

Pissed *at all of us* when he'd definitely seen me before this moment. I'd covered for his ass. He got to us, eyes narrowed. "The fuck you guys doing at a college party?"

Oh, yeah. Shit.

Charlie definitely was the most responsible of us, and I could imagine, since he was on his way to Pembroke in the fall, he thought him being here and *us* being here was different. I mean, it was, but I wasn't about to bust myself out.

Charlie eyed the guys, frowning. He eyed the girls, frowning deeper. But when his dark gaze fell on me, I saw nothing but hot fire beneath it.

"You're baked as hell," he drummed, and I rolled my eyes.

I wrestled with my hair. "You want to make something of it?" I asked, the audacity of him talking down to me right now. I'd covered for his scandalous ass. "It's not as bad as other things that are probably going on here tonight."

I put that out there, his eyes expanding. Swallowing, he passed a look over the other guys, and considering how confused my friends appeared to be about what I said, that told Charlie all he needed to know. I'd kept his secret.

That didn't mean he wasn't still pissed at me.

A muscle feathered in his tight jaw. He faced Ares. "You baked too?" he asked. "Wasted?"

"Sober." Ares shoved his hands in his pockets. "Had like half a beer."

"He's the designated driver," I informed, and Charlie weaved his fingers through his hair.

"Good," Charlie said. He jerked his chin in the guys' direction. "Take those girls and get yourselves home."

He must have recognized the girls from school. Us guys obviously brought them.

I started to go with the group, but Charlie got a hold of my arm.

"You're coming with me," he said. "I'm taking you home personally."

He let go of my arm, passing us all before I could protest to any of that, and my friends whistled, laughing. They probably thought Charlie was going to own my ass so my parents couldn't, but I most certainly knew what this was about.

I tapped my buddies' fists, going along with the ruse. I got some jostling about how I was about to get my butt handed to me, but I took it. I was no snitch. If Charlie didn't want his business out there, I wasn't going to share it.

We were in his Lexus not long after that. He'd inherited a good portion of my grandparents' assets after they died. Grandma Helen had been a homemaker but Grandpa Lindquist had a lot, and the assets had been split half and half between my mom and Charlie.

Charlie had never gotten rid of their car.

He still drove the same thing Grandpa Lindquist did, his main car and not the one he'd been driving the night of my grandparents' accident. The Lexus he'd only used for in-town driving, not road trips like he did with Grandma Helen.

The soft leather seats warmed with heat when Charlie turned the car on, but the car didn't move.

We just sat here.

Quiet.

In fact, I only heard Charlie's breathing, husky and labored. He was still amped up but something told me not because he'd caught me tonight at a college party with my friends.

"It's wrong, you know," I said, starting right in on him. Just because I kept his secret didn't mean I agreed with it. I tipped my head back. "You shouldn't be doing this. Coach is a good man."

He was good to us, the best coach ever. He didn't deserve his wife to be two-timing him.

The declaration only made Charlie laugh, and that enraged me. I'd kept his fucking secret, hadn't I?

"You know nothing, Robin," Charlie informed me. He hadn't called me that in so long. Not since we were kids and used to play the superhero game. The other guys were the rest of the Justice League, a game we all used to love. Charlie wet his lips. "Coach hits her. Did you know that?"

I blinked, shaking my head. "What?"

"Yeah." He nodded. "Black and blue when he's angry, or just because he fucking feels like it." The back of his head touched the seat. "She hides it under her clothes."

Something I guess he would know.

The thoughts had me thinking about how messed up this was, but not just because the woman was married and in an abusive relationship.

I mean, Charlie was a student. She wasn't his teacher, but still, *a student*. I didn't know how old our principal was, but the age didn't matter in this situation considering their current roles to the other.

"Even still, what you're doing is wrong," I said, making him laugh again. "You're a student. You guys shouldn't be messing around."

"We are both consenting adults," he stated, facing me. He frowned. "And you got some nerve preaching your moral compass to me." He shook his head. "How much fucking shit do I keep from Royal and December about all the crap you get up to? All the girls you fuck around with at six-*fucking-*

teen. Coming to parties like this and getting baked and shit—"

"We're not even in the same ballpark," I seethed, making his eyes lift. "I'm not in the wrong here. The shit I get up to is nothing like what you're doing."

It was nothing like it—at all, and he had no right comparing the two.

"Well, aren't you just perfect, Robin." He angled around to look at me. "Just fucking perfect and have it all together."

"I never said that."

He laughed.

Until, well, he didn't.

Until he was in my face and giving me a look he'd never given me before. A look of darkness and laced with so much heat and aggression. Charlie had never stared at me this way.

"Newsflash, kid," he said to me, eyes scanning mine. "Sometimes shit isn't perfect. Sometimes it's hard for some of us to have it together all the fucking time."

I never said that he had to, and I *never* made him feel like it had to be that way. Shit wasn't perfect. Not for me either and especially not for him.

I knew that.

We all did, Mom, Dad, and the rest of our family. My friends and his friends… We all knew things weren't perfect for him.

We all knew he was hurting.

My grandparents' death left a void in my life. I mean, they were my grandparents, but even still, it was different for Charlie.

They were his parents.

Charlie put on a good front. I'd give him that. He never waltzed around angry or broken. In fact, he made it *appear* as if he were the epitome of the opposite. He was number one in his class, senior class president, captain of the football team.

Homecoming king.

He did have his shit together, and no one would ever question that.

Maybe we should have.

Mom, Dad, and even the guys and me checked in with him all the time, but that didn't mean he told us shit, and I wondered if Principal Mayberry was giving him something we couldn't. Maybe she wasn't pushing. Maybe she was letting him give in and just bury himself in other thoughts for a while. Maybe she was being different with him like we weren't.

Charlie blinked, like maybe he'd said too much. He faced away, putting the car into drive, and I didn't want him to. I didn't want to just leave like this.

That didn't mean he didn't do it anyway.

He started us off on that more than two-hour drive, a pregnant silence in the car, and I had more than a sinking feeling. If Charlie was bottling up all this stuff, it wasn't good, and the fact made me feel nothing but powerless. This wasn't like when we'd been kids.

Just tucking him in and telling him we were brothers wouldn't be enough this time.

CHAPTER
SEVENTEEN

Dorian - present

My dad dropped me off at the curb with a huff, and considering how pissed I knew he was at me, I just got out of the car. The other guys, Wolf, Thatcher, and Wells were out there too. They stood in their tuxes in front of the theater. They'd obviously been dropped off by their dads too.

We'd been set up.

I knew what had been coming on the way to the theater downtown, but still, seeing my buddies was a surprise. They eyed me as I exited the car.

Dad leaned over the seat, jutting his chin at my friends. "Boys."

"Sir," all three of the fellas proclaimed. We all had respect for our fathers. We referred to each other's with similar terms. Our dads had all been friends for forever, but I was the only one out of my buddies to know each of their dads as a godfather. Wolf's dad, Ramses, was closer with my mom and, from what I understood, became friends with my dad through her.

Wells's and Thatcher's dads were super close with my father, so they did call my dad godfather, though.

Keeping it all straight over the years really was something else, but at the end of the day, none of it mattered. All our parents held a deep bond, and that extended to us. We *all* were family, and the labels really didn't mean much.

Dad nodded at my friends. "Where are your dads?"

Wells pushed a thumb behind himself. "Parking the cars."

Dad acknowledged that once more with a nod, also in a tux like me and the other guys. I could imagine all the dads were dressed in a similar fashion.

An evening at the ballet usually warranted it.

We were obviously all dragged here tonight, but my buddies and I didn't complain. Never did. From the street, Dad mumbled about going to park too, and I got a moment to breathe when he pulled away from the curb.

The drive up here had been tense to say the least.

I turned, and the others eyed me. Wolf pulled a joint out of his pocket, lighting up right there on the sidewalk. I let him because I needed the hit. There were also enough people loading and dropping off that we blended in enough. Most probably just thought it was a cigarette.

Wolf passed smoke through his nostrils before handing me the joint. I took a good long hit before passing it off to my friends. Wolf frowned. "So now that we're alone, who fucked up?"

The question of the evening. If we were all dragged here tonight, *at the ballet*, someone had fucked up. Our fathers only took us to the theater when one of us kids was being an asshole. Trips to the ballet were reserved for special offenses.

Ones usually concerning females.

See, our fathers came up with it in their heads long ago that, when their sons were being dicks, we *all* needed a reminder to be better men. Something about the male dancers of the ballet treating women in softer ways, more delicate. Respectful.

Honestly, the shit just put my friends and me to fucking sleep, but when we were all dragged here, we knew the reasons. One of us had fucked up, a personal offense against a woman, and our fathers were now trying to teach us all a lesson about it.

It made me wonder what kind of men they either believed we were coming up as, or how they themselves had been in the past. The fact they felt the need to orchestrate a group punishment such as this (one including themselves) was suspect as hell. All our dads were so deliriously drunk in love with our mothers I couldn't even imagine they'd been any other way, but stranger things had happened.

Despite me obviously being the offender tonight (i.e. the whole Noa Sloane thing), I kept my mouth shut. I would have said something, but I spotted LJ coming around the corner.

Shit, they called him too.

LJ was my dad's other best friend. He was my last and final god dad and called Wells and Thatcher god sons as well. Our four dads used to be in a strong clique back in high school, something that obliviously expanded once my dad met my mom and Wolf's dad came into their circle.

All our parents were tight as hell now, the husbands and the wives. Again, labels didn't matter, but LJ and his wife, Billie, had no children.

That didn't mean he was exempt from this little punishment.

"Okay, which one of you boys messed up," LJ growled, and out of all of the dads, he was the only one who looked like a surfer. He wore his blond hair free in his dark tux, eyeing us all on the sidewalk. He must have arrived first since he was coming from the lot without the other dads, and since we hadn't been prepared, we tried to hide our joint. Thatcher had it, and LJ chuckled upon seeing it. "I know you kids smoke weed. Stop."

That didn't mean he didn't fucking take it.

He put it out under his shoe, mumbling something about it being a waste. Odds were, had the four of us not been here, he might have finished it off with our dads. We'd caught them more than once in the garage lighting up. I mean, they never did it in front of us, and whenever our moms found out, the arguments commenced. We'd yet to catch any of our mothers smoking weed, but again, *in front of us*. Let's just say my mom kept a lighter in her dresser, and she had not one candle in my parents' bedroom.

The fact only made me mentally give my mother cool points, though, and each of the fellas gave LJ a hug, myself last. I ended it with a handshake and a snap. "The other dads?"

"They're coming. Saw them behind me but I was ahead." LJ's eyes narrowed. "Was it you?" He directed a finger. "Because if so, you owe me a night with Billie in the Hamptons. I had to get on a red-eye to make this shit happen today."

He and his wife traveled the world without the ties of children. LJ was a businessman like the rest of our fathers. He even had a few businesses with Wolf's dad, Ramses.

Yeah, we were really fucked if they'd called LJ all the way over for this thing. He and Billie did nothing but party, living a dream life. His wife used to be a college professor but stopped teaching years ago to just live life and travel the world with her husband. None of us kids ever asked, but we assumed they either couldn't have kids or didn't on purpose. Either way it was none of our business. Not like our parents would tell us anyway.

"Uh," I started, and he eyed me.

"Mmhmm," he said, figuring it out, and my friends groaned in my direction. I hadn't told any of them what had happened the other day when my mother had stormed the end of football practice. Hadn't really had time. Dad had had a field day on my butt when I'd gotten home that night, and it hadn't mattered that I explained the situation, that a prank had been played on me and I *hadn't* gotten a girl pregnant. It'd all been a lie, and I explained that.

It hadn't mattered.

I knew that because us guys were being dragged to the ballet. My friends' eyes were on me when the other dads finally did come around with mine. They'd taken a beat to come back, and I wondered if they'd been *talking*. That wouldn't have surprised me. They all greeted LJ before us kids.

Our fathers and LJ all took the time to shake and hug it out, not having seen each other all together in a while. Everyone lived in Maywood Heights, but they were all busy men in their various businesses. Outside of his online security startup, Knight, Thatcher's dad, ran Reed Corp. His company mostly delved in real estate development like LJ and Wolf's dad, Ramses. Ramses's businesses ventured outside his company Mallick Enterprises, though. He ran several major art galleries all over the world and Wells's dad, Jaxen, had fast-food chains all over the country amongst other businesses. This basically allowed us guys to get free food anywhere there was a franchise, and we had when we'd gone on weekend trips without our parents.

Odds were, those trips were dead in the water. *Personal freedom*, at least right now.

"Brother." Dad shook, then snapped LJ's hand since they'd been the last to shake it out. They all called each other brothers, all of us family. I didn't have memories that didn't include my god dads or their wives. They were all like second fathers to me, to all of us, and their wives, second mothers.

Which meant I had five fucking fathers to own my ass.

Yes, the dads definitely had talked because when I got my

hugs from each of them, I got a *look* that accompanied it. It was official. Everyone's Saturday night was gone because of me. Even Ramses flashed me a look, and he was the nice one.

"Kid," Ramses said to me, grabbing my head before taking me into a hug. His was extra tight, and out of all my god dads, we were the closest. That was mostly because Wolf and I were so close. I even had a second bedroom at the Mallicks', and Wolf had one at my house too. Ramses pulled away. "You okay?"

And he checked in with me, something I had a feeling was coming from my own dad on the way home. He'd kept the drive to the theater quiet, but I thought mostly because he was considering his own thoughts. I'd figured out over the years, that was his process. He didn't like not having control and saw that as weakness in others. He'd never say that, of course, but I knew it in the way he handled what he obviously considered his own weakness. Dad had a temper, but he never, at least in my life, openly showed it.

That was one of the many things that made him so strong in my eyes, how he obviously dealt with shit, but had his own way of processing things. He always put his best foot forward.

But he still sure as fuck intimated me, his gaze studying me over Ramses's shoulder. My father watched on, and I knew a talk was coming.

Brilliant.

"I'm okay," I said to Ramses. I was okay. At least, right now. By the end of the night, I might not be, though.

I may want to plan my funeral.

A million fucking acts were in tonight's ballet. At least, that was what it felt like. Our dads had literally dragged us to this one a million times, and I think all the guys could probably do the moves on stage if it came down to it. That said something considering I'd never danced *ballet* in my whole damn life.

The four of us had to sit between our huge fathers and LJ, tucked *tight* between them. We couldn't even sit next to each other, a dad between each kid, and they'd even taken our cell phones. We literally had no fucking escape.

I thought I'd die by intermission, but at least our dads and LJ had given us our cell phones back. They said it was an act of mercy while they went outside the theater to talk.

Probably about us.

Most certainly about me, the star of this apparent fucking show. I'd caught more than one eye from my buddies between dance moves prior to intermission, a scowl from Thatcher and Wells on my far right. The worst had been Wolf.

He'd mouthed, "What happened?" at one point before Ramses had checked his son by putting a finger to his own lips. We'd all sat in a theater box, and Ramses had made Wolf switch seats with him at that point, so Wolf couldn't even mouth shit to me.

It was all an epic fucking disaster, and with our dads gone at intermission, I was immediately assaulted left and right by my friends. I gave them the rundown the moment I could.

It was a long story, and every word rehashed all kinds of fucking crap in *my* head. The girl had most certainly gotten into it.

And was still there.

Like my father, I didn't like losing control, and Noa had taken me there. I ventured a line I didn't like, an obsessive one, and an anger that made me want to wring her fucking throat and shove my cock inside her while I did. It was all sick and fucking confusing as shit.

And the look Wolf sported while I spoke wasn't nice.

He stayed dangerously quiet the whole story. Though, I left the part out about nearly fucking the girl on the bleachers. He might have had something to say about that, and I wasn't sure I wanted to hear what he had to say. He may say something about playing with my food again, or something else I didn't feel like hearing.

"Fuck, and I bet I know how she found out shit about your mom. Where to find her and send her shit?" Thatch gritted toward the end of my story. Our dads and LJ hadn't come back yet, but we probably only had moments before they did. He tossed his head on the seat. "Bow said Noa came over to the house the other day."

"The fuck?" I shot off the seat. "And you're just now mentioning that?"

"I just found out," he said, his look apologetic. "I was going to mention it today." He punched the ledge in front of our seats, and the only reason the noise probably didn't garner any attention was because we were in a private box and people were still milling around down below. Thatcher shook his head. "Bitch obviously used my sister. Bow said Noa came over to study. They got the same math class or some shit. I just found out Noa was over because Bow mentioned it at dinner last night, and I really didn't think anything of it until what you just said, D." Thatch huffed. "I bet if I ask my sister exactly what they talked about, some-thing tells me information about your mom may have come up. Bitch was obviously doing some digging."

"She's dead." Wells said it, but out of all of us, typically he wouldn't say that. He was more laid-back.

But this was a special situation.

This was Bow, our Bow and Thatcher's sister. Someone fucked with her, they fucked with all of us, and that went double when it came to Wells. He didn't like Bow being messed with.

At least, if someone else was doing the messing.

None of us guys talked too much about that. Wells's deal with her was his own deal, but when it came to Rainbow Reed, all of us had a stake there. She was our sister, and we protected her like we did each other.

Wells's jaw clenched. "What do we do?"

"Payback." Wolf draped an arm over the box's ledge. He nodded. "Penance. She can't get away with this shit."

He'd really been dangerously quiet while I'd been speaking, like he'd been simmering over there. Noa Sloane had never been his favorite person, made sense with how they'd met.

Wolf was really capable of some dark shit. He was filled with a lot of anger, like me, and together, we typically checked each other.

We did that to protect each other.

Wolf was my boy, and we often kept each other from going down some really dark paths. That came with the territory of us all being brothers. We watched each other's backs and would even go to the ends of the earth for each other if need be.

I agreed Noa Sloane needed to be handled, but I wasn't sure how at the present. I needed to act.

I just didn't know how.

"She needs to sweat," I found myself saying. "We do nothing for now. The anticipation alone will drive her mad."

I believed this to be true, but it did surprise me to hear the words.

As well as my buddies.

They gazed at me as if I'd lost my mind, but by then, our dads and LJ were making their way back.

"Phones." Wells's dad, Jaxen, had his hand out, grinning. "And don't worry, I'll keep good care of them."

Groaning, we all handed them off to Jax one by one, sitting back when our fathers and LJ tucked themselves tight between us again. I didn't face my buddies as the room darkened and the show began again, but I didn't have to. I could feel their eyes.

I could feel Wolf's the most.

It was that continued look that made me not look at my

friend for the rest of the show. The thing about Wolf was, he was my closest friend. He could read me like no one else. He *knew me* like no one else, and because of that, he liked to psychoanalyze shit, and he wasn't my fucking head doctor. I didn't need him in my head, so I purposely kept him out of it.

The show couldn't have ended quickly enough.

It did eventually, the fathers and LJ taking us boys outside and the telltale lectures beginning after. Us guys all got the same song and dance, how it was important to respect women and treat them well. The adults used no names, of course, or called anyone out, but everyone knew I was the party at fault here. The fathers and LJ all made sure to make their points directly to me when they spoke.

It all just shoved the metaphorical dagger in that much deeper, and Dad even bowed him and me out of the after-show dinner with the rest of the guys. The adults normally all took us to Jax's Burgers after.

"I need some time with my son," Dad said to his friends, giving them all hugs and shakes. He did the same with Thatcher, Wells, and Wolf. Dad saved Wolf for last, whispering something to him. No doubt he was asking Wolf to talk some sense into me, knowing Wolf and I were the closest.

I was sure Wolf would talk to me after he so obviously disagreed with my stance on how to handle Noa Sloane. My friend studied me good and hard before we all left each other, and I got into the car with my dad gratefully.

"So, you gonna level with me now?" Dad asked the question behind the wheel, swinging his gaze over to me. We probably had about fifteen minutes between the theater and home, but that was enough. His eyes narrowed. "What happened?"

I'd explained to him what had happened, told him and Mom what had happened. I shrugged. "I told you. Some bitch was trying to get back at me at school." Though, I hadn't told them the why or the circumstances surrounding it.

Dad sighed, heavily. He shook his head. "And that's why we all took—and continue to take—you to these things, the ballet?" He frowned. "You think we enjoy it any more than you boys?"

Doubted it. My dad *wasn't* a ballet guy.

His jaw worked. "You kids could do with a reality check. You don't treat women right. Women aren't bitches. They're *women*."

"I told you. She—"

"What I heard, *son*." His eyes flared in my direction, my lips snapping closed. His frown deepened. "Is that you wronged someone so much that they decided to do such a thing against you. And getting your mother involved?" He fingered roughly through his hair. "You obviously did something to this girl. Something she felt warranted such cruel behavior."

His words were heated, his cheeks flared. He was obviously placing the blame of what happened to Mom on me.

In fact, it was probably taking all he could to not do anything about it. This was *Mom* and so came my dad's heavy control. He was clearly trying not to fly off the handle right now.

"We worked so goddamn hard so you boys *aren't* like us," he gritted, his knuckles white on the wheel. "So that you don't make the same mistakes and aren't such little shits like we were when we were kids."

I shook my head. "You guys all turned out okay."

He and my god dads all had happy marriages, had built great lives for themselves, and the love they had for our mothers, well, anyone could see that. The devotion.

My dad loved my mother with a love I couldn't even fathom. He loved her like she was enough and would always be, and she did the same. She loved him at his core, saw him worthy of her love. He was *worth* her love.

Not all of us were.

Some of us were such fuckups that we deserved whatever shit we got handed. I'd had a goddamn easy life, and I'd taken that shit for granted. I didn't count my good fortune and walked all over it. I'd become weak to it and completely ungrateful.

Charlie wouldn't have been that way. He'd loved his life.

Loved…

Looking outside, I couldn't breathe, staring instead into the darkness.

"It wasn't without struggle, Dorian," my dad said, his reflection through the window. We'd been driving for a while, almost home. My dad was looking at me, and I saw his eyes through the window.

Why can't I fucking breathe?

I grabbed the seat, the leather tight under my hands.

Breathe. Fucking breathe *goddammit.*

It was like my dreams at night, the ones where I couldn't wake up. The ones where I was drowning, and no matter what I did, I couldn't get out of the nightmare. I just kept seeing Charlie's face, and the fear he must have had the last day I'd seen him. He had to have had fear.

How could he not?

I undid my tie in the car. My father sighed beside me. I wasn't brave enough to look at him. He psychoanalyzed worse than Wolf.

"I know you're not sleeping, son," he said to me. "I know you're working out at night and jogging in the evenings. Your mom does too."

I figured. I wasn't quiet about it.

Not that I could be with Chestnut, our chocolate Labrador, around. She took a second to get quiet whenever I came in and out of the house, not like her mom before that. She was the only one we'd kept from Hershey's litter, a dog my parents had had before I was even born.

I'd cried like a little bitch when she'd passed, but having Chestnut made it easier.

"No one expects you to be okay, you know," Dad said, his attempt at a talk. He didn't do them a lot. He knew they didn't work with me and I didn't like them. He sighed again. "Not after all this just happened. It's a lot. A lot for all of us."

I swallowed, gripping the seat again. Why couldn't I just fucking breathe? Charlie wouldn't have been this way. He would have been strong.

Why couldn't it have just been me?

I didn't want to die. I cared about my life, but Charlie shouldn't have died. It was before his time.

It was too fucking soon.

"I'm *fine*," I managed to struggle out despite the lack of breath. I wet my lips, staring outside. "I'm okay."

I'm okay.

I'm okay.

I'm okay.

If I said it in my mind enough times, I'd convince myself, my parents. If I said it enough, it'd become true.

I'm okay.

I'm okay.

There was silence in my dad's car, silence all the way through our neighborhood, then into our driveway. He said nothing once inside the garage, turning off the car.

He squeezed my shoulder.

It was enough for me to almost say something, but I didn't.

Breathe, you fucking idiot.

"You're not okay," Dad said beside me. Like he knew. Of course, he knew. He knew me. I was his son. He nodded, his reflection still in the window. "But maybe, once you want to be, you'll come talk to me and your mother."

I didn't want to tell him fat chance. Dad wasn't one to talk about his feelings either.

I'd probably gotten it from him.

Like he had his own process with his anger, I had mine. I could control it. I could if I just held on to it long enough. I had my own way of release.

I just needed the time to do what needed to be done.

CHAPTER
EIGHTEEN

Sloane

Word of what I'd done to Dorian Prinze (sent his mom) made it back to school somehow. I had no idea if he'd spread the information himself, or if it'd been his friends, but people found out.

Virtually overnight, I'd become known as the lying bitch amongst the halls of Windsor Prep on top of the terms Legacy bitch/Vapor. Worse, once people found out about the pregnancy prank (I'd gotten some pregnant lady at a gas station to pee on the stick for twenty bucks), I'd also been labeled as a Legacy groupie whore. People had assumed that I wanted the attention of the Legacy boys so bad, I faked a pregnancy just to get to their dark prince.

The halls of gossip and rumors ensued, and they quickly made it to my breakfast table. One of the things my brother, Bru, and I still actually did was eat together on the rare days he didn't have to be at school early for practice.

Even if we didn't talk to each other.

After the news had broken, he'd paid no attention to me,

but this morning he actually scoffed at me. I'd been pouring a box of Frosted Flakes into an empty bowl, and quite honestly, that pissed me off. My kid brother hadn't been in my corner at all since I made it to this school. Sure, I hadn't told him about many of the terrible things Dorian had done to me, but that didn't negate that he was *well aware* they were bullying me. He'd had to have heard about the pranks. Then, of course, there was the way things had started with Ares Mallick.

Bru hadn't gone to bat for me whether I left certain things from his attention or not.

"I still can't believe you did what you did," he mumbled, on his phone while eating a piece of French toast. God, as if he'd actually made the thing for himself. He had gotten Callum to arrange a food delivery service for him. The service made him special meals Bru *claimed* he'd needed to bulk up for his new sport. I'd overheard this conversation my brother had had with our guardian at the beginning of the month.

My brother truly was taking advantage of the situation here. Becoming one of those people at the school and milking our new guardian for all he could. It disappointed me as much as how he still continued to be friends with those terrible boys...

And their wicked prince.

I hadn't forgotten that day on the bleachers with Dorian. I mean, how could I?

He'd brought me down to my knees.

I'd sucked him off (openly) and for anyone to see. What was worse was I'd pretty much begged him to do it. He'd gotten into my head, and I hadn't liked that.

Even if I'd enjoyed his taste.

Even if I'd indulged in his power and who he clearly was around the academy's campus. How it'd all gone down had been sick, and I thought I truly would be ill the way he'd left me there. He'd said I had been a conquest, nothing but a mouth to fuck, and I'd fallen for the shit. I had become one of them, the girls who obviously fell all over him.

I was still waiting for *that* particular ball to drop. Either he hadn't told anyone about that day on the bleachers, or he was simply waiting to expose me. He may want to keep me nervous and at his mercy. There was no way he'd conceal that information on purpose.

He'd said he wanted to break me.

He'd said he wanted me to scream for him, and he'd be the one to deliver. He'd gotten off on breaking me down and turning me into someone I didn't want to be. I didn't want to think about him.

I didn't want to remember his taste.

Dorian Prinze was already enough in my head, in this house. He hovered in it with how my brother had become his own personal fanboy. I'd also caught Bru singing Dorian's praises to Callum when my brother had been updating our guardian about his football stuff on the phone.

Bru dropped his fork on his plate. "You just couldn't help yourself, could you?" Bru shot, really going there. "You can't let me have just this one thing. You know, I'm actually good at football?"

I did know that. I mean, of course he wouldn't *know* that I did. I'd snuck in on a couple of his practices, missing my brother and wanting to see what he'd been doing.

I moved my lips. "I know you're good, Bru."

"Do you?" He frowned. "How about how much I enjoy it? That I'm actually making friends—"

"Those *aren't* your real friends." And I'd stand by that. I didn't know the Legacy guys' angle (Dorian Prinze's angle), but I knew they were still playing him. Them getting close to Bru was nothing but a power play—point blank. I sneered. "They don't like you. They're letting you get close because they hate me."

"Look how you sound right now." He shook his head. He

pointed at me. "You know, I think you're just paranoid. *Paranoid* that I might be leaving and finding something for myself. I swear to God you're just like Dad—"

"Enough!" I growled, slamming my hands on the table. He wouldn't speak to me like that and not about Dad. I directed a finger at him. "Say what you want about me. Say whatever you want but leave Dad out of this. You know he was sick."

Our dad was a troubled man with problems we obviously didn't get. He'd never told us, but he had to have had them. He was guarded and so obviously missed Mom.

Bru wiped his hands off, apparently done with his plate.

"I'm going to school," he mumbled and then that was that.

I eventually got to school too, and though I normally didn't go around talking to too many people, I did stop Bow Reed at her locker.

I hadn't seen her around class.

In fact, she'd all but disappeared after the news broke of what I'd done to Dorian around the halls. She wasn't in our math class, and I didn't see her around. Not even at lunch, and I looked for her.

She wasn't with her brother and his friends when they actually showed up for lunch. Lately, I hadn't seen the guys either in the courtyard, and I considered that a blessing.

When they weren't there, I didn't get food thrown at me.

It was like the lunchroom acted on their behalf whenever they were around. Legacy boys never did their own bidding. They had minions to do it for them. I still found shit in my locker. Sex toys were pretty much the exclusive thing, but most recently, boxes of pregnancy tests had been added to the haul. They fell out into the hallway after that first day and hadn't stopped since.

I'd grown accustomed to simply throwing them away, an

act I'd just finished when I spotted Bow at her locker. I raised my hand to her. "Hey."

Her head had been in her locker, and she gazed over the door, full smile on her face.

But then, she spotted me.

The smile wiped away as if I'd taken an eraser to it. Next thing I knew, she was pulling things out of her locker in quick time. She filled her arms with books and ignored me standing not a foot away from her.

I eyed her. "Little rabbit?" She continued to ignore me. I frowned. "I haven't seen you in class…"

"I dropped it," she stated, more bite in her voice than I was used to from her. She huffed. "Well, I didn't drop it. I transferred."

"Why?"

"Maybe I didn't want to see someone who was taking advantage of me every day."

"What?"

She whipped from behind her locker, getting in my face. This was crazy since I had more than a few inches on her. Even still, she stood tall in her heeled Mary Janes. She shook her head. "You know, I didn't tell you any of that stuff *at my house*, Sloane, for you to go and use it against Dorian. Dorian is like a brother to me. All the guys are."

Fuck.

"My brother actually had to break it down to me what you did." She frowned, definitely not used to that from her. She was always so cheery. "How you took advantage of me with all that stuff I told you."

She had shared a lot, more as I poked.

I'd poked a lot.

I'd found out exactly where Dorian's mom worked, and that made it easy to send the note with the pregnancy test.

Her arms crossed over her books. "I kind of actually thought we were friends."

"We are friends."

She put her hand up. "Well, if that's a friend, I'll just take family." She closed her locker. "Which Dorian and all the other guys are to me." She leaned in. "I told you. Our families are close as hell, and I may not agree with a lot of the things the guys do around here, but that doesn't stop the fact that they're my family. Always have been. Always will be."

Her family.

"And you hurt them." Her face grew red in color. "You hurt Dorian, and what's worse is, you did it through me."

"Little rabbit—"

"It's Bow," she countered. "Not little rabbit. Just Bow, and tutor yourself from now on."

"Bow."

Her hair swayed when she charged in the opposite direction away from me, and I couldn't even be mad at her or blame her. I had used her, and if she really was as close as she was with the Legacy guys, she should hate me.

I'd hate her too if someone did that to my family.

CHAPTER
NINETEEN

Sloane

The impending feeling of doom I got every time I walked the halls of Windsor Prep made me feel like maybe my brother had something to his claims of me being like our father. Besides people staring at me and still not acknowledging me by anything other than Vapor or Legacy bitch, I had a sense of dread following me. Like the shoe was about to drop, and I was simply waiting for the crushing blow. It had started the day Bow had called me out about taking advantage of her.

It never left after that.

Legacy hadn't been shy about making their presence known in the hallways. Whenever I did see them, they made sure to pass me a look, to sit closer to my brother at lunch, or to sneer when they tucked Bow in tighter between them at their table. The one with the most heat in his eyes had been Thatcher. He always had his arm draped around his sister, a hate in his eyes whenever I saw them all eating at lunch. The worst had been Dorian actually. Because unlike Wells's and Ares's "looks" and Thatcher's protective hold, Dorian didn't acknowledge me at all. I got none of his attention when I probably should have gotten his the most. He made sure to keep it on his girls he always had around him. Never once looking at me.

It just made my paranoia worse.

I'd felt like I had a target on my head before, but now, I was simply waiting for the act of revenge. I'd made my statement with that pregnancy test pretty vocal. I'd drawn the line in the sand. I'd hit back when I had a feeling most didn't bother.

No one else had been dumb enough to try.

That sinking feeling of dread followed into the first games of the Windsor Prep football season my brother actually got to play in. He didn't at first. I figured that was because he was new out there, but once they had him on the field, he played quite a bit. He was out there with Dorian, Wells, Thatcher, and Ares, and shit did I get Ares's nickname after watching that barbarian play. He bowled down players like a madman, howling into the air after every successful play. The amount of fear he struck into the opposing team's eyes had been crazy. People merely got out of his way and didn't bother to do anything else.

He protected my brother out there. He did as his teammate, and the other boys did the same. They were the supporting force for Dorian being quarterback, but all these boys had each other's backs. They came at the other team like an unstoppable force of power and speed, and at the center was the dark prince himself.

I tried not to watch Dorian as he sped down the field during the games, *think* about him and what he'd done to me on the very bleachers I sat. He frequented my thoughts like a matinee quite often, all power out there on the field like he'd been above me that day. He caught passes with ease, a strong leader to his team. They all loved and respected him out there, and the fans went wild for him.

He led the team into yet another victory at today's game, and I'd seen a few.

I came to them all.

I did to support my brother, even though he never saw me in the crazy crowds. After today's game, though, I decided to stay and give him a shout-out. The coaches had let him play nearly the entire game, and he'd done a good job.

My brother didn't come out of the locker room by himself.

He was tucked between Thatcher and Wells, the guys hitting his chest, and Ares sprinted backward in front of them. I heard the words "Good job" from Ares, and Dorian came up behind my brother.

"You killed it out there today, bro," Dorian said, strong-arming him like an actual bro. Wells broke away so Dorian could sling his meaty arm around my brother. Dorian grinned. "Didn't I tell you you'd rock that shit out there?"

"Yeah, man. You did," Bru said, being modest. I knew because a bunch of red crept up his neck. He never liked being acknowledged. Not even when it came to academics, which he'd always rocked at in the past. Bru shrugged. "I did okay."

"More than." Dorian tapped his chest. "Coach will have you playing in every game now."

"Yeah, man. You really brought it today."

That one came from Ares, really surprising me. He was obviously the most vicious out of all of them.

But not only was he acknowledging my brother, he got in on the bro fest too. Thatcher made room for him to get in, my brother now tucked between Dorian Prinze and Ares Mallick. These guys actually looked like his friends.

"Bru?"

My brother glanced in my direction when I ventured out of the shadows, and my appearance put an ice bath on the moment like I'd never seen.

The guys dropped their arms from around my brother,

Dorian stopping in his tracks. He stared right at me, full on, and I didn't know what to do. I'd managed to escape those dark brown eyes in recent days. He'd been all but ignoring me since the "incident."

He wasn't now.

Those ebony pools charged black like hot coals. His chin lifted in my direction. Honestly, with that heated look, I wasn't sure whether he wanted to strike me or kiss me. It could have gone either way.

But the thought of the latter…

Truly, it made me uncomfortable. How my thoughts could even *go there* after what had happened between us and what I'd ended up doing. It was like he'd brought me down to my knees again.

And the others noticed.

Most especially Ares. He passed a glance between us, his arm coming around his buddy. That one move blinked Dorian out of whatever trance he'd been in, and I took the opportunity to approach my brother.

"Good job today," I said to him, noticing his teammates backing off. Ares kept Dorian real close, and suddenly, Dorian was on his phone. Apparently, my appearance really meant nothing to the dark prince. After what had happened, I was beneath him, hate or otherwise.

Why I felt anything about that I didn't know.

My brother nodded at me.

"Thanks," Bru mumbled, gazing back to his friends. The Legacy boys had moved on to their fangirls. They and the other football guys had groupies who stayed after the game to see the players. I knew because I saw them whenever I came to a game.

The groupie bitches had called me all kinds of things when I waited today, joking that I'd been waiting for Dorian to give him another pregnancy test. I put up with it so I could see my brother.

Deciding to speed this little visit up, I reached into my pocket and gave my brother the gift I'd gotten for him. I had told myself I'd give it to him once they really started to let him play.

"It's not much," I said, referring to the football key chain I ordered a couple weeks ago. I shrugged. "It's to go on your key ring for your car."

It really wasn't much, just a little football with his initials: BHS. His middle name was Henry.

He smiled a little, the chain on his finger. "You didn't have to do that."

"I hoped for an olive branch, idiot," I said, tapping his shoulder with my fist. It made him laugh a little, which was good. I shrugged. "And maybe dinner. We could go someplace and celebrate."

His smile fell a little. He pointed his thumb back. "Actually, the team and I were going to go to Jax's. It's a burger place in town."

I'd seen them but had never gone there.

Bruno stared at me. "I mean, you probably could come. If you want."

His teammates behind him maybe had girls in the distance, but I was well aware *I* wasn't invited to this shindig.

And Dorian stared at me again.

His inky-dark pools eased away from his cell phone, almost a dare in his eyes. Like he dared me to come and possibly get in his way again. I really didn't know what this guy's problem was. What I'd done so badly by simply *existing*, but I didn't want to make more trouble for Bru than I already had. I did care about him, and his happiness far outweighed mine. That was just how it was. I was his sister.

"Actually, that's okay. You go ahead and have a fun night," I said, facing him. "You know how I bury myself in my work."

Whenever he found me, I was in my art room Callum had

arranged for me. I was a frequent flier since I had zero social life since coming to this town.

Bru nodded. Though, he had actually looked a little disappointed. That made me feel like maybe we were getting somewhere, that maybe we could get back to being Sloane and Bru. Not just brother and sister, but friends.

Rather than make this whole thing more awkward than it already was, I let my brother go and headed to the parking lot.

As I made it to the Chevelle, my cell phone rang, and I was surprised to see Callum's number on the front. I didn't go out of my way to call him. He checked in, of course, but not often. He really was leaving Bru and me to our own devices here, which was something I appreciated. Callum had promised me he'd only be our guardian on paper, and he'd been keeping to that promise about letting my brother and me live our lives.

"How have you been, Sloane?" he asked after I picked up. I leaned against my car to take the call. "Bru tells me he just won the game tonight."

Which meant Bru either called him in the locker room or after he just spoke to me. Odds were, it was the former.

The fact my brother was obviously talking more to a virtual stranger than me didn't necessarily make me feel good. But with as turbulent as our weeks here in Maywood Heights had been, I supposed I wasn't surprised. My brother and I had basically been strangers ourselves with the exception of a few moments ago.

I pushed my hair out of my face. "Yeah, I just saw him. He's doing well."

"Sounds like really well," Callum said. "Seems like a future in football may be for him."

That shocked me, that maybe Bru was even telling him that when he clearly hadn't been talking to me.

What's happened with us?

We were acting like we weren't even siblings anymore. The kid used to be my best friend, my *good* friend.

"I wouldn't know," I passed off, more so in my own thoughts. I obviously said it out loud, though. I shook my head. "I just mean he's been really busy. We haven't talked a lot. You know, his football and stuff."

I obviously downplayed what was going on. I mean, I still didn't know Callum. Not really. He was keeping me alive and well, that was where it ended.

"He asked about football camp," Callum stated, again surprising me. "He says it's over the summer. Sounds like he's making plans."

My chest hurt. *What the fuck?*

"Yeah?" I rubbed my face, ignoring what suddenly felt like a gaping wound in my chest. "That's awesome. He's really good. You should see him play."

I managed to make it come out like my brother's absence in my life didn't hurt. Like I didn't completely not know him anymore.

I didn't know how good I managed to do that, but Callum did move the conversation on.

"I plan to see him play before the end of the season," he said. "Promised him that."

"Good. I'm sure he'd like that." I knew my brother had taken a liking to him, and Callum had been kind to us. Really, he was the only decent break *I'd* had in the last few months, his kindness.

Though, he had brought me to this stupid town.

My life going completely belly up wasn't Callum's problem, though. He hadn't started a fight in the parking lot and egged on the popular clique. *He* hadn't made himself an enemy to Legacy, which led to making the entire school hate me. Callum also hadn't sent an innocent woman (Dorian's mother) a used pregnancy test claiming her son had knocked up someone. Even if her son had been a complete dick. No, Callum hadn't done that.

You did.

"You never said how you were, Sloane," Callum chimed during my thoughts. "Every time I call you, though, it sounds like you're in your art studio, keeping busy. I'm glad you've been able to utilize it."

I had, cupping my arm. "I really thank you for that. It's been nice."

"And how are classes, school?" It sounded like he was moving around somewhere. Maybe outside and going into a car. "I haven't really heard anything outside of your art."

That was because I hadn't said anything. I'd promised Callum we'd be okay out here on our own, so he wouldn't need to disrupt his life to take care of us.

He was already doing so much.

Knowing I had a safe haven outside of the hellhole that was school told me that. Callum's shelter and luxury had been the one thing I had to escape it. How ironic since I'd been so resistant to it at first, the changes.

"It's been fine," I said, but even I didn't believe it. "School's school, you know? Been to a lot of schools. It's all the same thing after a while."

"I know you have," he said. "You know, I did see your records before I had them sent to the academy. I know about your and Bru's history. All your different schools and moving." My lips parted. "Your, um, fighting. Heard about that too."

I closed my eyes. "Well, my brother and I have been to a lot of schools." I shrugged. "Bullies come with that. People don't always like the new kid."

And Bru was right. It made me a little combative. I tried to get in people's faces before they got in mine, the best way to make sure Bru and I were taken care of. It hadn't mattered since we had moved all the time with Dad's job situation. If one person handled me, it didn't matter if I pushed back. I'd be gone soon and moving on to the next.

That obviously wasn't the case here.

"I see." The movement had stopped in the background, and I assumed he was driving at this point. "It's been a while since I've been in school, but I imagine that would be hard. I'm aware my old friend, your dad, had a lot of issues. Having problems both finding and *keeping* a job. I'm sure that was hard too, all that moving around."

He put that mildly. I said nothing.

"That was a big concern for me regarding you children. You've both been dealt a pretty tough hand. I hoped coming to a new place would help. Has that not been the case?"

The last thing I needed was for him to hop on a plane and decide to take the reins out here. Especially since Bru had been okay.

"It's been a change but a good one," I said, hoping he believed me. "As you heard, Bru's thriving. Me too."

Please believe me.

I wasn't sure if he did, and in that moment, my attention was distracted.

Whispering.

It came from my right, a few cars over in the parking lot. I noticed red hair, a woman.

Principal Mayberry.

She was talking to someone, some guy who looked sketchy as hell actually. She kept looking around, her head low, and suddenly, he was handing something to her. I couldn't see what he handed her, but she handed him something as well. She kept it concealed under her handbag.

What the fuck?

"Well, that's good, Sloane. Very good," Callum informed, and apparently, I'd been pretty good at fibbing. "Things are actually wrapping up around here with this deal, so I plan to visit you both in person real soon. I blocked off some time, and I hope, once summer hits, you'll consider a trip. I'd like to gift you with a holiday to Paris for graduation."

My lips parted. "Paris?"

He laughed lightly into the phone. "Once I found out you were an artist, I couldn't help myself. Of course, if that's not where you want to go, we can negotiate. We can talk about it more when I come to town."

Murmuring in the background sounded. Callum was obviously busy. He must have called me on the fly.

"Anyway, be sure to check in," he said. "And tell Bru good job for me again."

"I will, Callum, and thank you." I mean, what else could I say? Paris? Wild.

I never would have dreamed to be able to take such of trip. I'd never had the option. Bru and I were just two poor kids.

Who apparently suddenly had a fairy godfather.

I didn't know Callum to have a family of his own, so maybe, with his obviously lavish life, he just wanted to help out his old friend, my father. He was giving my brother and me more than we could ever ask, and after I let him go, I nearly forgot the fact my headmaster was across the parking lot.

What's she doing?

Principal Mayberry was doing something that was for sure and whatever she gave the sketchy guy, he didn't seem satisfied with.

"That's not enough, bitch," he growled at her, looking around. "You still owe me from last week."

"I'll get it to you," she whispered. The woman actually looked kind of all over the place, hair disheveled and bags under her eyes. "I'm good for it."

"Mmm. You better be," he said, but some shuffling took both their attention.

"I said back off," came from my other side, Bow Reed, but

she wasn't by herself. Two dudes flanked her, one wearing a letterman jacket, but neither were on the football team. Since I watched enough games, I knew who ran the field. The guy must have played some other kind of sport.

The guys surrounded Bow, cutting her off in the lot. One of them smirked. "Don't act like you're too good for us. You should be fucking lucky."

The second guy tugged the other. "Back off, she could go tell her brother."

The boy growled. "That motherfucker and his boys got me cut from the team so that Sloane kid could join." He faced Bow. "This is nothing but revenge."

What the hell?

The guys continued to surround her, and the guy with Principal Mayberry hushed.

"Someone's fucking coming," the sketchy guy growled, going one way, and Principal Mayberry went another. I had no time to figure out what they were doing.

Those guys continued to follow Bow deeper into the lot, and shaking my head, I headed toward the back of my dad's Chevelle. Apparently, this old bat was really getting some use since coming to Maywood Heights.

Safe town my ass.

Principal Mayberry looked like she was in the middle of some drug deal and now two creeps were going after the little rabbit.

Bat in hand, I ran toward the scene.

"I said back off," Bow said, and one of them attempted to grab at her hand. She shoved him. "Leave me alone."

"Her brother, man," one of the guys started to say, the same one who appeared to be the voice of reason before.

The guy in the letterman jacket waved his friend off. "You go and be a little bitch, then," he gritted. "I'm going to get mine."

His friend lifted his hands. "Fuck this, man."

The guy ran off, hands in his pockets, and that made me feel a little better as I ran up on the other guy with Bow. Dealing with one asshole would be easier than two.

Bow had her hair up, spirit paint on her face. She must have gone to tonight's game. "I said leave me alone!"

The guy didn't listen, backing her up against the car. He grabbed for her, and she screamed, kicking at him.

"Back off," I yelled, the guy whirling around. I readied my bat in the air. "Get away from her or I'll knock your fucking head off. I swear to God."

I had confidence since this tactic worked the first time, but what I hadn't expected was the guy to wield a knife.

Which he did.

He flicked a long blade out, coming at me. "Well, if it ain't the Legacy bitch." He grinned. "I ain't Legacy, but I'll make you mine."

I sneered, waving the bat higher. Noticing Bow cowering, I jerked my chin at her. "Get out of here. *Now.*"

She didn't. She ran at the fool, and if that little rabbit didn't launch herself at his back.

"Fucking bitch!" he roared, grabbing at her hands on his back.

In a crazy-as-fuck turn of events, Bow jerked his head back, making him drop the knife. Deciding to double-team, I slammed the bat into the guy's legs. He fell to the ground, fury in his yell as he took Bow on the ground with him.

Rushing, I grabbed for her, helping her up so we could run.

Suddenly, we weren't alone.

Four dudes came into view, one of which was the guy who'd run off like a little bitch earlier.

Apparently, he was getting reinforcements.

He was the one to run up to the guy on the ground, who Bow had basically took out by herself. He tried to help his friend up, but the asshole was ungrateful and pushed his buddy off him.

"Don't fucking help me. Get them!" the guy on the ground growled, directing his finger at Bow and me. The reinforcements his friend had brought were clearly drunk, stumbling over with beers in their hands. They also wore spirit paint on their faces, obviously spectators too from tonight's game.

They were coming up on Bow and me.

"Bow, *run*," I urged, but she shook her head. The little rabbit stood with me, backing up with me. I raised my bat to the boys. "Back off and leave us alone."

"Last I checked, it's five against two, bitch." Boy with the knife had it out again, his blade gleaming under the parking lot lights. He grinned. "Now, maybe we should try this again?"

I tucked Bow behind me, hoping with maybe me in front, she'd get some sense. She'd *run*, but she didn't move. She stayed with me.

We were screwed.

"Actually, it's seven against five, bitch."

Ares Mallick bounded over the hood of a car, tall enough to do that very feat. That put him right in the middle of the action, cutting those tools off from Bow and me.

He hadn't come alone.

Dorian was right behind him, Thatcher and Wells too. My brother, Bru, brought up the rear and seeing her own brother, Bow immediately ran over to him.

Thatcher grabbed her. His eyes were fire, and the guys about to come at us looked like they were about to shit their pants.

Ares grinned. "Actually, there's eight if you count Thatch's big ass."

"Fuck you," Thatcher growled at him, but all that heat he kept reserved on the boys who'd messed with Bow and me. He hugged Bow close. "You messing with my sister?"

"Nah, man." Guy with the knife put it away. He tucked it in his letterman jacket. "This was just a misunderstanding, and that bitch with the bat egged it on." His chin jutted in my direction. "Ain't that right, Legacy bitch?"

He thought he was being funny, clearly expecting laughter from the Legacy boys themselves.

They weren't laughing.

And neither was Bru, who came over to me. He stood by me, Ares and the other guys in the center.

Dorian made the peak.

He was the tip of their arrow, the male power like he always was on the field. He braced his big arms, in *his own* letterman jacket. He bared teeth. "You got five seconds before we break your legs."

They didn't wait for five.

The assholes stumbled off in a pack, and something told me, it hadn't mattered it was seven against five.

In fact, Dorian probably could have been standing there by himself.

That was how much power he exuded, *Legacy* exuded, and with the assholes gone, Thatcher grabbed Bow.

"Why didn't you wait in the fucking car like I asked you to?" he ground out, but even as he did, he hugged her. It looked so funny since she was so much smaller than him. "You never fucking listen."

"You guys were taking a long time," she said, and good for her standing up to him. She laughed. "You're choking me, jerk."

"Good." He let go. He messed with her hair, a grin on his face, and Bow groaned.

Beside me, Bru studied me. "You okay?" More than his eyes were on me, though.

In fact, everyone's were.

My gaze flitted over them all, especially Dorian. He had

this way of stealing way too much of my attention, and I didn't like it.

I lowered the bat. "Fine," I said, then directed a finger at Bow and crew. "Just get her out of here. There's obviously creeps about."

I'd seen more than one tonight, whatever was going on with Principal Mayberry included. For all I knew, she could have just been buying weed or something. That was her right, but still.

It was weird.

Maywood Heights was proving to be more trouble than I wanted to handle. If I had wanted this much action, I could have stayed in Chicago.

Bru started to say something, but I said I had to go. He let me, but everyone's eyes were on me as I left.

I felt Dorian's the most.

CHAPTER
TWENTY

Sloane

I was surprised when Thatcher Reed dropped his linebacker
self at my lunch table the very next school day.

In fact, I looked around.

Needless to say, my table had been barren since I'd estab-
lished war with Windsor Preparatory Academy's elite.

And Thatcher was royalty. He caught several eyes upon
making it to my basically abandoned table, looking extra
pretty with his dangling earrings and hair in a messy tousle.
He was beyond attractive, and that may have been something
I noticed from the jump…

Had he not basically assaulted me in a swimming pool.

I hadn't forgotten that day, stiffening when he placed his
big self on the other side of the table. He may be a junior,
younger than me, but he was still *bigger* than me. I eyed him.
"What do you want?"

He studied me, my straw between my lips. I'd stopped
sipping the milk from my carton, basically stuck. His strong
chin jutted in my direction. "I heard what you did." He

looked around, his royal-blue eyes narrowed to slits when they returned. "For my sister? Bow told me how you stood up for her at the game."

Did she now? Removing the straw from between my lips, I set my carton on the table. I laughed. "Well, did she tell you what *she* did?" I stated, thinking about that night. I tilted my head. "She basically tackled that motherfucker like a little monkey before you and your boys showed up."

She'd been completely badass. She obviously had a little fire cat in that tank. The little rabbit surprised me. I'd come to save her, and she'd ended up getting me out of a scrape.

Thatcher smirked. "I taught her well," he said, but as he said the words, his gaze circulated. It landed on a couple of guys coming into the cafeteria.

One had his arm in a sling.

A fresh cast was on the tool's arm from the football game, and seeing Thatcher at my reject table, the guy's eyes basically bugged out of their sockets.

Tool-burger shielded his eyes before skirting past my table. The guy behind him I recognized as well. I recognized him as his friend from that evening, but he didn't have a broken arm.

"We promised him we wouldn't break his legs if he left," Thatcher said, and I blinked. He took one of my fries out of my basket, dipping it in my ketchup before chewing it. He smirked again. "We didn't say we wouldn't break his arm."

Holy fucking shit.

That guy definitely had a cast as he cruised into the lunch line.

I supposed Legacy wasn't playing.

These Legacy boys weren't just all bark, sheer power, which made me really look at the guy sitting with me. I saw none of his friends around.

But that didn't mean they weren't nearby.

That didn't mean Dorian Prinze wasn't somewhere, the

dark ruler himself. I still was at war with these guys, obviously thugs at this school.

"Why did you do it?" he asked, eyeing me again. He frowned. "Stand up for my sister. I mean, we know you used her. To get to D?"

I had used her and was well aware of it. I'd messed up, done her dirty, and I was woman enough to admit that. I shook my head. "I didn't mean to use her," I said, opening my hands. "I fucked up, and she didn't deserve that."

The words tasted sour coming out of my mouth, but not because I didn't feel that way. I had messed up. I didn't mean to do such a thing to Bow. She'd always been nice to me. A little all over the place, but always nice.

It was saying all this shit *in front of the enemy* I didn't like. That I was bowing down to the force that ran this place.

"So you felt guilty?" Thatcher cocked his head at me, really trying to figure me out. I shook my head, and his eyes twitched wide.

I shrugged. "I may have fucked up when it came to your sister, but I'm not an asshole." My eyes narrowed. "I stepped in because it was the right thing to do. It wasn't guilt. It was just the right thing. She was in trouble, and I wanted to help her out."

Thatcher leaned back, his beefy arm on his chair. "Surely, you knew you couldn't have done much with those guys." He leaned in. "Even with that little bat of yours."

That didn't matter. It was the right thing to do. Call me stupid, but I stood up for the little guy. Maybe because I knew what it was like to be the little guy. I hugged my arms. "I don't like bullies."

Thatcher's eyes returned into slits, this boy seriously serpent-like. He was as lethal as he was pretty, deadly. Wetting his lips, he kicked his chair from underneath him, rising to the sky. He waved a hand. "Come on. You're coming with me."

I shot up. "Uh, no." *How about a hell no?*

He shook his head, then pointed at my food. "Your food is garbage, and I'm not going to be an asshole and let you eat it." He popped a big shoulder. "Come. I'm going to get you a decent burger and fries. It's the least I can do for you helping Bow."

I tilted my head. "Like… off campus?" I said, but he was already leaving. We weren't allowed to leave school for lunch, one of the academy's rules. I read that in the handbook the first week. I sat up. "Like we're leaving?"

He turned around, his arms open. "You coming or not, Pretty, Pretty Princess? Where I come from, we take care of those who take care of us. I owe you a burger. Let me do that for you."

He put a hand to his chest, and though he appeared genuine, I wasn't so sure. I stood. "I didn't help your sister for a favor or anything."

He was backing away. "I know," he said, then paused to flash a cheeky grin. "That's exactly why you're about to get one."

———

How I ended up in Thatcher's Audi was beyond me, and I'd gotten more than a few looks before we drove off school property. Ironically enough, attention we *hadn't* gotten had been that of the school security.

"They don't care what the fuck we do," Thatcher said, his thick arm hanging out the window. "Our parents own this school. This town."

Apparently, they really did. He went on to say how much their parents donated to the school and the influence all their parents had on the school board because of it. Actually, once Thatcher got talking, he couldn't stop, and I was surprised he relayed this much information about his family. Well, Legacy's families. I supposedly was the enemy.

I guessed I wasn't today.

This "favor" Thatcher seemed obligated to fulfill, and he chatted my ear off all the way to the closest Jax's Burger franchise. As it seemed, the Legacy boys owned this too.

"Wells's dad is Jax," he stated, his tongue out in a gleeful fashion as he unstrapped himself. "We basically get all the free shit we want. Come on."

Eh, big spender, huh?

I rolled my eyes, unstrapping myself. I wasn't surprised to see more than one academy jacket donning both guys and girls in the lot. This must have been a hot place to sneak off to during lunch, and it was close, so I'd give them all that.

Still, this was awkward as fuck flanking behind Windsor Prep elite. Thatcher threw out his large wing span to anyone who gave him attention, the life of the party and vain as complete fuck. The amount of kisses he demanded on his cheek on the way inside alone told me what he thought of himself. And some of the chicks he passed were with guys.

This guy really was something else, but he made me laugh surprisingly enough. His arrogance alone I found laughable.

I wasn't laughing when we got inside.

One booth specifically held all *his* friends, Dorian and Ares eating from their Jax's haul. Wells sat on their opposite side. Dorian and Ares specifically had Bow tucked between them, and she was the one to spot me.

"Sloane!" She waved in my direction like the spirited little rabbit I'd come to miss. This action completely got the attention of her "brothers," and each one of them whirled their heads in my direction. Wells arched his neck, Dorian sat up, and Ares…

"The fuck she doing here?" Ares sneered and even did one better to put a protective hold around the little rabbit. Like I'd eat her or something if I got too close.

Bow picked up on this action and shoved him off her. In fact, she shoved him so much she eventually got him to get out of the booth and let her out.

"Come sit with us," she chanted, definitely in a different place than the last time I'd seen her. Last couple times. I wouldn't mind sitting with *her*, but the rest of the guys not so much.

Ares was currently looking at me like he wanted to strangle me when Thatcher brought me to the table. Wells appeared to be indifferent, and Dorian, well, I had a hard time reading him. He sat there observant to it all but gave no input. He had his big honking fists together as he analyzed the situation.

"I owe her at least a burger, don't you think?" Thatcher stated, taking one of Ares's fries out of his basket. The whole table was filled with empty baskets, and I wondered how much food these guys had already consumed before we'd gotten there. Dorian had a couple of stacks with different colored wrappers, and I noticed the basket in front of him held some kind of wrap instead of a burger. Maybe he had different tastes than his friends. I didn't know.

Nor did I care.

I was too busy trying not to watch him while Thatcher pleaded his case for me, the big guy shoving himself into the booth on Wells's side. The table jutted forward, and Wells smirked.

Thatcher shoved Wells's head before throwing an arm behind the booth. "She saved Bow. I'm buying her a meal."

Ares's expression darkened. "None of us pay for this shit, you asshole."

"Yeah, my dad's footing the bill." Wells chuckled. He put his hands together. "Anyway, Thatcher is right." Wells eyed me. "So you're pretty good with a bat, then, huh?"

I didn't know about all that, both Wells and Thatcher jostling each other like they had some kind of joke going on between them. This made Ares roll his eyes, but Dorian didn't appear so amused. He was chillingly calm while he sat there next to Ares, silent.

Dorian shifted his broad body left. "Wolf, make room."

Ares's jaw dropped. "Are you fucking kidding me?"

Dorian shot him a look, definitely not kidding. Anyway, after the command, the dark prince faced forward, shoving his wrap into his mouth. He stared outside the window, and one would have thought someone had shoved a scoop of pure lard in his mouth with the way he sneered around his lunch.

Dorian may have invited me to sit, but he hadn't wanted to. In any case, Bow seemed ecstatic to have me there today. She sat across from me while I occupied the little space Thatcher left for me.

"You're going to love the food," she said, ringing the buzzer. Apparently, this was a sit-down place once inside. A guy came up and took my order, and despite being a meat eater, I decided to try the vegan chik'n wrap. Since that was the only wrap on the menu I assumed that was what Dorian was eating, and I wondered if he was a vegan.

I didn't know why I ordered it, for something different I supposed, and Ares had something to say about it the moment it arrived.

"You would eat that shit too," he grumbled, getting a wrapper thrown at him from Wells. It seemed Wells took pride in all the food that was on the menu, seeing as how this was his dad's burger franchise. Wells even mentioned his dad put the vegan option on the menu because Dorian asked him if he could. I was right in guessing Dorian was vegan. Ares tossed a hand. "I'm just saying. This girl just can't help but be fucking different." He showed his wolfish grin. "A little fucking noisemaker."

"Aww, isn't it cute how the two of them always fight?" Wells crooned, and Thatcher busted out laughing.

Thatcher tipped his chin at Ares. "Like an old fucking married couple. Right, Wolf?"

Ares's sneer deepened. "Fuck you," he gritted, but then growled at me. "And I'm not into chicks who look like they could be my goddamn twin," he said, surprising me. He threw a balled-up wrapper at Thatcher. "I'm not as vain as you and wouldn't date myself."

I wouldn't date his ass either, the sentiment shared, and I so did *not* look like him. I mean, we were both tall, I'd give him that. We had dark hair and similar skin complexions too, but in his case, his attitude alone made him unattractive to me.

"Your thoughts are shared," I said, making him bare his teeth. This guy really didn't fucking like me, but since I'd called him a bitch on that first day we met (and maybe a time or two since), I'd also give him that. He didn't have to like me, and I didn't have to like him.

And Dorian was staring at me again.

His chocolate-brown irises didn't lift from my direction, watching the exchange between his buddy and me with interest. Maybe he was noting what his boy said about us looking alike, and he was deciding that was just another reason to tuck me farther into the back spaces of his mind. I mean, who'd want to pick up something with someone who looked like his fucking friend.

And why are you thinking about that?

Dorian Prinze was a fucking asshole too, and I wouldn't entertain anything with him either. He was a bully, point blank.

"Sorry I'm late. You guys save something for me?"

I whirled around at the sound of my brother's voice, and his eyes shot out of his head upon seeing me.

"Sloane?" he asked, nearly laughing where he stood. He was obviously shocked. "What are you doing…"

"I owe her a meal, buddy, for saving my sis." Thatcher

tapped Bru's fist. "Pick up a chair and sit on the end. You had Jax's food before?"

So this was my brother's first time here at their meeting spot.

Interesting.

I cataloged this in my mind as my brother did pull up a chair and something else I remembered. That tool with the knife had said it'd been Dorian and the rest of the guys to kick him off the team. They'd done that for a spot for my brother. Now, this could have just been because of Dorian and his hate for me, though.

I assumed as much.

Anyway, I watched on as they all greeted him, welcomed him. Even Dorian smiled at him.

"Good to see you here," Bru said to me, sitting on the back of a chair. He stole one of my fries. "It's nice to each lunch together."

I silently agreed, but playfully shoved him to let him know I did. I'd missed my brother, and I guess I could put up with a lunch for him.

It was nice chatting with Bow too, and she made sure to talk my ear off. I'd be lying if I said I hadn't missed her.

I'd be lying if I said I hadn't missed people.

CHAPTER
TWENTY-ONE

Sloane

I didn't get another invite out to lunch with Legacy. This wasn't surprising, but what had followed that impromptu lunch date was.

I got free food.

Every day at lunch, Thatcher would drop off a sack. Sometimes it'd be from Jax's Burgers. Other times not, but he always made sure to drop something off. Sometimes the drop-offs even included his company, and when it did, Wells tended to join him. The two seemed to move as a unit like Ares and Dorian, and suddenly, I found myself with free food every day at lunch. I never asked for this food, nor did I want it.

I got it anyway.

It seemed Thatcher felt he had a debt to pay, and it extended well past that first lunch. On days he either couldn't make it or didn't make it, Wells entertained me with his company. He'd give me the same food, mentioning Thatcher had a previous engagement. Wells always made sure to wink at me when he said that, and I assumed Thatcher was probably off getting some afternoon delight somewhere. Thatcher was known as a huge ladies' man around the school. Wells too, and I found out he was bisexual. I'd assumed as much. Thatcher never brought his dates to our lunch, but Wells always did. Sometimes he'd have two or three of his groupies, his followers feeding him food while I rolled my eyes from the other side of the table. The days Wells did appear were the most awkward, but not because of who he brought. Bow too had returned to eating lunch with me, and whenever just Wells and his groupies arrived, it put her off. She'd clam up and get all silent, which was the exact opposite of the little rabbit.

I asked her once what the deal was, but she got all shy about it and passed it off. Her cheeks grew incredibly warm, though, and considering Wells typically had his tongue shoved down the throat of one of his minions, I understood why. I forgot sometimes she was just a sophomore, and after I did see he was bothering her, I asked him to tone down some of the PDA.

"Sure thing, Pretty, Pretty Princess," Wells said to me, something both him and Thatcher had started to call me. I'd take it over *Vapor* and *Legacy bitch* any day. Hell, I'd take my name back.

That came the following week.

The Legacy effect was something else. People definitely took note of Thatcher Reed's and Wells Ambrose's sudden attention. They made known their gifts of food and attention, and with that came people actually looking me in the face again. I got greetings from people I hadn't seen the eyes of in weeks.

And teachers actually called on me again.

That last bit I could have done without. I mean, I wasn't a brain like my brother. I wasn't always prepared to answer questions in class, but it was nice that I existed again. The little "gifts" in the form of pranks deposited inside my locker also stopped, and I found my little brother without his attitude in the mornings. He was smiling at me again. He was acknowledging me, and though I definitely thought he'd been an asshole to me in the time we'd been here, I did know my place in our feud. I promised I'd make things easier for us, and I definitely hadn't done that by starting a war with the boss dog clique. I'd gotten myself in a mess and him by association, and I completely acknowledged that. I also hadn't told him a lot of things that had been done to me.

Again, something I acknowledged.

Those dark days seemed to be long in the past as the days continued on. The leaves on the trees started to shift and change, the breeze sharper as Maywood Heights hinted at a change in the seasons. We were still well away from winter. Thank God. Chicago didn't play when it came to Midwestern winters, but I did have to wear a jacket sometimes with my academy uniform. I also stopped wearing knee-highs and shifted to trousers. Girls were allowed to wear them when the colder weather hit.

I was grateful the day I fell.

I tripped on a floorboard literally in the middle of the hall. Had I been wearing a skirt, my lady bits would have been all over the place. My feet left from under me and everything, and I might have hit the floor if not for a set of strong hands.

And a solid chest.

Dark brown irises came with it, those big arms and firm hands bracing me close. The dark prince had caught me like a football on the field, quick and agile.

Damn-near unmovable.

No shake rattled his meaty arms in his embrace. This boy was unshakable. Dorian wet his lips as he brought me to my feet. He and his bastard friend Ares were two members of Legacy I actually hadn't seen lately. The gifts of food and attention stopped at Thatcher and Wells.

Dorian and Ares had been noticeably absent.

They may have let the younger of their ranks indulge in my company, but they sure as fuck weren't doing the same. This was something I'd definitely noticed too, which annoyed the ever-loving fuck out of me. Of course, I wanted nothing to do with Ares "Wolf" Mallick. I mean, the guy hated me as much as I did him. I wanted nothing to do with Dorian either, but for some reason, I always made note when the two Legacy juniors showed up and Dorian didn't.

This was something I simply stopped questioning, accepting it. I cataloged it as I noted all the different shades of brown in his eyes while he held me now. The hallway's fluorescent lights seemed to make them appear more hazel instead of the dark brown. They hinted at a lightness inside him, but I knew this to be a lie. There was no light inside this boy.

He stabilized me.

"Watch where you're going," he grumbled, point proven. His jaw tightened. "This floorboard sticks, always has."

I noted his warning, and I almost told him I knew about it. Though, I didn't. I mean, I never tripped on this floorboard but suddenly I felt like I should have known that. Like there'd been a space in my memory reserved for that very thought.

Shaking that off, I nodded at Dorian. He passed nothing more than a hard glance my way before he stalked down the hallway like a Neanderthal. He filled up so much of the hall it was crazy, and the students around him parted like the Red Sea for him to pass. They all filled in after that, everyone always shifting in his wake, and I shook my head.

Dick.

He still was, and I glanced down, seeing a sharp piece of metal on the locker. Had I actually fallen (had he not caught me), I would have hit that, punctured myself or even worse.

I played with my sleeve, rubbing beneath my forearm. The

ghost of a feeling caused me to turn my arm around, and I unbuttoned my sleeve.

A faded scar faced me on my skin. It was something I'd always had. In fact, I'd had it so long I didn't even remember when I got it. The weird thing was, had I fallen into the metal shard on the locker, I would have hit that same place where my scar was located.

I guess I should thank the dark prince.

He probably saved me some more damage to my skin.

I buttoned my sleeve. I was already late for my next class but stopped when I noticed a glint of something between the lockers. It was something metal, small, and I didn't even know how I spotted it.

I placed my books down, getting on all fours. I had long arms, so I was able to touch the back of the wall pretty easy. I couldn't see for shit, though.

I pressed my face to the dirty floor, well aware of how stupid I looked but whatever that was beneath the lockers was within reach. I just had to get it.

"What the fuck are you doing, little?"

My jacket ripped.

Like literally, I ripped my sleeve at the hem, the voice surprising me. The lockers caught on my sleeve, and when I slid my arm from underneath them, I made the tear worse.

"Nice," I grumbled, forgetting about whatever was under the locker when I analyzed my jacket. I shook my head at the hole. "Really nice."

"Well, what were you fucking doing?" Ares cast a dark look down on me, a wash of dark curls shrouding his face. His hair was more feathered some days, and odds were, he normally put something in it to tame his curls. Today, they were on full display. His big shoulders popped up. "Tell me it hasn't gotten to the point where you're rooting around for trash to get by? You see some food down there, yeah?"

This guy's asshole energy was off the charts. I flipped him

off, and he chuckled, backing off so I could get up. I noticed he didn't offer to help. I brushed myself off. "No, I thought I found something."

"What kind of something?" He angled a look down. "Something where?"

It was probably nothing. I shrugged. "Just something. Doesn't matter."

It probably was nothing, and I managed to look like an idiot in front of the guy who'd bullied me from day one, the one who'd started this whole thing.

Well, technically you did when you parked in his spot.

I didn't care what I'd done. It gave him no right to treat me the way he had, nor to continue talking to me like I was his personal piece of shit.

He was still staring at the floor and the area I'd been searching but stopped when I started to pass him. He put a hand out. "Wait. I want to talk to you." He directed a finger. "And it's Sloane, right? I heard that's what people are calling you."

Wow, he had a couple of brain cells up there.

Though I wondered why he actually bothered to learn something about me. I lounged back against the lockers. "What do you want? Or is my breathing bothering you now?"

I'd done less before.

He smirked at me. A couple of thirsty bitches passed him in the hallway, and he merely whipped those curls in their direction to get a giggle and red cheeks. This guy was just as full of himself as the rest of them, but I didn't have time for it. I started to go again, but he cut me off with that long wingspan.

I frowned. "Let me by."

"If her highness would come down from her ice castle for all of a second, I might be able to tell her I'm offering an olive branch," he said, and my eyes twitched wide. He nodded. "This shit between us I'm over. I'm sure you're over it too."

His eyes narrowed. "I figured we should squash it before we killed each other in the end."

He hadn't cared about that before, until this moment anyway.

He scrubbed into his hair. "Believe me or not. I don't care. But here I am, and I can say I tried."

He started to walk away now, but I cut him off this time.

He shook his head. "My time's better spent on the field or in my art. I don't have time for anymore sophomoric shit, despite what you may believe." He eyed me up and down. "I also know this tense shit has become a thing between us guys. Thatcher and Wells are obviously taking up with you, and I too have to acknowledge you did Bow a solid. That girl's like my little sis, and I'm tired of whatever this shit is between us making D look at me funny."

Dorian was looking at him funny? I wondered why.

And he said he did art? I jerked my chin in his direction. "What kind of art?"

"What?"

I laughed. "What kind of art do you do? Painting? Sculpting?"

He studied me. "Sketch work. Specifically, I like to design."

"Design what?"

"Stuff."

Well, sorry. Jesus. I smirked. "I never would have taken you for an artist."

"Well, you don't know me. Do you?" He angled a look at me. He put a hand out. "So, are we going to squash this shit or what? I don't want to hear it from my boys anymore."

Honestly, I didn't care about him or the situation with "his boys," but I did care that, with our war, a line against the Legacy was still drawn.

That alone had me giving him my hand. "Fine."

"Fine," he said, a more than tense truce. But at least it was one. He let go. "I'll see you around then. Maybe at my party tonight."

"Party?"

He nodded. "I do them sometimes." He eyed me. "Give me your number. I'll text you the deets."

I let him because I honestly was having an out-of-body experience here. No way was my luck suddenly changing like this, where Ares was acknowledging me and actually inviting me to his party. I didn't care about this shit, but I was shocked he'd come forward.

After I gave him my number, he shot me a text. "There you go. See you tonight."

Nodding, I backed away from the conversation, leaving him there.

"It's a lingerie party, by the way," he said behind me. He dashed up his thick eyebrows. "If you dare to show up now, that is."

And he just couldn't help himself, more than a dare in his voice. He probably thought I wouldn't show up now. I hugged my books. "That's if *you* dare to show up."

He tugged up his dress shirt, displaying his washboard abs. "I ain't got nothing to hide, little. You be there, I'll be there."

I rolled my eyes, hearing him chuckle as I walked away. God, he was such an arrogant fuck. I really couldn't stand that dude.

But what could I say? I couldn't help a good challenge.

CHAPTER
TWENTY-TWO

Sloane

The fucker *Legally Blond*ed me.

I showed up to Ares's little party, and not only was I the *only* one in lingerie, I was also the only person who decided to wear a fucking feathered mask.

Like a goddamn idiot.

I'd wanted to make a statement, and I definitely managed that, my kitten heels taking me across a lit entryway. The curvy letters A and M brightened coral flooring, this guy extra as fuck to have his insignia highlighting what were obviously his parents' floors. Ares lived in some kind of manor on the north side of town, mansions everywhere. The roads had been filled down the block for this party.

And here I was half naked.

My feathered, black mask matched my laced boy short panties. I didn't have a lot of sexy things, but that seemed appropriate for what was supposed to have been a lingerie party. I showed up in this bitch looking like Elle Woods minus her bunny ears.

I might as well have had some with the way everyone stared.

I had a spotlight on me the minute I showed up thanks to Ares's lighting effect. The curly letters shone bright over my body, my coat in my hand and jaw dropped to the floor. I'd come inside with a bunch of people wearing coats, and I figured they'd all been wearing the same thing underneath.

I was so terribly, *terribly* wrong.

The snickers ensued, as I forced my coat on but not quick enough to avoid catching the eye of several partygoers. Two of which were Bow and my brother. They were in a small group of others I recognized from school.

Bow gasped, and my brother nearly dropped his drink. Both came over to me, as I secured my belt, but the damage had been done.

"No one told me Ares was getting prostitutes!" some dick roared nearby, and my brother shoved him.

"Shut the fuck up, asshole," Bru gritted, and by then, Bow had grabbed my arm.

She shook her head. "Sloane, what the hell?"

What the hell indeed, my face shooting up a million degrees in heat. I let that rich fucker Ares Mallick embarrass me.

Olive branch, my ass.

All that shit had obviously been a setup, *this invite* a setup. I fluffed my hair over my coat. "Don't ask."

"Well, I'm gonna." It seemed Bru had gotten those tools to watch their mouths because he now joined Bow's side. He studied my coat. "Why are you only wearing that under there?"

Because *his friend* had once again gone out of his way to make me look like an idiot.

"Ares," I hissed, looking for him around the foyer, but this was impossible. Ares's house pumped full of people. So many, in fact, I was quite surprised not to see them hanging

off the chandeliers. My view from even the entryway gave
vantage to a full house, and the pool outside had even more.
The DJ was out there, raising his hands amongst dancing
teens, but his beats played in the house.

I assumed Ares had some kind of speaker system set up
inside. My brother touched my arm. "Wait. Ares did this?"

"Asshole told me it was a lingerie party," I said, his eyes
widening, and Bru's reaction to that actually surprised me.
He had not once stood up for me when it came to these boys,
but his face definitely shot red in color after what I said. He
even started to drag my arm away.

"We're getting you home," he stated, but I slipped my
arm out.

"I'm fine."

"You sure?" he studied me, really concerned, and I smiled.

"Yeah, dweeb. I'm okay. I swear." After all, I did have my
coat, and I wasn't about to let Ares get a reaction out of me.

Well, actually…

A reaction might be just what I needed in this scenario. In
fact, it felt like the perfect thing. I looked around for Ares
again, and while I did, Bru asked me if I wanted a drink.

"Nah, I'm okay," I told him. "Go mingle or something."

He didn't look like he wanted to. I mean, his sister just
walked in here half naked, and only after assuring I was okay
did he decide to go off to find some friends. I was really
happy to have him in my corner again, and I hoped I did after
what I was about to do.

Fact of the matter was, I needed to stand up for myself.

I purposely took my coat off.

I got right back down to my undies, striding with nothing
but self-assurance when I dropped my coat and my purse off
at coat check. Yep, Ares Mallick actually had coat check at this
party. They had a guy in a suit taking everyone's stuff in the
foyer.

Bow's jaw dropped.

"What are you doing?" she gasped, her cheeks warming. The way she stared at my boobs, one would have thought she didn't have any herself, but then again, I did have pretty big boobs for my size. I was lanky, but easily fit into a D cup.

"I'm going to make a statement," I said, confident as hell. Well, at least I tried to put that off. I got more than a few catcalls as tool-burgers passed me half drunk. I threw my cheap mask at one of them. "Take a picture, it'll last longer."

"No problem, baby." Dude snapped that picture, and I growled. The guy scampered off, but I didn't have any time for him.

I faced Bow. "Where's Ares?"

The asshat was here somewhere, and he was about to answer to me.

Bow shrank in her little jeans and T-shirt. Really, we were yin and yang, and how we'd been able to establish some kind of friendship was beyond me. There must have been something about the two of us that went together, though, and like the rest of Legacy, I somehow felt like I had a long-lost little sister I never had. She was just cute like that, and you wanted to protect her.

She hugged her arms. "Depends. What are you going to do with that information?"

"What's necessary," I said, honest. "Where are they?"

Because where he was, I was sure I'd find the others. Those four traveled in a pack like an actual wolf pack.

"Probably hanging out in his dad's lounge," she mumbled. Though, obviously she didn't want to tell me. "But no one else is allowed in there." She leaned in. "They take girls."

Meaning they were getting their dicks wet.

Perfect.

Some thought really should have gone into this next move. I mean, I probably should have reconsidered before I stormed the house looking for this lounge. I found it easily.

Everyone apparently knew where Legacy like to have their fun.

They even had a dude at the door.

The guy hadn't even bothered to question me when I swiveled my hips and scampered inside a room reeking of weed and *flesh.* Actual sweat clouded my nostrils, and I was sure the goon at the door thought I'd fit right in for what I'd been about to see.

I definitely did.

I was as scandalously clad as some of the other chicks in there. Thatcher had two girls in iridescent cat suits on his lap, bra and panties on full display. The girls made out in front of him, his hand on the ass of a *third* girl kissing his neck.

He paid no attention as I waltzed past him, clearly busy, but the other three played poker. They passed a blunt around. A couple of topless chicks felt each other up while dancing for the guys who barely even looked at them. The girls appeared to be partygoers who simply looked thirsty as hell, and Ares had been taking his hit when one girl pushed her tits in his face.

"Back off," he grunted, making the girl whine. Wells gave her a nice place on his lap instead, and that seemed to appease her. Ares passed the joint off to Wells next, and he started to take a drink.

That was until he saw me.

The guy literally blew the alcohol out of his mouth, spraying it all over the poker table and the remaining girl who vied for his attention. She made the mistake of trying to kiss his neck, and he got it right in her face.

"Ew, yuck!" she squealed, getting up, and Dorian and Wells threw up their hands.

"What the fuck, bro?" Dorian charged, growling. It didn't appear Ares had gotten him too, but his buddy had just spat alcohol all over the place.

Ares howled boisterous laughter.

"Holy fucking shit. This is amazing," he stated, clapping, then directed his finger toward me. "You actually fucking fell for it."

Dorian and Wells whirled in my direction, Thatcher too.

Thatcher's women nearly fell off his lap. He actually had to do a double catch just to keep them up there. His jaw dropped. "What the fuck? *Sloane*?"

What the fuck indeed.

I pranced over, tossing my hair around and looking like an idiot. I propped my hands on my hips. "Hey, guys. Got room for another?"

Wells cleared his lap, Thatcher too, which caused all three of their girls to moan and groan. Thatcher waved a hand. "Come on, baby. I'll take care of you."

"Only after me." Wells was more delicate about it, taking my hand. He kissed it. "I'll say. You certainly like to make an appearance."

"Yeah, she does." Ares was still roaring, but Dorian was not.

Dorian shoved him. "What the fuck?"

"Chill, bro." Ares threw a hand at him, finally calming down a little. "She can take a joke. Why can't you?"

"Because she shouldn't have to." Dorian stood, and it was like the record stopped. All laughter completely left Ares's lips, his smile wiping away.

Dorian never had one.

The dark prince was steamed for some reason. Red was chasing up his neck, and when Ares opened his mouth to say something, he never got the chance.

His buddy was too busy taking me away.

Dorian literally jerked me by the arm out of the room, being more than forceful about it. I threw him off me outside the door. "What the fuck?"

"*You*, what the fuck?" he growled, then snatched my arm

again. I punched at his big, meaty grip, but this guy gripped footballs for a living.

He wasn't letting go.

"Get your hands off me," I bit out, then he physically picked me up. He tossed me like a fucking sack of potatoes over his shoulder. I got nothing but the sight of a muscled ass as he walked me up a spiral staircase.

I kicked and screamed the whole way, physically punching at his perfect ass, but that only made him slap mine.

"Hit me again, little fighter, and I'll be owning this," he warned, his hand cradling my ass still. He squeezed, his palm rough through my underwear, and I thought he'd rip them off.

He gratefully didn't.

He just continued to walk, and people passed us like this wasn't unusual. Like this ape of a boy did this all the time, and this was simply normal. Eventually, we stopped at some room, but he didn't set me down.

He threw me on a bed.

Fear caused me to back up on it, not fucking playing anymore. This guy had come at me before, and he'd definitely do it again.

Dorian smirked at me, as if I was an idiot for the thought when he studied me on the bed. He shook his blond head before heading over to a set of dresser drawers.

"Can't help but make noise," he gritted, seemingly to himself as he rooted around in it. Next thing I knew, he was tossing clothes at me. Boy clothes.

I eyed the shorts and top. "What's this?"

"Put it on," he ground out, then turned around.

Like a gentleman.

I almost laughed, thinking he was joking. On my elbows, I did nothing.

He cuffed his arms, head raised. "Do it, or I'll do it for you." He eyed over his shoulder. "And you won't like it."

My eyes lifted, putting his stupid clothes on. They were of course way too big, and I looked even more of an idiot than I had a second ago. Once I stood before him fully clothed, he turned around. I raised and dropped my hands. "Happy?"

"Actually, no." He got in my face, not shy about it. He bared his teeth. "I'll be happy when you stop making noise. When you stop getting in my way and fucking with my boys."

You got to be shitting me.

I directed a finger at the door. "*Your boy* set me up, dick wad."

The wrong thing to say.

I knew because he turned the tables around on me.

He whirled me around by the hips, locking me ass-first to that same dresser. His hand braced my throat, and I gasped. "Let go."

He didn't.

His hold tightened, and a madness danced about his ebony eyes. Like he was teetering a line of destruction and pain.

"What did my mom do to deserve what you did?" His eyes scanned mine. "What did my mother do to deserve to cry from your *noise*?"

He was obviously referring to earlier acts, things I did to get to him.

"I didn't mean to make her cry." And I meant that. "I didn't mean to use Bow either. I didn't mean to do anything to either of them."

"Then what do you mean to do?" He got up in my face, but he didn't let go. His irises simmered. "Tell me. What are your intentions, Noa Sloane?"

"Sloane," I corrected and wouldn't back down from this

jock. I wriggled within his tight hold. "And I'll do whatever I have to in order to stand up for myself."

"So, you're not sorry." Breath to breath. Scowl to scowl. He was so close I tasted his wintry breath again, cool winds passing roughly over my lips. "For making my mom cry? For betraying Bow?"

Of course, I was. I didn't mean to upset his mother. I didn't even *know* his mother, and Bow was my friend. Of course, I hadn't wanted to hurt her.

This boy made me do things, *got in my head*, and I made mistakes I couldn't take back.

"*Fuck you*," I emphasized, and I didn't care that it was the wrong thing to say. I didn't care if it set him off. He wouldn't get his way with me. I shook my head. "You touched me. *Tackled* me."

"And like you didn't like it." He was too close now. He placed a hand on either side of my face, his dark eyes flaring. "Like you weren't *begging* to suck my cock."

I reared back to slap him, but he caught it. Stupid fucking football player.

"Like you didn't gag around me," he heated over my face, my insides churning, my lower lips *surging*. They buzzed like my clit between them, my thighs hugging together. Dorian wet his lips. "Like you didn't want to taste me." He angled forward. "Like you didn't want me tasting you."

His chest pressed close to mine, my nipples hard and erect, and as if to make his point, he reached between my legs.

"Dorian…"

He shoved his hand down my shorts, cupping me right through my panties, and I gasped.

My pussy lips ignited against his rough fingers, the heat beneath my legs easily soaking his fingers.

He knew.

I watched as that awareness drove his madness across the line, the dark prince taken to his brink.

"You're so wet for me, Noa Sloane," he said, ignoring what I wanted to be called. He eyed my mouth. "I'm in your head just as much as you're in mine."

What?

He bit my lip, the thoughts gone when his big hands drew my face up to meet his. Our teeth clacked, all tongues and pants.

"Fuck you for getting in my head." He sounded angry, enraged, and he bit my mouth so hard I cried out. "Fuck you, Noa."

"Sloane." I shoved at his beefy chest, a weak attempt at best. "Get off me."

"You want me," he gritted, almost smirking as a simple tongue flick caused me to open my mouth for me. "You want me filling all your holes. Making you scream."

He had such a disgusting mouth. My panties were completely wet as he manhandled me. He shoved my shorts down to my ankles. And whoever's shirt he gave me, he ripped off.

His went next.

Beautifully tanned skin hugged muscled flesh, no doubt from all those days he played football shirtless in the sun. His hair caught that same sunlight, streaked and trapped in every strand.

He drew his fingers through them, looking crazed and deranged as he ground his cock against my mound.

"Stop fucking fighting it." He dragged my arms up, knocking off candles and a display of framed art off the dresser. Whoever's room this was, he was trashing it. He tangled our arms. "Stop *fighting me.*"

He made it hard not to. I was in a constant fight with him basically since I'd set foot in this town. He'd placed a target on me and set quickly to break me.

I moved my mouth away, and all that did was cause him to fasten his full lips to my neck. His teeth bit my pulse, canines piercing the skin. My breasts sagged, heavy and weighted through my lace cups.

"You'll hurt me." I trembled beneath his mouth, I think my real fear. This boy drove me insane. He made me not think for myself. I didn't think clearly.

His hand captured my throat, his tongue dragging up my quivering pulse. The mere action alone caused weakness to hit my legs.

Dorian was there to keep me upright. Hands on my thighs, he picked me up and looped my legs around his waist. His hands braced my ass, and he kissed me so hard and fast I forgot what I'd just said to him.

I forgot that he could hurt me.

"You'd do worse," he panted, our tongues dueling, his taste full and explosive with heat. "*You're doing* worse."

He made it sound like I was getting to him too, in his head just as bad, but I found that hard to believe. This boy was unshakable, impenetrable. He'd gotten me literally down on my knees for him in multiple occasions.

The bed was soft.

He set me down on high thread count sheets, and I disappeared into it. It sunk deeper with Dorian's weight, a smirk on his lips when he tugged my kitten heels off.

"These are dangerous," he growled, tossing them to the floor. Like an animal, he then proceeded to bite my naked toes. Seriously, it was like the hottest fucking thing he could have done, and not once had someone ever done that to me.

The dark prince wasn't just anyone.

He was a man god, a boy making the transition into the fullest potential of himself. He exuded power, all raw sex and muscled flesh. Those around him bowed down, and those far beneath him didn't even bother.

They couldn't get low enough.

This boy had broken me, trembling at just the anticipation of him inside me. That was no doubt where this was going. I mean, he had me half naked on a bed. There were candles in the room, and he put them out with his fingers. The room dimmed to nothing but the moonlight streaming in.

He really did look like a god now, a beast of a man on his knees in front of me. The room's dim shadows hugged his bulky frame, large biceps and thighs.

He jerked me to him, and since making out his expression was hard with the low light, I had to literally wait with anticipation as he felt me up.

As he tasted me.

His tongue flicked me through my underwear, and my thighs hugged his face. He forced them apart, the growl from his lips buzzing my pussy.

"What the fuck? Why do you taste like this?" He sounded drunk below me, and since I couldn't see his face, I had no idea if this was a good reaction to the way I tasted or not. It might have been strategic, him taking away the light. He didn't want to expose himself to me. It made him vulnerable.

And something told me the dark prince didn't like being vulnerable.

He shredded my panties, ripped them clean off with his teeth, and his hands did the rest. Bracing my thighs, he drank from my center. My fingers gripped his hair as I called out, and he chuckled against my pussy. "I'd like to keep some of my hair, Sloane."

"Fuck you." God, we were so dysfunctional. I mean, who made love like this? We weren't making love actually—at all. This was just sex between us.

Hot. Fucking. Sex.

Dorian knew how to eat pussy, nearly feral about it when he drove his tongue into my core and probed me deep. He hit me with piston-like precision, his hands digging into my ass cheeks.

"I told you. You *wanted* me to taste you." He buried himself between my legs, his big arms sliding beneath them. Bracing them to his shoulders, he blew heat on my sex. "You're a goddamn liar, Sloane."

I was a liar. Everything he was doing to me felt so good.

"Don't stop," I called out, nearly there, but Dorian didn't make anything easy. He left my sex, and my body sagged without his mouth.

He was such an asshole, arrogant, and I made out nothing but a dark smile on his lips when he wiped his mouth with his arm. He loomed largely over me, my sex still vibrating with need.

"Beg for me," he said, guiding my mouth up, but he didn't kiss me. His eyebrows narrowed. "You don't get it until you tell me you want it."

I had told him.

And he was playing games again.

He liked to win, and apparently, this went far beyond the football field.

I turned my face away, equally frustrated as I was annoyed. But then he played with me, his hand at my center. His fingers buried inside me, his hard body pinning me down.

"Sloane."

I faced him, his eyes like ebony pools. They scanned mine with interest, analyzing like he was trying to figure me out. He did kiss me then, hot and hard, and I ached beneath his mouth.

"You can do worse to me," he said, something he had said before. He turned me on my front, unstrapping my bra, but then, he crowded me.

His big hips drove into me from behind through his jeans. His growl touched the air when he tugged my hair back and bit my neck. He was going so slow, controlled, and I nearly came with him just grinding on top of me.

"Beg me," he said again. Slowly breaking me down. He had broken me. I was fucking shattered. He laced our fingers, pinning them to the bed. "Tell me to fuck you."

"Fuck me, please," I cried, nearly in tears. The frustration claimed me, anger buckling me and making me want to knock him off me. I didn't understand why he needed me to be like this, why he felt the need to control me and take whatever he wanted.

He stripped me raw, and upon turning me around, I saw him through clouded eyes. He was a beautiful monster, all darkness and little light.

I wondered how it had happened.

I wondered what had happened to him to make him feel the need to have such control. He seemed to enjoy taking what he needed, power and control meaning more than everything else.

He saw my eyes. Curling a finger, he flicked my hair away from them. He bowed his head then, kissing my eyelids. His mouth moved like he was speaking words over them.

Breathless.

Gentle.

Words.

But he wasn't gentle. He was calloused and hard like his rough football hands.

In the next seconds, he stripped himself bare down to nothing but his muscled form. Like the rest of his body, he was powerful, chiseled everywhere from his thick torso to his bulky legs. He sheathed himself with a condom before palming my legs apart and made no apologies for those tears he clearly saw. He said he wanted me to scream for him.

I did once he entered me.

I called out at that first thrust, flesh tearing, my body filled to the brink. I wasn't casual with sex. I only did it with people I trusted or had an emotional attachment to.

Needless to say, that hadn't been many.

Dorian Prinze was only the third boy I'd been with, and he filled me so largely it was as if he were the only one. He stretched and pulled me from the inside out, the expression of awe on his face telling me he felt the same tension in my core.

"Shit, you're so tight," he said, kissing my mouth open before bowing his head and tonguing my nipples. He sucked one in, and I screamed again, his thrust hard and fast between my legs. "You're mine."

He said the word *mine* as if claiming me. Like he had any right to brand me. His words heated over my moist flesh, Dorian's warm body slick over me. We were both sweating, his body powerful and unrelenting.

"*Mine,*" he repeated, feral and completely maddened. Drawing back, he watched himself enter me again and again. My muscles expanded and contracted as I hugged my thighs to his hips. He faced me. "You're mine. You hear that, Noa?"

I'd say whatever he wanted…

As long as he didn't stop.

As long as he gave himself to me for as long as these few moments in this bed lasted. They would end. I'd get up and realize what a mistake this was. He probably would too, but would most likely still believe his words of ownership.

But I couldn't be owned. Not by him at least.

I mean, there wasn't a place for me anyway.

Dorian was consumed by something, and I wasn't about to fuck with whatever it was. I had my own life, my own family and myself to take care of.

I didn't have time for the heartbreak.

I cried out again as Dorian took me to my brink, and he roared, the bed slamming against the wall as he fucked me into submission.

"That's it," he coached, pumping once, then twice before his eyes rolled back. His cock spasmed inside me, emptying himself into the condom, and the fact he was ridiculously beautiful (even as he came) made me want to touch him.

He let me, my fingers dancing in that lovely blond hair. The tendrils slid through my fingers like shimmering silk, his hair sun-kissed and glowing in the moonlight. He let me play with it for longer than I thought he would before kissing my fingers. He sucked one into his mouth, biting me.

My flesh burned beneath his teeth, my body wriggling below him. I wanted to kiss him again, and I hated myself for it. I hated my draw to him.

But then, he kissed me first.

He bent that big body, crowding me in. He took my mouth like he did everything, no apologies from his full lips.

He kissed me so long I forgot where we were and, eventually, how I'd ended up in his arms. He hugged me to his big body like a teddy bear, playing with *my hair* as he kissed me.

It felt too good to tell him to stop.

CHAPTER
TWENTY-THREE

Sloane

I woke up the next morning in a bed and a room I didn't recognize.

Oh, yeah. Right.

I'd had sex with Dorian Prinze, then *fallen asleep* with Dorian Prinze.

Not that I had a choice.

His big bear hold had felt really good, and I was a girl with hormones.

Stupid big football player.

He hadn't let go of me, so I'd stayed snuggled tucked inside his mighty embrace. At some point, I'd realized he'd fallen asleep too, and there was no escape then.

He'd held my ass all night. He'd kept me close like he didn't want to let go. Like I was his like he said. He might have felt that way, but I didn't belong to anyone.

He was gone.

He'd left me in this big bed by myself, and right away, I

thought about Bru. The last time I'd seen him, we'd both been partying, and it wasn't like me to just not check in.

He's probably worried sick.

My brother and I had our problems, but we still cared about each other. I'd worry too if I hadn't seen him at all after that first run-in we had.

Pressing soft blankets to my boobs, I whipped my bare legs off the bed. I started to look for my bra and panties, but they'd been folded and placed on the bedside table.

With my purse and cell phone.

They both literally sat on top of my folded panties, my trench coat beneath all that.

It'd been folded too.

I found this rather odd, but Dorian had obviously gotten my stuff from coat check. I was just surprised he'd even bothered.

Putting that out of my mind, I opened my phone, and naturally, I had messages from Bru. He'd wondered about me at several points in the night, but then his texts stopped at some point.

Me: I'm going to an after party. Might be out all night.

I'd sent that text at around three apparently.

What the fuck?

Bru's return text told me to have fun and that he was glad I was doing that for once. My brother was literally happy I was staying out all night and not coming back home.

And Dorian Prinze had lied for me.

He'd covered, which was good, *I guess*, but a severe invasion of privacy.

Again, I wondered why he'd even bothered. The boy was callous, cold and after getting his dick wet with me, I found it very peculiar he'd actually looked out for me afterward. I mean, why would he care?

This was all terribly confusing, but I had to pee and maybe roll something around in my mouth so it didn't smell like death. I also had school in like an hour, so I should probably get home and get ready.

Whoever Ares's parents were, they obviously were really lax or just not around. Considering what a wild child he was, something told me it was the latter. He seemed to be more dysfunctional than even Dorian managed to be and that was saying something.

I'm not going out there in a bra and panties.

I had my coat, but I put the shorts and top on that Dorian had given me over my underwear. I just needed to pee, then I was getting the hell out of Dodge.

I started to put my heels on but decided against that if I was trying to be stealthy. Even still, I kept my heels gripped in my hand and the rest of my stuff under my arm when I toed out of the bedroom in search of a bathroom. There was no doubt several around in this big-ass manor. Ares's house made Bru's and mine look like a small cottage.

I got down the hall and simply started trying doors (not smart), but I figured eventually, one would be a bathroom. I found a couple bedrooms, one of which still had several partygoers in it. Some had been in the bed while others were scattered across the floor like the discarded clothing in the room.

Apparently, people just staying over at Ares's place was old hat after one of his parties.

I closed that door, then started to open another with gold handles.

The voices behind the door stopped me.

Actually, *his* voice in particular stopped me. Dorian was speaking to someone on the other side of the door.

"I just need you to cover for me today," he said, his voice low, tense. He always sounded on edge, but the rough timbre of his deep voice rattled with heat. "I won't be long. Just for the day, but my dad's starting to get suspicious. If he or my mom, or anyone else asks, I was at school all day. I paid my butler off to call in sick for me."

What the fuck?

I pressed my ear to the door. I probably shouldn't be listening but...

"This is fucked, man." Thatcher. Thatcher Reed. "I hate that you're even telling me this. I hate that *I know* this."

"Me too." Wells was in there with them, maybe Ares too, but I hadn't heard him. "What the fuck? This is so fucked."

"I know, but I wouldn't be telling you if I didn't have a choice. I need an excuse for today, and Wolf won't understand," Dorian said. He sighed. "I just need you to cover for me. Say whatever you have to say, and if Wolf asks, tell him I went out of town. It's the truth."

Apparently, he was going somewhere and needed them to back him up. It just didn't make sense he was keeping Ares out of the information. I mean, he was his friend. Probably his closest the way they interacted.

"Of course, he won't fucking understand. *We* don't understand," Wells gritted. "And you're making us an accessory."

"And keeping shit from Wolf." Thatcher sighed now. "We don't lie to each other, D. We don't keep shit from each other."

"I think you know, in this case, it's necessary," Dorian continued. "You know this will all set Ares off and I... I have to protect him from that. He doesn't need to know."

"Charlie wouldn't want this," Thatcher gritted, and some shuffling sound. I didn't know if Dorian got up or what, but for whatever reason, Thatcher stopped talking.

The room silenced.

"I'm doing this for him," Dorian said. More silence. "Remember that."

"So you're a little fucking spy now?"

I whipped around, the boy his friends were *just speaking* about in front of me now.

He had a black eye.

Ares literally had black ringing one of his dark eyes, his expression heated on me. He wore a silk robe and matching bed pants like some kind of prince, his familiar white tank on beneath. His curls were wet too. Like he'd just gotten out of the shower and was possibly attempting to get ready for school. He stared at the door, then me. "What are you doing?"

I was too busy looking at his eye.

Someone had obviously hit him. I folded my arms. "Nothing." I frowned. "What happened to your eye?"

Like he remembered, he touched it, wincing a little. It was definitely fresh, and since he hadn't had that shiner last night, something had happened recently.

"Ask your brother," he said, surprising me, and my jaw dropped. He shrugged. "It seems he didn't like the little joke I played on you last night." He nodded. "I have to say, I respect it. If you were my sister, I would have done the same."

I felt like I was in an alternate universe right now. My mouth parted. "Bru hit you?"

"Yeah." He faced me, eyeing the hallway like he didn't want to admit it. He started to say something, but he possibly thought better of it because he closed his mouth. He eyed the door again. "Stop being a nosy little shit. It's rude when you're in someone else's fucking house."

Had he known the conversation behind that very door included him, he might have felt differently.

Ares passed me with a huff, and I cursed when something in his pocket punctured my thigh.

"What the hell?" I gazed down, seeing blood. A small dot of red expanded on my thigh. "You scratched me. What the hell is in your pocket?"

Ares appeared aloof as he turned around. He shrugged. "I'd be careful snooping around hallways, little," he said, frowning. "Some things you hear can't be unheard."

Sneering at him, I studied my thigh again. I didn't know if

it was a pen he had or what, but he obviously hadn't cared he'd stabbed me with it. It wasn't bleeding a lot, so I just rubbed it away with my borrowed shorts.

Ares sauntered away while I tended to myself, crazy fucker.

"What are you doing?"

Dorian was coming out of that room behind me, Wells and Thatcher behind him.

All three boys stopped.

Wells and Thatcher eyed me, Dorian too. The dark prince frowned. "Well?"

I said nothing, clearly caught outside the door. I'd heard every word behind it too. At least, what I'd walked in upon. Dorian started to say something, but Thatcher placed his big hand on his shoulder.

Thatcher pounded his fist. "We got you, man," he said, then pulled him into a hug. This surprised me. Boys hugged? I supposed close boys did.

These boys did seem close.

Wells did the same after Thatcher let go.

"Be safe," Wells added, as if Dorian were about to go to war or something.

Dorian's tense expression during the exchange hinted it may be something similar. He pulled away from his friend, then pounded Wells's fist. The two juniors acknowledged me with a chin tip before heading off in the other direction down the hall. They left Dorian and me standing there.

Dorian closed that door they'd all come out of.

"How much of that did you hear?" he asked me, angling closer. He was dressed in his uniform, ready for classes unlike me.

I shrugged. "I was just passing by," I said. "You're going somewhere?" I mean, that was all I heard.

The uniform must have been a front.

He obviously wasn't going to classes today. I'd heard him say the opposite.

Dorian outlined his firm jaw. "Yeah," he said, his hands shoving into his pockets. His chin jutted in my direction. "You miss your uniform or something?"

He studied my clothing under more than an observant gaze, and seeing all my own shit in my arms, he smiled for some reason. His eyes lifted to the ceiling, then next thing I knew, he was squeezing my shoulder. He directed me right back to the room from which I'd come.

He drew open the curtains once inside, letting the light in, and his next move consisted of pointing toward the fireplace.

A school uniform hung there on a special hook for hanging garments. It wasn't a male uniform, though. The skirt and tights gave that away.

I headed over to them and blinked when I noticed they weren't only my size but *were mine*. Academy uniforms all had our initials sewn into the collar, custom made, and I'd found that laughable when I'd first discovered that little tidbit upon coming here.

Dorian also had a pair of polished pumps beneath them, also mine, and the overnight bag toward the right, really made me scratch my head.

Upon further observance, I noticed it was filled with my toiletries. Like my actual stuff from home and my makeup. I frowned. "What the fuck? Did you rob my house?"

And how in the fuck had he gotten into it?

The dark prince chuckled, lounging his big body back against the fireplace. Could this guy be more of a god? He looked as if he could break the bricks out of it one by one. He grinned. "I had Wells and Thatcher go over to your house this morning and get it," he admitted, shocking me. He lifted a hand. "And before you ask, your brother let them in. They didn't break inside. From what I hear, your brother even got your stuff together for you."

My stomach soured. "Bru knows I stayed over here?" I recalled the texts, but they'd been a lie, not my actual location.

Dorian opened his hands. "I'm sure he guessed," Dorian stated, pushing off the fireplace. He smirked. "You ashamed of me, little fighter? Our night together?"

I was shocked by him if anything. I shook my head. "Why did you do this? Get my stuff?"

"Why not?" He shrugged as if it were casual. As if what he'd done wasn't a completely nice and *normal* thing. Tugging my T-shirt, he brought me forward.

I went.

He exuded heat, *sex* and had I not still had to go to the bathroom, I might have considered doing something really stupid. Something like kiss his face off until we both couldn't breathe and be underneath him until I didn't know where he ended or I began.

"So cautious of me," he said, playing with my hair. His rough fingers barely grazed my neck, and my flesh heated. He smiled. "Do you ever let your guard down?"

"Do you?" An honest question, and had either of us given each other a reason to? We fucking hated each other.

But right now, we sure weren't acting like it.

A tense muscle feathered Dorian's jaw after what I said. He wet his lips. "You should get dressed. If you need a bathroom, this room has one. I should know, this room's mine."

My mouth parted. "You have a room in Ares's house?"

Dorian popped up his big shoulders again. "I'm over here enough." His hands palmed up my arms until he found my neck. He tipped my chin. "Wolf's my brother. Thatcher and Wells too."

I almost asked a stupid question in that moment. He'd mentioned another name behind that door. I wanted to know if this Charlie person was also close to him.

His fingers flicked my hair out of my face. He pinched my shorts, summoning me to come close.

I went again.

I was stupid *again*, letting his finger curl beneath my jaw.

"You're a head fuck, you know that?" He scanned my eyes. His hand covered my throat before he forced a kiss so hard on me I nearly shattered again. He'd broken me last night. He'd broken *us*, whatever we'd been before gone.

And he called me the head fuck.

CHAPTER
TWENTY-FOUR

Sloane

Dorian never told me where he was going, and I didn't ask after he left the room. He let me get ready, and after, I went to school.

I didn't even see him on the way out.

I did see Thatcher and Wells, though, before I left. They were in the kitchen, basically raiding Ares's fridge. Apparently, his parents were out for the week on business, and those particular weeks were the ones where he always threw his parties. They told me all about it while shoveling frozen waffles and microwave hash browns between their lips. They offered me some, but I only took a waffle because I was hungry and didn't have time to go home before class. I also wanted to get the fuck out of there.

Last night and this morning had been weird enough.

I had to say I was glad I hadn't drunk any alcohol last night because coming to school with a hangover would have just been the cherry on the weirdest fucking night ever in recorded history. Actually, upon getting to school, I questioned if I'd had an out-of-body experience. I questioned if last night had happened and if this morning Dorian Prinze had actually been *nice* to me.

With school came the stares.

They occurred once I entered the familiar halls of Windsor Prep. People were talking. I also got more than a few catcalls. They'd all obviously heard about me having my own personal costume party last night, and I got the usual song and dance of people talking about me. More than one creep tried to fondle my ass, and after fighting off a third, I came across Bru at his locker. He had a curious brace on his hand and a more than knowing expression on his face when he looked at me.

He smiled a little. "So, um..."

"Don't." I shoved him, making him laugh.

He lifted his hands. "I wasn't going to say anything," he stated, but he most certainly was going to say something. He hung an arm on his locker. "Do I take it that this war with you and Legacy is over? Wells and Thatcher never said who they were getting your clothes for this morning, but they don't move unless Dorian tells them."

Sounded like Wells and Thatcher had never revealed my dirty laundry, but my brother was intuitive. He'd guessed it was Dorian I'd stayed with last night.

"I don't fucking know," I admitted because I didn't. Dorian Prinze was a special egg. A *dark* special egg. I grabbed my brother's arm, lifting his brace. "Anyway, it sounds like you're starting your own war. Wolf mentioned you slugged him."

It'd been freaking weird too. The guy didn't even seem mad about it.

My brother grinned. "He actually said I had balls after I did it. Standing up for my sister and all that."

He said as much, and I threw my arm around him, pulling

him down with me. I gave him a noogie. "I can fight my own battles."

"I know," he said, wrestling me away. He smiled. "But I've been a little shit to you recently, and I think we both know that I owed you."

I was happy to hear him say that. I was happy to hear we were *cool* again.

He lounged back against the lockers. "Anyway, I think I got lucky hitting Wolf this time. He said he'd kill my ass if I tried something like that again. Pretty sure this was a one-off." He chuckled. "It was kind of weird actually. It was almost like he let me punch him when I found him last night."

Again, an uber weird morning. The guy had fucking stabbed me, but thought it was cool that Bru was standing up for his sister?

Epically.

Fucking.

Weird.

These Legacy boys were most certainly a special breed.

"So are you and Dorian a thing?" I gazed around after what my brother said. He laughed. "Sloane, that's a good thing. It means you're basically shielded around this place. You know that, right?"

I could assume that was probably a given *if Dorian and I were a thing*, but I wasn't his property.

"He doesn't own me," I said to Bru, and he merely laughed again.

"You're going to get me killed one of these days," he said, but did toss an arm around me.

Gratefully, my brother hadn't fucked his hand up enough not to play. He went on to explain he got the brace from the school nurse this morning, and it was temporary. He just needed to rest and ice it until the swelling went down, I guess.

He'd still be able to play ball, and I was glad he wouldn't suffer again for another one of my stunts.

My brother ended up walking me to my first class, and though we chatted for a little bit, he didn't bring up anything about Dorian or Legacy. I was glad. I wouldn't talk any more about it if he did.

Last night and this morning were just all too weird.

———

Dorian wasn't at lunch.

In fact, none of the Legacy boys were. According to Bow, they'd gone to Jax's Burgers today. They'd invited her to come along, but she'd opted to stay at school. She apparently wasn't much of a rule breaker, and I guessed they'd been dragging her along to eat with them when they had gone.

I supposed they trusted me enough not to take advantage of her now because none of them were there in the courtyard that day. Of course, many of their legions of fans still were, and I noticed Bru out there with them.

I wondered if that burger invite they'd given him that day had been a one-off, or if Bru had simply made enemies with Ares when my brother had decided to defend my honor this morning.

Odds were, that probably wasn't the case considering how lax Ares had been when it came to the whole thing, and really, any distance between my brother and that psychopath Mallick I was completely okay with anyway. The guy was fucking crazy.

I mean, he'd stabbed me this morning.

The little rabbit talked my ear off now that she was back at my table, and I didn't mind because I really had missed her. Call me crazy, but I really did want to protect this girl. She just had this innocence about her, and it couldn't be helped.

"I can't believe you just *walked in there*," she said, truly awed after I told her about busting up the guys' poker game. "They just let that happen?" She shook her head. "That doesn't happen, Sloane."

Well, they'd let me. At least, Dorian had. Again, the whole thing had been unusual. Telling the story back, it almost seemed like he'd stood up for me for a hot minute before dragging me away.

"Who's Charlie?" I asked, casual about it. The name had been a buzzword in my head through my first few classes. For obvious reasons, I hadn't asked Dorian about it when he'd asked what I heard.

Bow stopped eating.

Like she legit stopped, the fry falling out of her mouth. She rubbed salt off her lips. "Charlie?"

"Mmhmm." I took a drink. "Dorian mentioned his name."

Now, she coughed. She full-on choked despite not eating any food, and I handed her the soda in front of her.

She patted her throat after a drink. "Dorian mentioned Charlie to you?"

I sat back, figuring the truth was better. I was serious that I didn't want to do her wrong again. "No, he didn't. I over-heard. He mentioned the name Charlie."

Her lips immediately closed like I'd known they probably would, but I didn't regret being honest. That was what sepa-rated me from the boys themselves. I didn't just stomp around all deceitful and caveman-like when I wanted something.

I didn't just take things from people.

Dorian had done that last night, but I knew he was still in my head despite him being an asshole.

I knew because I was asking about Charlie.

I knew because I cared Dorian wasn't here today and off doing whatever the fuck he was doing. He wasn't at lunch with the other boys, and I knew this as fact.

Bow didn't, though. She couldn't have. Dorian had been

rather tight-lipped about that with Thatcher and Wells. Bow laced her fingers together. "Charlie is Dorian's uncle."

"His uncle?"

She nodded. "He died last year," she said, my lips parting. She frowned. "He was like a brother to Dorian. He was like a brother to all of us really. He was close in age. Only nineteen when it happened."

"What did happen?"

She appeared hesitant again, her throat working. Her expression shifted, and she appeared pained.

"Someone hurt him," she said, nodding. Her cheeks flushed, and when she blinked away, I realized I triggered something.

"I'm sorry." I didn't know what else to say. Nineteen was so young.

She moved her shoulders. "The boys took it pretty hard. All of our families." She leaned in. "Charlie grew up with Dorian. Same house and everything."

Yikes.

Lunch ended at the bell, and she sat back. Bow grabbed her stuff.

"Probably not mention Charlie again?" She wet her lips. "It messed with our families pretty bad. The boys and me." She nodded. "Broke Dorian, though. Broke Dorian real bad. He took it the hardest."

For obvious reasons. Especially if they lived together.

I nodded, of course, lifting my hand. "Of course. I'm sorry I brought it up."

"You didn't know." She forced a smile I knew she didn't really mean when she turned with her things and walked away.

Why else would she hide something she normally loved to do?

CHAPTER
TWENTY-FIVE

Dorian - age 17

"Hey, you fellas got room for another player?"

I stopped mid-shot, and Wolf, Wells, and Thatcher stood tall on the court. We'd been joined by a fifth.

Charlie.

My uncle came waltzing onto the community park's basketball court like we'd seen him every day. Like he hadn't been away at classes, and we all hadn't been missing him. He raised his arms. "What do you say? Or am I too fucking old to hang out with you guys now?"

Grinning, I ran, the other guys too. I tackled Charlie's ass, and he caught me.

"Dude," I said, catching his hand first. I held tight as I hugged him, the other guys crowding around. I pulled back. "When did you get in, bro?"

"Just now. Just now," he returned, smiling wide. He looked good. Hair slicked back and rocking a little style with his bomber jacket. Charlie looked like a college boy through and through. He put out a hand to Wolf. "Wolfy!"

Wolf grinned, taking him in, and Thatcher and Wells did the same. We'd expected Charlie home for the three-day weekend, but not until Saturday.

It seemed he wanted to see us early.

I'd welcome that, always. I missed my uncle, my brother. Home life had been different since he'd been gone for the past few weeks. I was used to always having access to him, down the hall and in my life.

He punched at our chests, asking in on our basketball game again. My buddies and I all welcomed him with open arms.

We played into the night.

We played like we were kids again and not divided by years or miles. Wolf and I were juniors this year, Wells and Thatcher sophomores. We'd all been really coming into our games on the football field, and I hoped were making Charlie proud. He'd left quite a legacy on the field himself after he left. He'd been quarterback before I took over.

Charlie told us all about his first semester so far as we played. He was a freshman at Pembroke University. I could imagine most of us would be going there too. Pembroke was kind of like a sister school to Windsor Prep, and many of the guys and girls who matriculated through the academy's halls ended up there.

We all played so long Charlie and I ended up sitting down for a drink, letting the guys play for a bit. We sat on the benches, chugging water while the other guys just dicked around.

"You look good, man," I said. Charlie did look good, amazing actually.

Charlie smiled a little, sitting back. "Thanks. I am good. Stressed to fucking *hell* already with classes…"

I chuckled.

"But good, Robin. Real good."

I'd missed that too, being the Robin to his Batman. I shook

his leg. "How's the female situation?" I asked, the first shit he should have led in with. What the fuck did I care about school and academic shit? "You should have started with that shit, by the way."

The jostle had Charlie shaking his head. He was pretty modest when it came to women, didn't talk about them a lot. He laced his hands. "I'm sure you can imagine."

"I can." I grinned. "But stop leaving me hanging like an asshole."

"Your ass needs to be focused on school." He brought me under his arm. "Not girls."

Who did he think I was? I mean, he *knew me,* right? We had the same blood.

I wrestled with him a bit but didn't leave from under his arm when he stopped. He patted my chest. "How have things been here? In school?"

"Okay." I was top of my classes. Not a wiz like Wolf or even Thatcher, who was brilliant too. I shrugged. "I get by."

"Mmm." He grinned at me, but his smile faded a little. In fact, it wiped away completely. "How is she?"

She.

I was surprised he hadn't led in with that.

I'd never asked Charlie about him and his relationship with our headmaster Principal Mayberry after the party he'd caught my friends and me at last year.

But that didn't mean I wasn't aware of the fallout.

The guy had been a wreck when he left for college, and though he hadn't talked about it, I knew that'd been because of her. From what I understood, he'd ended things with her. I hadn't meant to, but I'd stumbled across one of his text messages before he left. He'd been wishing her well, ending things because he was going to college.

It should have ended sooner.

I assumed, since he had ended things, what had been

going on had just been a temporary infatuation. Charlie was dealing with personal shit and needed a release.

I supposed she'd been good for at least that, and Charlie did seem happier now. Lighter. I picked up the spare ball the boys and I'd brought, spinning it around with my fingers. "She's fine, I guess." I shrugged. "She and Coach—"

"Wait. Coach?" Charlie raised a hand. "She and Coach are a thing?"

I frowned, confused. "What do you mean? They're married."

"Still?" He sat back, looking thoroughly thrown by the information. Shaken. He outlined his lips. "You mean to tell me they're still together?"

"Yeah, why? Are they not supposed to be—"

"No." He pulled a joint out of his pocket, lighting up in front of me, which was something he never did. I mean, I knew he smoked weed. I wasn't a fucking idiot, but he tried not to do it around me. Something about wanting to be a good example or some shit. He blew smoke through his nostrils. "They're not. She was supposed to leave him. She said she was."

I watched him, red creeping up the side of his neck. He drew another hit, and with the tension, I wished I hadn't said anything. I knocked his knees. "How about we do another game? We can do two on two. Have Thatch sit out or something."

Thatcher never liked playing as much as us anyway.

In his own thoughts, Charlie had to come out of them just to look at me. But once he had, he wrestled my hair, grinning in the way he always did. He passed it off like what I said didn't bother him, but that grin didn't quite reach his eyes.

"No, y'all play," he said, letting me go. He jutted his chin forward. "I'll watch you guys."

He leaned back with his blunt, and though I didn't like that, I couldn't tell him what to do. I tossed him the spare ball, then headed back out there with the boys. We played for a little bit before I noticed Charlie over there on his phone. He was just playing on it, his fingers scrolling, but then out of nowhere, he was standing.

I stopped bouncing the ball. "Charlie?"

He was putting his bomber jacket back on when I came over, something he'd taken off when we'd started playing. He popped his collar. "Hey, Robin. I'm gonna take off."

My eye twitched. "Take off where?"

"Just to go visit some friends." He put his blunt out under his sneaker, tapping my fist. "I'll be back for dinner, though."

My family tended to eat pretty late. I usually came home when Mom shot me a text, and since I hadn't gotten that, I assumed food wasn't ready.

I studied Charlie. "Charlie—"

"I'll be right back. Gotta go." He was rushed, an urgency in his voice I didn't like. He started to walk away but I grabbed him.

I hugged him.

I didn't know why. It was like I felt compelled, and the gesture definitely threw him off. He frowned before folding his big arms around me.

"Dinner," I made him promise, pulling away, and he nodded. He wrestled my hair again like he liked to do, making me smile, and next thing I knew, he was disappearing into the park.

I lost him through the trees.

———

Wolf and I played hoops long after Thatcher and Wells left. They were tired, but I simply wanted to tire myself out. I had stress in my muscles I didn't like, so I played hard. Wolf was with me. I could tell he was tired too, but he kept playing.

I was like my dad in that way. He tended to work out too

when he had thoughts roaming his mind.

The hour got so late. So late in fact, Wolf and I both decided to call it. My mom definitely should have texted me for dinner by now but might have gotten word Charlie was back and wanted to do things big.

I went ahead and asked Wolf if he wanted to join us. He or the other guys often did and Wolf never turned down my mom's pot roast. My mom and I weren't meat eaters, but she made it for Dad.

Wolf and I could smell the roasted meat all the way down the block, the pair of us walking home from the park since it was so close. We got pretty close to my house before we noticed the cop car outside it.

And my god dad's Mercedes.

"That's my dad's car." Wolf noticed at the same time as me, the pair of us picking up the pace. We got to my house, and I opened the door, placing the basketball down beside it.

"Mom?" I called.

"Dad?" Wolf asked, not far behind.

We heard no answer.

A buzzing hit my ears I didn't like, a tension. In our search for our parents, I felt a tightness in my chest. It was an anticipation of something, a ringing in my head.

We found our parents in the kitchen.

Like all our parents, my mom and dad and Wolf's. My god dad Ramses and Wolf's mom, Brielle, were both there. Brielle had been headmaster of our school before we'd enrolled and Principal Mayberry had taken over.

The cop was with them.

The officer was talking to my father, my dad's hands in his pockets. Brielle was holding my mom with Ramses right beside them.

The familiarity of it all twisted sickness into my stomach.

The last time I'd seen my parents like this...

"Mom?"

Our parents and the cop saw us when I called for Mom. They must have not heard us come in.

Mom immediately went to me. She *immediately* placed me in her arms, and Brielle did the same with Wolf.

"Oh, God," my mom gasped in my ear, shaking the fuck to hell. "Baby. My love…"

"Mom." I gripped her shirt, staring at my dad over her shoulder.

He was more than tense.

In fact, he appeared to be having a hard time keeping eye contact with me.

"What's going on?" I asked, those words familiar too. The difference was it'd been Charlie to say them.

Where's Charlie?

He should have been home by now. He promised he'd be here by dinner, and he always kept a promise.

"Where's Charlie?" My immediate next question. I pulled away from my mother. "Mom, where's Charlie? He said he'd be here for dinner. He came home early—"

"Son." My dad cut me off, coming forward. He lifted a hand. "Son, there was an accident."

"An accident?"

At this point, my mom started to cry. Like full-on sobbing in the kitchen. She immediately left the room, and my dad started to go after her.

"Royal, I got it," Ramses stepped in, my mom's best friend. My mom and Ares's dad had been best friends since high school. He touched Brielle's shoulder. "Honey, Ares?"

Immediately, Brielle took Wolf off to the side, and I had no idea where they were going.

I was too busy freaking the fuck out.

I was shaking and my dad had to physically take me out of the goddamn room. When we ended up in the hallway, I struggled away.

"What are you talking about an accident?" I shot, louder

than I should toward my father. "I *just* saw Charlie. Charlie's fine."

"But that's what I'm saying. He's not, Dorian." He tugged me over. "Listen to me—"

"I just saw him, Dad," I croaked. "Dad, I just saw him."

Dad placed cautious hands on my shoulders, and from somewhere I could hear my mom still, my god dad's whispers. Ramses was telling her it would be okay.

Why was he telling her that?

They were both acting like someone died. They were...

"Dad, where's Charlie?" If he was at the hospital or something... If there was an accident, we should be there, not here. "Dad..."

"He was jogging, son," Dad said, and at this point, the officer left the room. He tipped his hat at my father before he left, the door clicking closed behind him. Dad faced me. "You know how he liked to jog in the high hills."

I did, but that had always been the excuse. Charlie used to use that as an excuse to go over and see Principal Mayberry behind Coach's back.

I knew because I always covered for him at home.

"He was in that neighborhood tonight, and he heard something. Screaming." Dad rubbed his mouth, his words and expression pained. "He was passing by Principal Mayberry's house, and he heard some shouting. Elevated voices."

My breath left me, thoughts completely escaping me.

"Apparently, there was an altercation between her and her husband, Coach Mayberry," Dad continued. "And according to the officer, things got aggressive. He hit her."

He hit her.

"Charlie heard the screaming from the street, and he broke in."

I faced him, the color completely drained from his face.

"Coach was armed."

Armed.

My lips parted. "Dad…"

Dad shook his head. "According to Elaine Mayberry, her husband believed Charlie to be an intruder. He shot on instinct." Dad's voice thickened, pained. "He shot, Dorian, and Charlie didn't make it. He passed away at the scene."

No…

No.

I didn't believe it, backing away.

"Dorian."

"No." I raised my hand. "It's not true. I just saw Charlie, Dad. I just saw him."

"But it is true, son." Dad's voice boomed in the room, his face entirely red. Dad didn't lose his composure. He was completely in control always.

But this shook him.

It had to have shaken him at his core because he even placed a hand on the kitchen island to stabilize himself.

"The man was clearly troubled," Dad stated, his jaw tense. "Because after he saw what he did, that it was Charlie and not an intruder, he turned the gun on himself. Blew himself away right in front of his wife."

I couldn't hear this. *I didn't believe this.*

It was bullshit.

I refused to believe it and left the room.

"Dorian—"

I ignored my father, taking my keys. I got into my car and drove all the way to the high hills.

I was there in moments.

It was like a police shootout had occurred there, cop cars everywhere and news reporters filling the streets. The scene was a nightmare, a cluster fuck, and I honked my way as close as I could get. I ended up leaving my car in the street and hadn't cared if someone stole it or did whatever the fuck they wanted.

This is a lie.

This was my recurring thought as I ran, *lies* everywhere. It was a lie that Charlie was dead. It was a lie that all this was happening.

I stood at the yellow tape. The scene was completely blocked off by the cops. Suddenly, the shutters flew, and the reporters and photographers redirected their attention to a pale woman being escorted out of the house. She was underneath the arm of a female officer, the woman guiding her off the property.

They had Principal Mayberry under a blanket.

Her eyes were red, her expression vacant. Tear lines tracked down her face, and when the female officer placed her in a cop car, my headmaster stared out the window. Principal Mayberry blinked amongst the lights and shutters of the cameras. Her expression was blank.

But then she spotted me.

Her mouth parted, her eyes wide. She stared at me like all the answers were there, and I merely had to see them in her eyes to decipher them. She sat there like there were far more answers inside that house than what I'd been told.

She was a lie.

She was *lying*, and I stared at her now. Charlie had been thoroughly shaken after finding out Coach Mayberry was still with his wife. After finding out *his ex-girlfriend* was still with her abusive husband. He hadn't come over to this neighborhood tonight to jog.

I knew that in my gut.

That woman had something to do with this. She did something, and I watched as the cops drove her away. She shifted in her seat, staring at me through the rearview mirror. There were more answers that needed to be found out here and once I found them…

I was going to end her.

CHAPTER
TWENTY-SIX

Dorian - present

The text came from Thatcher as I reentered Maywood Heights's city limits, but I didn't check it until I stopped at a streetlight.

Thatcher: Did you do it?

I had, picking up my phone off the seat.

Me: It's done.

I tossed the phone after that. The light changed, but the phone flashed again, and I couldn't help but look over.

Wells: You okay?

Word certainly traveled fast between my friends. Thatcher had obviously texted Wells.

I had no more words for my friends, so I let the text go.

I drove home.

I took the long way, scenic until I got so lost in my thoughts I had no idea how I'd gotten there. I sat in the driveway for what felt like forever. Meanwhile, my phone blew up beside me.

I hung an arm over the wheel, staring at the phone on my

seat. Texts from both Wells and Thatcher rolled in, but I didn't move an inch.

Thatcher: D, wanna talk?

Wells: Wanna meet?

They were in a group chat at this point, and I'd obviously figured out they'd been talking to each other first. How else would Wells know to ask if I was okay?

I wasn't.

I was man enough to admit that what I'd done today had affected me. I was goddamn human.

And what I'd done was fucked.

It'd been necessary, though, which was why I'd done it.

I started to pick up my phone, but wasn't man enough to admit my feelings to my friends. They weren't going to know.

Me: I'm fine.

I wasn't fine.

It didn't matter.

What was done was done, and now that tonight was behind me, I could move on.

I was free.

I could sleep well tonight knowing I'd stepped up and done what I'd needed to do. My father also wouldn't have to worry any longer about things he shouldn't have been close to knowing about. I'd admit I'd gotten sloppy in the past, but this time, I'd used cash during my stops upstate.

Not that I could stop and fucking eat anything.

I'd ended up pulling over at a truck stop halfway between here and my destination just to make good use of the toilet. I'd hurled my fucking brains out like a little bitch, nerves.

On my return trip, though, there'd been nothing but stomach bile in my gut. I'd managed to at least keep that down. I'd driven all the way back to Maywood Heights with my stomach clenched, my chest tight.

I just didn't know why.

I'd stared a monster in the eyes tonight, taken care of shit, so I shouldn't have felt anything about what I'd just done.

Thatcher: Talk to us, D.

Wells: Should we call your parents? Wolf?

God, fucking no.

Me: I told you I'm fucking fine. Stop worrying.

They didn't stop.

They continued to blow up my phone for the next few days.

I didn't go to school.

I had Ronald call me in after my parents went off to work, and he could probably get fired for such a thing.

I stopped caring about stuff I used to care about. I stopped being a decent fucking human being. Wells and Thatcher continued to text and even showed up during those few days I cut class and needed time to my fucking self.

I had Ronald send them away.

I'd never been more grateful to not share events of my life with my other best friend, Wolf. One person who wasn't blowing up my phone had been him, and oddly enough, he'd been very quiet. I got one or two texts asking if I was still living since I was calling in sick. But nothing after that.

It was just Thatcher and Wells who were hovering. Like they themselves stated, they felt they were accessories to what I'd done. They knew about shit, but they were sworn to secrecy—by me.

Eventually, I did leave the house to drive and did plan on going to school tomorrow. Currently, I sat in my car picking at food I'd just gotten from Jax's Burgers. I still had no taste, but Ronald had urged me to go out and get something to eat. He'd said I hadn't been looking well.

He didn't know the half of it.

My food had gotten cold in my lap, and I just sat in my parents' driveway with it. It was starting to get late, and I probably should go to bed. Not that I could sleep either.

My mind was a cluster fuck, but I had to get my shit together. Things still weren't done, not by a long shot, and I'd just mustered up the energy to go inside when I got a weird text.

For once, it wasn't Thatcher or Wells.

Unknown: Hey, this is Sloane. I'm not sure if you're still out of town. It's been a few days, but if you are back, are you with my brother? I can't find him.

Sloane.

What the fuck?

Me: How did you get this number?

She shouldn't have it. I'd never given it to her.

Sloane: Went through Bru's phone one night.

She pinged.

Sloane: Swiped his contacts.

She pinged again.

Sloane: I didn't trust you.

She shouldn't. She shouldn't trust me at all.

I was a monster.

My trail of dark deeds would only grow as the days progressed. That I knew. Sloane's text message bubble surfaced again, and I waited.

Sloane: Also, if he was hanging with you guys, I needed a way to contact him in case I couldn't find him. Example: tonight. Are you with him? Are you back?

I definitely was. Had been for days.

Me: I'm back, but I'm not with him. Sorry.

I tossed my phone, my headache a mile long.

My phone rang.

I started to shut that shit off, but then Sloane's number showed on the front.

Christ.

I answered despite myself. Why did I always fucking cater to this girl?

I sat in silence when I answered, hadn't even said her

name when I picked up.

"Hi."

Her hurried voice slid into the line, breathy, panting. It reminded me of when I'd made her come.

Instantly.

Fucking.

Hard.

This girl had a fucking effect on me I couldn't stand, and she was obviously moving around somewhere.

"What do you need?" I asked her, doing my best not to sound like a fucking dick.

Why do you care?

For some reason, I did, waiting. But when she didn't say anything at first, I sat up. "What are you doing?"

"I'm trying to look for Bru," she huffed, more than aggressive about it. It was one of the things I liked about her. Noa Sloane put up with no shit. She stood up to me, stood up to all of us, and not a lot of people around here did that whether because of fear or intimidation.

We'd attempted both on her, but to no avail. She'd handled her own.

And got in your goddamn head.

I blamed that on only her taste, something I'd made myself truly believe. I didn't have time for anything else.

"The Find My Phone app said he's at Murphy Park," she said. "But I think I'm lost. That's why I called you. I have no idea where the fuck I am."

I smiled. "I know it. Where did you just pass? Anything identifiable?"

"Actually, yes." She stopped, then chuckled. "You probably won't believe this, but there's a tree that looks like a fucking dick."

I laughed.

Actually laughed.

This girl managed to get laughter out of me, go fucking

figure after the week I'd had. I nodded my chin though she couldn't see. "Doyle's Cock."

"What?"

My smile widened. "That's its name." Well, at least that's what me and my asshole friends named it. "We had a teacher named Mr. Doyle in the seventh grade. Total dick. We named it after him."

"Hence, Doyle's Cock." Her own laughter sounded into the line, like those little birds that flew around in spring.

What the fuck? Little birds? Really, D?

This chick was way too into my head, and I knew because I was now backing out of my driveway.

"Stay there," I said into the line. I had my speakerphone on at this point. "I'm coming out. I'll find you."

"What?"

"I said I'm coming to you. What, you don't want the help?" Not to mention she was fucking lost. "Just stay there. Don't get yourself lost any deeper."

"Okay." Her voice had been light, hesitant. Noa Sloane still didn't trust me.

She really shouldn't.

I got to Doyle's Cock, and Sloane sat on a picnic table beside it. She had her phone in her lap, the light from it contouring the soft shape of her face. My Audi lights flooded the grass in front of her, and she lifted her head, all that dark hair sliding off her shoulder when she stood up.

This girl was a goddamn goddess from her little shirts that hugged her perfect tits to the shorts that barely covered her ass cheeks. She had these dark nipples that I loved too, like chocolate fucking kisses.

But then she fucking looked at you.

Borderline knocked me out more than once, and I was man enough to admit that too. I had no place in my life for Noa Sloane.

Yet, here she was.

She strode over to me in her high-top tennis shoes, eye level to eye level with me when she got there. I still couldn't get over how tall this girl was. I had a good half a foot on her, but it was rare I actually stared into a girl's eyes without looking down at her. Sloane stood toe to toe with me.

She always had.

"Hi." She said this timidly. Not like herself at all.

But then again, last time you saw her you fucked her and she made you come like a goddamn virgin.

This girl continued to be a complete head fuck, and as she showed me her phone, her skin smelling all sweet and shit like cookies, I tried to focus on what she was showing me.

"Find My Phone says he's here," she said, long dark lashes flowing at me. She gazed around. "I just don't know why."

"He won't pick up his phone?" I typed his number, calling him. Her phone app wasn't saying much. Just had a dot on Murphy Park.

The number went right to voicemail, no ring at all.

"Just voicemail." She turned, confirming what she'd obviously gotten too. She messed with her hair. "I'm trying not to worry."

She was, her face flushed and cheeks rosy. How was it this girl had not a stitch of makeup on and managed to look like a complete fucking wet dream?

Focus.

I wasn't acting like myself either, coming out here and shit.

Mentally, I blamed that on my last few days. I pocketed my phone. "Come on."

"Where we going?" she asked, but she followed.

"Obviously, to look for him." I turned around. "You don't want the help?"

I was being an asshole because I was an asshole.

She noticed.

Her eyes narrowed into hard slits, her nostrils flaring. "Don't pretend like you want to help or anything."

"I won't," I stated. Though, I was doing the exact opposite.

She must have wanted the help because she followed along with me. I got to watch her little ass cheeks as we delved deeper into the park, using nothing but our cell phones and the park lights for guidance. The park's lights were few and far between, though. We were pretty much in the dark out here.

"Any reason why my brother would come out here?" she asked me. "After all, you and your boys are his new besties, right?"

Hardly. I smirked. "I think we both know why I was hanging out with your brother."

I'd done it to get to her, point blank. Me hanging with Bru pissed her off and was completely intentional.

She silenced as we walked through prairie grass. It was reaching up to our knees at this point. "You're full of shit."

"And I'm sure you're about to tell me about it." I used my cell to push some grass away. "Less talking. More moving."

"You know what? I am going to tell you about it."

I lifted my eyes but did smile. I really liked bugging this girl, getting under her skin. I turned around. "Give it to me."

She frowned. "You put off this big dick energy." I started to bow for the compliment, but she shoved me. Laughing, I stumbled back. She growled. "But you're full of it. I know you are."

"You do?" I cuffed my arms, and she nodded.

"I know for a fact you got Bru on that football team. A permanent spot, and you wouldn't have done that unless he could play."

"He can play." And I had no problem admitting that. "So what?"

"So you *care*," she ground out. "You may act like you

don't. That you're just some vapid dark prince who has no soul."

"Dark prince, huh?" I danced my eyebrows. "Be careful, Noa Sloane. You might be accidentally complimenting me."

"I'm not." Her face hardened. "Because behind that dark prince is just some little boy who's completely scared of his feelings." She homed in. "Even though they all show all over his face and in everything he does. You do care. You care about my brother. I've seen your friendship. I see how you treat him."

I eyed her, letting her talk but merely out of curiosity now.

She got in my face. "And you wouldn't be out here helping if you weren't his friend. Then there's what you did for me."

"And what's that exactly?"

She chewed the inside of her cheek. "There've been things. Little things I've noticed."

I noticed she didn't delve into those. Was it possible the little fighter was scared of some feelings too?

You sure are.

Her throat moved. "You wouldn't do any of that stuff if you didn't care. If you had no soul—"

"That's where you're wrong." I got in her face. "My soul died. Just this week actually, so congratulations. You have your dark fucking prince."

I had nothing to lose anymore, no more sins to leave out on the table. I'd done the worst thing a person could possibly do.

And I'd do it again.

She scanned my eyes and didn't fight me despite the fact I had her arm. I must have grabbed it when I got in her face.

"You're a bad liar, Dorian Prinze," she said, smelling too sweet this close. She wet her lips. "And what have you done?"

I didn't like how she said that, cautious as if I were that

tiny boy she spoke about. Like I was a little kid who needed coddling and protecting. I let go of her, and she grabbed my arm.

"Little fighter," I warned, her hand coming up my chest. She touched me, my heart fucking pounding into her hand. Her fingers burned through my shirt, and I peeled them off. I dampened my mouth. "Sloane."

She came closer, timid like she was worried.

But not for herself.

She got right into my space, our energies colliding.

"Do you ever let your guard down?" she asked, turning the tables on me. She frowned. "Or is it just so comfortable there in the dark?"

It was comfortable.

It was all I had.

It was me and my revenge, but somehow, this girl continued to fight her way through the layers of it.

My hand moved to her hip, and I opened my mouth. I had no idea what I was about to say.

The screams cut me off.

CHAPTER
TWENTY-SEVEN

Sloane

Dorian bolted, and I almost lost him in the tall grass.

That said something considering he grabbed me.

He dragged me literally alongside him. Two boys ahead of us were yelling and screaming. I didn't recognize either one, and when the pair of us got in the clearing, I identified them as two boys from school. I didn't know their names, but I recognized them as kids from the Court, Dorian's posse.

The guys were shouting in the direction of a lake and where Dorian and I'd been searching, I hadn't seen it until now. It'd been hidden behind the tall grass.

One of the boys was completely wet, like he'd gone in the water, which was crazy. The waves of dark water lapped in the night breeze, and it was basically pitch black out here.

"The fuck's going on?" Dorian's voice boomed in the air. He finally let go of me, and I nearly stumbled. He went so fast. Both boys shot around, and Dorian's eyes expanded. "Ryder, what the hell?" he said to one of them before facing the other. "Josh, that you?"

The guys ran toward Dorian and me. The one he called Josh was wet, completely soaked when he got to us.

"It was an accident, Dorian," Josh panted, his face completely red. "I went after him, but I couldn't get him."

Dorian's face twitched. "Who?"

"That kid Bru from the team." Josh shot his finger in the direction of the water. "We were trying to initiate him and—"

"Initiate him into what!" I screamed, but Dorian was shaking Josh.

"Bru's fucking out there?" Dorian shot out, but when Josh nodded his head, he let go. He ran toward that dark water.

And went in.

He hiked his thick legs until the water got him to his waist. He glided in then, pulling broad strokes while the water lapped and chopped around him. He called Bru's name, turning and going deeper into that dark water. The waves covered him, and I screamed, racing out toward him.

Ryder jerked me back.

"Don't," he urged. Josh took my other arm. Ryder's expression turned grim. "You'll get lost too."

Lost.

This isn't happening.

My brother wasn't out there right now, and Dorian hadn't just gone underneath the dark water to get him.

I couldn't even see Dorian now. He'd *disappeared,* and I shoved both the guys off me.

"Bru!" I went into ankle-deep water, cupping my mouth. "Dorian!"

My gaze searched rapidly through the moving waves, but no words returned to me. The lake was so dark and completely unsteady.

No.

Sickness swirled my gut, and I honest to God thought I'd be sick all over myself. I couldn't breathe, but I tread deeper into the water. I couldn't just stand here and do nothing.

"Bru!" I swam up to my waist, whirling around. "Dorian!"
"Sloane!"

Dorian's voice shot me in his direction, his voice and his voice alone. I couldn't see him. It was too dark, but a large shadow was coming closer and closer through the dim water.

He was dragging something.

Dorian was on his back, physically dragging another body with him. He labored, pulling his arm through the water while his other one grappled around another. I recognized my brother under his arm.

He wasn't moving.

My brother was chillingly still, his eyes closed and his limbs simply wading in the water.

"Bruno!" His name shrieked from my lips as I stroked out to meet the pair. At this point, Ryder and Josh caught wind of what was going on, and both boys swam out to assist.

With Dorian's help, they were able to get my brother onto the shore, but as soon as they laid him down, my brother lay limp. Panicked, neither Josh nor Ryder knew what to do, but Dorian dove in.

"He's not breathing," he said, and I almost did throw up then. Dorian cleared the way and out of nowhere, he started performing CPR. He began chest compressions, performing mouth to mouth right after. The first set did nothing, and I watched in horror as my kid brother continued not to breathe.

"Bru," I gasped. My brother was completely ghost white.

"Come on, Bru. Fuck," Dorian gritted, his blond hair soaked and sopping over his brow. He pressed his big hands to my brother's chest again, and out of nowhere, my brother gasped and coughed up water.

Oh my God.

"Bru!" I reached for him, but Dorian guided him to his side. My brother spat out more water then, gagging on it.

"Get it out, man," Dorian called, and I didn't know what to say.

He'd just saved my brother's life.

He'd just done that. *Right here* in front of me. Able to breathe again, my brother looked at me, and I nearly decked him in his face.

"Bruno Sloane, what the fuck were you thinking?" I chose to say to my brother instead, shaking. "Why would you go out there? Why would you do that?"

"I'm sorry," he panted. His hug was so weak in return. "I was stupid. I'm sorry."

He needed to do better than that. I pulled back, and Dorian and I helped him sit up. At this point, Dorian was on his knees, but he was shouting.

Ryder and Josh were the victims.

"What was this?" Dorian roared, his face completely red. He shot a hand toward Bru. "Tell me this isn't what I think it is. You know that shit is *fucking banned*—"

"What shit?"

Dorian whipped around in my direction, his big body panting with heavy breaths. He pulled back his hair. "A haze," he said, nearly growling at Ryder and Josh. Dorian frowned. "We used to do them a long time ago."

"Who's we?"

Dorian's expression traveled grim. He outlined his lips. "Old members of the Court. Not us, but our fathers and their fathers. It used to be a way they used to initiate new members."

I faced Bru. "Is that what this was?"

Bru said nothing, rubbing his arm. "Sloane..."

"What is the haze?" I asked Dorian. I raised and dropped a hand. "Go and kill yourself?"

"I had to just make it across the lake," Bru admitted, frowning. He couldn't even look at me at this point. He put a hand on the ground. "They told me if I made it across, I was in."

I couldn't believe this. All of this was so ridiculous, and

Dorian was seething. He shot a finger toward Bru, but faced the other boys. "This shit is banned, bro. Fucking *banned* for a reason."

He started to grab Ryder since he was closer, but the boy raised his hands.

"Wolf told us we had to," Ryder shrieked, turning his face before the blow that was obviously coming. He waved his hands before Dorian could strike. "He said we had to, or the Sloane kid couldn't get in." He frowned at him. "You didn't know?"

By the look of shock that struck Dorian's lovely face, it appeared he hadn't.

But that didn't mean much to me.

This was how he operated, him and his crazier-than-fuck friends. They did this shit to people. All bred from the same cloth.

And I was apparently very, *very* wrong about him.

I was wrong about everything. It didn't matter if Dorian Prinze had a soul or not. It didn't matter if he cared. This was still the wicked Legacy he came from, and there was no place for Bru in it.

That went double for me.

The result would be nothing but poison and most certainly would end in my brother's death. I started to help Bru up, putting my shoulder under his arm. I got him to his feet, but when Dorian started to assist, I raised my hand.

"Stop it," I said, his eyes twitching. I shook my head. "Just don't. I appreciate what you did. Saving my brother, but don't."

I did appreciate it. He did save my brother's life, but we couldn't do this shit. This was some fucked-up mess.

Dorian raised a hand, like he actually did care. "Sloane…"

I raised and dropped mine. "I just can't with you, okay?" I studied the area, all of us drenched and two of us almost dead. That was the result of him and *his* people. All of this was on them, on Wolf. My jaw clenched. "I can't have anything to do with this toxic, *elitist* shit."

It really would kill us in the end, and it might kill Dorian himself.

And how beautiful he was. Dorian stood still in that dark moonlight, his wet T-shirt clinging to his big body, his jeans damp and doing the same. He really did appear that dark prince.

But it wasn't a compliment. He was toxic, and he came from cruelty. It didn't matter if he showed me flashes of something else.

Dorian's hands clenched at his sides, like he was doing all he could not to do something else. I carted my brother away, no time to see what he'd do.

I didn't care anyway.

"This wasn't his fault," Bru said, angling a look back. He shook his head. "Sloane—"

"Don't." My brother hadn't listened to me at all since we'd gotten there.

He was going to listen now.

CHAPTER
TWENTY-EIGHT

Dorian - age 17

Thatch had asked me to meet him at the computer lab today, and it couldn't have been good.

He had asked me to come alone.

He'd only do that if he wasn't sure about my reaction to something and wanted to spare me from showcasing that reaction to our other friends. This was his way of looking out for me.

I didn't ask for it.

We were all in this together, but I showed up alone like he'd asked. He was in front of the computer when I came to him, his permanent place as of late.

He'd even been skipping classes to do research for me, research for Charlie. These days, our search was feeling very much like the first forty-eight hours of a murder.

Except it had been months.

The time between Charlie's death and today had been far too long, and the trail on figuring shit out was getting cold.

Thatch's face was grim.

"I can't find her, man." He had his hands together, laced on the computer desk. He eyed me over his shoulder. "I've tried everything. All my contacts have led to nothing." He sat back. "I even reached out to my dad's contacts."

Thatcher had a few, all of us did, but we could only do so much poking around before our fathers caught wind of what we were doing. The four of us did what we could with names we'd heard over dinner conversations throughout the years and only made contact with them anonymously. We did nothing in a way that could be traced back to a pack of high school kids.

We couldn't take the risk.

No one was stopping us. No one was stopping *me* from gaining the truth about what had happened to Charlie last year.

Not even our own goddamn parents.

They might put a hold on this whole thing knowing we were trying to work up shit. Our parents were trying to move on after what had happened, but they wouldn't be able to completely unless they knew the truth. The four of us didn't have enough evidence to give that to them unfortunately. So, at the present, we were conducting our own research.

Which was apparently turning up dry.

I wet my mouth. It was goddamn dry like the fucking Sahara. I touched my lips to my fist. "There has to be something else."

"I'm telling you there isn't." He looked pained, his brow twisted with frustration and anguish. No one wanted this to work more than him. All of us were equally invested. Charlie Lindquist was our brother, *all* of ours. Not just mine. Thatch shook his head. "I'm fucking sorry. I fucking suck—"

I rubbed his shoulder. The guy had dark circles under his eyes and shit. I wondered if he slept, his nights spent pacing like I did. We were too young to be putting ourselves through all this stress. Especially Thatcher and Wells. They were barely sixteen, sophomores.

I only knew Thatch in particular was giving himself a hard time because he was a computer wiz and should've been able to find anyone. He'd learned from the best. His father's internet security company reached all over the world. We should have been able to find this bitch.

"Mayberry's wiped off the face of the earth." Thatcher sat back. "I can't find her. Not without help."

Our dear headmaster had skipped town after what had happened to Charlie. She'd claimed it was the stress and strain from witnessing the murder-suicide that had happened as a result of her abusive husband.

Except we knew the truth.

We'd found out the truth through Thatcher. At least, in part.

Charlie had been very careful about his contact with Principal Mayberry. In fact, once the police had issued my parents Charlie's personal belongings, we'd searched, but there had been no conversations with himself and that bitch Mayberry.

But thanks to Thatcher, not all of Charlie's secrets had died with him. Thatcher had been able to get us into Charlie's social media accounts. One in particular showed a direct back-and-forth exchange between Charlie himself and an anonymous handle. The conversation discussed running away together. No names were given, but whoever it was had specifically asked Charlie to be with them.

He'd obviously decided to.

This wasn't enough to implicate Mayberry, though. The bitch had obviously deleted her account. Nothing but a blank profile picture made it look like Charlie had been talking with himself that day. The pair of them also had been very good. They'd used no names or identifiable information. Neither Charlie nor Mayberry wanted anyone to know what they'd been planning.

We needed the source herself to admit her sins. She needed to admit what had really happened that night, but all leads were turning up dry and our hacker, Thatch, was getting defeated.

"I don't know how much more I can do," he said, swiveling back around to the computer. "Maybe if we had our dads' contacts."

That'd fix everything *if* our dads would have been on board with our theories.

We didn't have enough evidence.

There simply wasn't enough, and I personally couldn't drag my family back into the media circus that had been the last year. The news reporters had *just* stopped stalking our house.

No, we couldn't involve our parents. I couldn't pull anyone else into this shit. It was bad enough that Wells and Thatcher were in this too. They should have been enjoying their sophomore year, and Wolf should have been enjoying our junior year. No one else should have had to deal with this.

This should have been just my burden.

I hadn't been able to convince my friends of that, so they helped, and now, they were strained just like me.

You're such a fuckup.

I kept fucking up.

Blinking, I patted Thatcher's shoulder. "You need to get out of here. Go home early. Get something to eat. Sleep."

"I'm not tired," he gritted and went back to his searching. "I'll find her, D." He faced me. "I won't give up. I promise."

My stomach twisted.

Because I knew he wouldn't. My friends continued to labor over something only I felt personally responsible for. My guilt ran completely heavy, but I let my buddy stay in the lab. This was his free period, so he could spend it how he wished.

I stayed with him as long as I could until I had to go to class, and on my way out of the school that day, I found him still sitting in here. Wells had joined him. In our group text, I knew they both planned to do some late research tonight. Wolf was even going to join them after an art thing he couldn't get out of. We all had keys to the school, and the coverage of the academy was a nice way to keep our parents from asking questions.

I left my friends that night, but only because I had to go home and check on my mom.

She was where I'd left her.

I found her in the parlor, sipping tea and staring out the window. She'd returned to work after everything, but work was all she'd allowed herself to do these days. As soon as she came home, she was right back here. Last to leave, first to show up.

She told me it was just because she needed the quiet, and though I never bothered her, I did check on her. She'd kick my ass if I didn't, claiming she always wanted to see my face.

"Hey, Mom." I put my arms around her, and she smiled, twisting in her seat to hug me. My mom had a smile like the light, like the daytime and sunshine daisies.

It reminded me so much of Charlie's smile it killed my fucking insides. Charlie was her half brother. The pair of them looked so much alike despite having different moms. Mom had obviously taken Charlie's passing pretty hard. Especially since she'd lost a sister before that. It was a long time ago and before I was born. I'd never met my aunt Paige, but she'd been another casualty to this town. She'd been killed, murdered.

It was like my family was cursed. It was a curse I'd never seen due to privilege and my own self-involved shit. Before Charlie and my grandparents passing before that, I'd never really experienced loss. At least not like my mom and my dad had.

Mom hugged me tight. "Hey, baby."

She just held me there craned over her, held me for so long. Eventually, I stopped paying attention to the time and took a seat beside her. I texted my buddies that night.

Me: Mom's having a bad day. I can't make it.

She was the only one I'd make the sacrifice for. She needed me.

All the guys got back to me that the absence was fine, but it wasn't. It ripped me raw apart. It killed me she was this way.

Because of you.

The thoughts chilled me, each moment of every damn day. I stayed with my mother in silence until eventually, I gave her the space she liked. She'd never tell me. I always had to gauge that on my own.

She twisted in her chair. "Can you give the mail to your dad? It's on the table there."

We always ended the same way. I came in, gave her a hug and sat with her, then she asked me to bring the mail to my dad. I'd do that, then normally do more searching with the guys, but it'd gotten late tonight.

I nodded, telling my mom I loved her before I left the room. She spent evenings with my dad, quiet dinners during which he held her and told her everything would be okay. I didn't always make the dinner with this constant searching for Mayberry, but I'd come in one night and saw that was what my parents had been doing. My dad was my mother's rock.

And she was his.

I'd seen that on more than one occasion too. There were many secrets in this house. My dad was never vocal about the things that sometimes plagued him, but I'd caught my mother consoling him on more than one occasion. My dad wore his heart in a steel vise, and only my mother had the key.

"Dad." I knocked before I came into his office, mail in hand. Dad was over by the fireplace, a brandy in his hand. "Mom asked me to give you the mail."

I did, coming over and giving it to him. He started to filter through it, asking about my day. We did this banter too after Charlie passed. My dad was always busy, but it was like time had stopped after Charlie died. Like we'd all realized how truly fragile life could be.

Dad stopped on a letter, eyeing me before studying the door. "Your mom saw this?"

I started to look at the letter, but Dad took it back.

He cursed and, without warning, threw the envelope into the fireplace.

Shocked, I took a step toward it, watching the light catch it. A name on the front highlighted in the rapid flames.

To: Mr. Dorian Riley Prinze.

"Dad?" I questioned. He placed a hand to my chest before I could save it, shaking his head. I frowned. "But—"

"Don't, Dorian." My father lounged against the fireplace, watching the letter curl and burn. "Some things are just better left in the fire." His hand folded on his face. "I wish your mom hadn't seen that. I try to take those out before she can see them. They upset her every time."

I blinked, confused. There'd been more than one letter? To me?

But from whom?

I walked over to my dad, standing with him by the hearth.

A large sigh left him. "It's your grandfather," he stated, causing me to blink again. Dad nodded. "Grandfather Prinze. For some reason, my father thinks he has the right to speak to you."

I twitched. *Grandpa Prinze?* I shook my head. "I thought he was dead."

Or maybe I'd hoped he was. We never talked about him in this house.

Another secret.

For a long time, I hadn't known the truth about my father's father, and once told, I'd never heard the words again. The man had become a ghost, and I never pushed the issue after my parents finally did sit down and explain to me why I'd never *ever* in my life meet him.

My lips parted. "What does he want?" The letter had been to me, not my dad.

My father's face hardened, then with his big hands he squeezed my shoulders. "My father is cancer," he said, sighing. "And it doesn't matter what he wants."

He left me after that, his hand rubbing the back of his neck. His office door clicked behind him, and I simply stared at the letter in the flame. The letter curled, off to the side, and for some reason, I grabbed the poker off the fireplace.

I pulled the thing out, half of it burnt to hell, but I blew the ash away.

I didn't know what made me pocket it or take it out of my dad's office, but I did note one thing.

This was the first time I'd ever really defied my father.

CHAPTER
TWENTY-NINE

Dorian - age 17

I really had no idea why I stole the letter, but I did read it that night. It talked about me, how my grandfather wanted to see me.

"I think the boy has a right to know who his grandfather is, son," the letter said. *"Maybe you should let him decide whether or not he wants me in his life."*

The man was a rat fucking bastard if he thought he had any rights to me, not after what he'd done to our family. That was even outside of the abuse I knew he'd subjected my father to. There was a reason my dad never *ever* put hands on me. I hadn't even gotten a spanking growing up.

And that was because of Grandpa Prinze.

The man was an abuser, and the admittance had made me respect the hell out of my father. He told me himself why he didn't and never would put hands on me, and really, he'd never had to. My father's presence alone had been enough to keep me in line.

He'd never had to hit me.

The physical abuse of my dad, though, turned out to only be the cusp of my grandfather's dark deeds. There was a reason he'd been in prison a good portion of my life. My parents kept the reason as to why close to the cuff until I was about thirteen. They'd wanted to protect me from the reality of what my grandfather truly was.

A monster.

I knew that as true as I was reading the letter he'd sent me. As I took in the fine cursive, I realized exactly why I had taken it. I needed to know about the man's audacity, why he could possibly think he could or should see me. Fuck no, I didn't want to see that motherfucker, and I actually ended up starting my own little fire in my bedroom's fireplace that night. I got it nice and big, ready to see that letter turn to nothing but ash. I had full intentions of burning the letter and even held it over the flame.

Something had me squeezing the remains, though, and eventually pulling it back and putting out the fire. I later found out what that something was when I found myself outside of Wolf's room that night.

I tapped the window like I always did, and he woke up, letting me in around 3 AM.

"You know you can use the goddamn door," he said, rubbing the sleep out of his eyes. I half-expected to find a girl in here with him. He tended to bring them up and sneak them out before morning.

I dashed my eyebrows. "This is way more dramatic, don't you think?" I stated. Plus, I didn't have to wait for his string bean ass to pull himself out of bed and come downstairs. If I was pounding at his window like a motherfucker, he let me in right away.

"Right." He smirked, then sat on his bed in his boxers. I took a seat on his desk, trying to find his eyes under all that hair. He got all that curly shit from my god dad.

I folded my hands on the desk's edge. "I was thinking about something."

He put his hands together, his smile fading. "What kind of something?"

Something he wasn't going to like, but I took the letter out of my pocket. I gave it to him. "It's from my grandfather."

"The fuck?" When he ripped it out of the envelope, I thought he'd tear the remains in two. His eyes blazed. "The fuck?"

"Right?" I braced my arms. "He wants to see me. Bastard must be crazy."

"Fuck, yeah. He is," he said. Wolf shook his head. He lifted it. "Why is it burnt?"

"Dad. Threw it in the fireplace right in front of me. Told me about it after."

Wolf fingered his curls, pulling them out of his face. "Deep, man."

"Yeah."

"Well, what are you thinking about?" He lounged back, but then my buddy's eyebrows dashed up. "You don't *want* to see him do you…"

"Fuck no." I hopped off the desk, taking the letter back and sitting beside him. "Not ever in my life."

"Then what?"

I faced him, forcing myself to brave the fuck up. Ares wouldn't like this *at all*.

But I wasn't sure we had a choice. We'd reached a dead end in our search for Mayberry. "I was thinking maybe we could use him."

"Use him?"

I nodded. "Use his resources, I mean." I gazed around, restless. "He has a lot more pull than we do, and we can't find that bitch Mayberry."

Wolf looked at me as if I'd lost my goddamn mind, and maybe I had. I was desperate here.

I was more than desperate.

What else would actually compel me to even think about asking the man who'd caused so much terrible shit in my family's life? I didn't feel I had a choice here.

Wolf frowned. "D, what are you talking about?"

"Just hear me out. I make him think I want a relationship with him. I even go see him a couple of times." Wolf was already shaking his head, but I kept on. "We use his ass. You know how powerful my grandpa is."

We were Prinzes, part of the foundation of this town. We did what we wanted, and prison time wouldn't have hurt my grandfather. It was a media circus once he'd finally gotten out. My parents had actually taken me out of town for the weeks surrounding it. They'd wanted to protect me.

Grandpa Prinze was a powerful man, and it'd been the relief of I think all of us that he'd chosen to stay away. My grandfather had ended up making roots outside of Maywood Heights gratefully.

He'd gone upstate.

"I know how powerful he is." Wolf's eyes had gone hard, his frown harder. "Mine is too, but you don't see me going to see him."

His words sobered, chilled. He got up, and I followed him with my gaze. "Wolf?"

"We'll find another way."

"Ares—"

"I said we'll find *another way*, Dorian," he gritted. He directed a finger toward the letter. "Going anywhere near that guy would be like unleashing Pandora's box. Not to mention hurting your dad. *Your mom*."

I knew what he was saying. I knew that, and I'd never in my life want to hurt my mother. I was doing this *for* my mother. She'd want justice for Charlie.

She'd want the truth to come out.

That bitch Mayberry was running around like she hadn't

done anything. She looked like nothing but the suffering widow and not the filth who'd gotten Charlie killed.

That was only the last of her sins.

She'd been with him when she'd had no right, a secret affair, but the world was going to know who she was. *They'd know* about her place in all of this. The bitch had gotten off completely scot-free and left the rest of us to suffer the fallout. I had no uncle because of her.

My brother was dead.

Coming out of those thoughts, I got up and joined Wolf by the window. He was framing his face.

"They'll understand once we find out the truth," I said. "I'm not sure what other choice we have, Ares."

Slowly, he looked at me. He swallowed hard. "We do have a choice," he said, leaning in. "Just like he and my grandfather had a choice back then. *Like my great-uncle* had back then."

I chilled again. "This isn't the same."

"But it is, man." He got in my face. "My great-uncle Leo *murdered* your aunt Paige, Dorian. That was a choice, and you know what else was one?" His eyes scanned mine. "The choice our grandfathers made to help him cover it up."

I stiffened, my buddy speaking hard truths.

Wolf wet his lips. "That's our reality, that's the backlash from what the patriarchs in our families did. You don't think back then they all had a choice to do something different?" He shook his head. "Thank God my great-uncle is serving double life for that shit. He may be a monster. *Our grandfathers* may be monsters, but I refuse to be that way too."

But it was different. His great-uncle killed my aunt because he was psychotic, facts. He'd believed she'd gotten in the way of his jealous rage involving another woman. These details were cemented in the town's history, any paper readily available with the information.

It was Wolf's and my dark legacy. Even made worse when

our grandfathers had helped to cover it up to serve their own self-interests. They'd believed, at the time, the scandal could damage our families for various reasons. They were all monsters, but Wolf and us guys weren't.

We were the ones making things right.

We were the ones finally righting some wrongs in our families. Our grandfathers had served some time, but not nearly enough for what they'd done.

Wolf and us guys were the good ones.

I swallowed. "I wouldn't even be proposing this if I didn't think we had another option." I pointed a finger. "We have to get that woman. We have to find her. *I* have to find her. I have to make this goddamn right. Why can't you fucking help me!"

I said the words before they could be taken back.

The reality of them shone all over my buddy's face. His eyes twitched wide, shocked by what I said.

But I wasn't.

I knew the truth and my place in this whole thing as well. I knew *my* reality.

Wolf squeezed my shoulders, and it took me a moment to realize something.

He was keeping me standing.

My buddy had his hands on me, and the only reason I wasn't falling was because he was keeping me eye level with him. He swallowed. "We're going to make this right, D. I swear to God we will."

I shook, no words.

He scanned my eyes. "We're going to all do this together, and I *promise you* we won't have to be monsters to do it." He shook his head. "We don't have to lose our humanity, and I refuse to let you lose yours. Not while I still have a breath. I won't. Sorry."

My throat constricted, his hands leaving me.

He stared out the window.

"We'll find another way," he said, and I stared out the window too. There weren't a lot of times Ares was wrong. He was brilliant, completely owned school academically, and was like my god dad in that right. They were both incredibly brilliant men, but my buddy was wrong tonight. He couldn't keep me from losing my humanity.

Because I already was.

CHAPTER
THIRTY

Dorian - present

"Where's Ares?" I'd driven too fast over to Windsor House.

It was necessary.

I'd stopped by Wolf's place first, but his parents had said he'd gone to Windsor House, the meeting place of the Court and where those of us affiliated liked to unwind. Basically, it was a place for Court members to get away from our parents. Older Court members, like my father, never came to Windsor House unless there was official Court business going on. This made the aged building always a nice place to release for the younger generation.

Apparently, Wolf had wanted to get away.

Tucker, another Court guy, directed his finger across the clubhouse. This particular area of Windsor House was where the boys of the Court liked to mostly dick around. Women were allowed, but they never came in here. They had their own places they liked to do shit around the old castle. Us guys mostly played video games, billiards, and whatever in here.

Wolf sat in front of the fireplace.

I stalked over in a red haze, still soaking *fucking* wet from physically jumping into Murphy's Lake. Tucker and the other guys in the room eyed me along the way, and I found Wolf working his hands. He stared aimlessly at the fire, his hands moving restlessly. He didn't even hear me come up.

I shoved him off his chair.

He hit the floor, his chair with him, and I tossed it out of the way to get to him. He threw his head back. "Dude—"

I socked him, right in the goddamn face, and the follow-through sprayed blood from his mouth like an ocean spray. He roared, grabbing for my fist, but not quick enough.

I hit him. Again and again, I hit him. I didn't stop, determined to make his other eye match the one Sloane's brother had done a good job on. Wolf's first black eye had, again, been from his own antics. He'd tried to embarrass Sloane that night.

I slugged him once more, blinded, but Wolf anticipated my swings this time. Wolf got my wrists. He struggled with me until he got me off him enough to look at me. His eyes twitched, his lip busted from where I'd hit him. He shook his head. "D, what the fuck?"

I'd come at him so hot he apparently hadn't been able to take in who his assailant was until now.

Fighting his hold, I attempted to hit the son of a bitch again, but we were equal strength. He had height where I had muscle, but for the most part, my best friend and I were evenly matched. I threw his hands off me while guys shouted around us.

We apparently had an audience.

I'd been so focused on Wolf's ass I hadn't cared, and currently, some of them were using the break in our fight to cut in. Two grabbed me. Others were on Wolf pulling him away.

"What the fuck is wrong with you!" I shot, fighting both

the guys until they got their fucking hands off me. They *weren't* evenly matched with me, and no sooner had I shoved them off than I was back on Wolf. I pushed at the guy holding him until I got my buddy's shirt in my hands. I got in his face. "You trying to fucking kill someone? Huh? Are you?"

Because he could have. Bruno Sloane could have died tonight and would have had I not saved his ass.

I snorted like a bull. "Bruno Sloane could have died, you asshole!"

"D, stop it!" Wolf growled, grabbing my wrists, and we both tumbled to the floor. Gaining the upper hand this time, Wolf got me to my back. He held my arms above me while the other guys continued to chant and yell.

Mostly for us to stop.

Fights weren't respected amongst us. They were trivial, ridiculous. When they did start, it was usually Wolf or myself breaking it up. The Court was a brother and sisterhood of respect. We didn't turn against each other.

Which was why I was currently fighting my best friend.

He'd gone too far tonight, too *fucking* far, and I kicked at him on top of me. Wolf had me pinned, and I roared, bucking beneath him. I was acting out of character.

Even for me.

I knew that but didn't care. I still tried to fight my best friend.

"Stop, D. Stop!" Wolf roared, but I couldn't. I continued to growl and rage at him. I was acting like a complete maniac, but he'd set me off and I wasn't stopping.

My buddy had my hands real good. In fact, he had them so good I didn't know why I was still fighting. I was blinded, *enraged*.

Wolf obviously saw that. His expression changed. The next thing I knew, he was shouting at the other guys to leave us. They appeared hesitant before dispersing, but they did.

"And close the fucking door," Wolf yelled after them, but he'd made a mistake in that distraction.

He gave me an opening.

I took it. I shoved him so hard off me that he went flying. He backed into a chess set, and the pieces flew everywhere.

Getting up, I steamrolled him, and he grappled me around the chest like we were on the field. "Dorian!"

I tossed him off me, then shot my shoulder into him so hard he hit one of the bookcases. Books fell off the top shelves, landing at our feet. Wolf gauged his time between dodging both them and me.

"You've gone too far!" I was barely able to even hear myself and all I was saying. It was like I was a fly on the wall watching all this shit happen. I was punching at my best friend's arms, Sloane's voice playing in my head.

The way she looked at me tonight…

She'd called me toxic, me and mine and everything I was associated with. She'd basically called me a monster.

You are one.

The rage inside blinded me, but this time, Wolf was ready. He blocked every punch, his hands ensnaring my wrists. "Dorian, stop this!"

"Is this about me?" I asked, ignoring him. "Did you find out what I did? Is this revenge for that?"

Why else would he do such a thing? I knew my friend. I *knew* Ares. He'd never pull the shit he'd done tonight unless provoked.

He wasn't a monster.

This had to be because of me, all of this. I sneered. "Did you pull that haze because of me?"

"What?"

"Bruno!" I shoved until he stumbled off me, space finally between us. "Ryder and Josh said *you* called a haze to get him into the Court when you know we don't fucking do that."

We didn't. That shit was explicitly banned. It'd been a

haze that led to my aunt Paige being killed years ago, and he knew that. She'd been doing one to get into the Court the night she died, then was murdered by *his* great-uncle who was still in prison for the crime. She'd been in the wrong place, given the guy an opportunity. She'd been tied down to railroad tracks when his great-uncle had gotten to her.

The man had taken it from there.

The Court didn't do that shit anymore after my aunt Paige. It was dumb shit, and it shouldn't be done.

Wolf knew that.

"How dare you?" I growled. "How fucking dare you, Ares!"

"I forgot I planned it, man!" He tackled my arms. "I completely forgot about it. I meant to call it off, I..." He blinked as if lost for words. His mouth parted. "Sloane and her brother were getting in our way. Bru had been bugging me about getting into the Court, and I thought a haze might scare him off. Scare him out of town maybe once he knew what it was. I never thought he'd fucking do it."

He eyed me then. I was still wet from going in the lake after him. Bru had obviously tried it.

Wolf twitched. "Is he okay?"

"Fucking barely," I ground out, shaking him. "He almost died and *would have* had I not gone in after him. He didn't make it to the other side."

I let go, mostly out of shock. I could have died tonight too.

That might have been best.

The war inside me still raged on, and I turned my back to my friend. He came upon me, nearly silent.

"D, I'm sorry. I..." he started. "I honestly thought I was doing the right thing. I never—"

Whirling around, I grabbed him again, and this time, he didn't fight me. I got him by the shirt, backing him to the bookcase. I snarled. "If this is some sick revenge against me…"

He studied me, still not fighting. "What revenge?"

I had to admit my friend was good, but he played me for a fool if he didn't think I'd caught on to the real shit this was about.

"This is about me, right?" I said. "You coming at me because of what I did? I'm assuming Thatcher and Wells told you about where I went a few days ago. *What I did?*"

I'd been ignoring their calls, their texts. They'd even come by over the last few days, but each time I'd had them sent away. They probably had told Wolf's ass about everything because they were worried about me.

I was worried about me.

I was worried that I currently had my friend against a bookcase, at war with one of the closest people in my life. I was worried how my life was turning out, and as each second passed, I lost more and more of a grip on it.

Wolf eyed me. "Where you went?"

My hold tightened on him. "Don't play fucking dumb."

"I'm not." He placed his hands on my arms, cautious as if he were coming at an animal. "D, I set that haze up weeks ago."

Weeks ago…

"Like I said, I meant to call it off. I set it up before I realized…" He started to say something, but then chose not to. He studied the floor a moment before facing me. "Where did you go, Dorian?"

Nausea surfaced within me, my paranoia actually bringing me here.

He didn't know.

Wolf had no idea, and now, I just outed myself. I let go of him, but he got me by the arm.

"What did you do?" He spoke my own words back to me. He wet his lips. "Bro?"

The better question was: what hadn't I done? How had I gotten to this place?

I had no words for him, pushing him away, but he had me good.

He gazed around the room this time before bringing his attention back. "Whatever it is, we'll make it right, okay? But I can't help if I don't know."

There was no one to help me.

It was already done.

I did what I had to do.

"I already took care of it," I said, forcing myself to look at him. "I took care of him."

"Who?"

I closed my eyes. "I did what I had to do." My jaw clenched. "And you wouldn't have agreed."

He shook me to make me keep focus on him. He was one of a few who could get to me. Not even Thatcher and Wells could get me to face them full on and stare whatever it was in the face like Wolf. We'd been boys since the womb. I folded my hand over my face.

"Hey." He leaned in. "What happened?"

"I got him involved, that's what happened," I said, nodding. "And you were right. It was Pandora's box."

It was a box I couldn't close, but I'd done what I had to do.

Cringing, I shouldered Wolf away, but he got me back.

"You didn't," he said, looking at me, but when I said nothing, he paled. "Please tell me you…"

"I did." The truth. I faced away. "Why do you think Mayberry suddenly came back into town this year?"

I hadn't exactly lied to my friends at the beginning of the school year. I'd told them I had a contact who'd suddenly come out of the woodwork to help us. That contact had been able to find Mayberry and even get her to come back into town. As it turned out, our principal had needed money. She'd spent all her late husband's life insurance on a recent drug habit, pharmaceuticals and other shit. Our dear headmaster had turned into nothing but a drug abuser after she'd left this town and racked up quite the bill to back it.

It'd been too easy really, for that new contact to find her. That contact had power, influence.

He'd even arranged for her to get her old job back.

He had pull with the school, got them to even give her a bonus for coming back. The amount had happened to be just what she owed all those drug dealers.

How could Mayberry turn that offer down?

Yes, my contact had arranged that. He'd forced our headmaster to come back and to the mercy of my friends and me.

I just hadn't told my friends who that contact was.

Wolf swallowed, looking at me. "I told you we'd find another way. I told you it didn't have to come to that."

He'd told me a lot of things.

I just wished I would have listened.

I left him, staring at the same fire I'd caught him looking into when I'd arrived. "I did what had to be done." I placed my hand on the fireplace. "I did what I had to."

Wolf moved with stealth in the room. I knew because when I looked up, he wasn't where I'd left him.

He was beside me. His hand came down on my shoulder. "What did you have to do?" When I said nothing, Wolf shook his head. "What did you feel you had to do?"

I did what he would have done too, what had to be done to protect my family. Had he been given the opportunity, he would have done the same. "I had no choice, Ares." I cringed. "He threatened me, *my family* and our way of life." I swallowed. "I couldn't let that happen. I…"

He angled me around, but I couldn't look at him. Next thing I knew, he grappled me with his long wingspan.

And I was holding on to him like a little bitch.

I couldn't stop myself, two fucking seconds from breaking down. "I had to."

"What?" he questioned in my ear. "Say it, D."

I couldn't, my hands gripping his shirt. He said we didn't have to be monsters. But how could a monster be anything other than what it was destined to be? We were Legacy, and this was mine.

It'd always be shrouded in the dark.

CHAPTER
THIRTY-ONE

Sloane

"I told you he had nothing to do with it," Bru spat. He dropped onto the couch beside me, his hair wet and clothes changed like he'd showered. "And *I* wanted to get into the Court. *Me*." Bru frowned. "All Dorian did was save my life."

Dorian had saved his life. But he was also associated with Ares "Wolf" Mallick. I played on my phone. "Dorian did save your life and I appreciate that, but—"

"No *but*." Bru stood, his hands up. "He saved my life. He stood up for me." Bru heaved a dry laugh. "And you threw that shit into his face so fast it was ridiculous. He had nothing to do with Wolf wanting me to do that haze. Also, did you forget that I crossed Wolf first? I mean, I punched him in the fucking face over you."

"So that gives the guy every right to try and kill you?" I asked, both appalled and shocked. "You really are desperate for friends."

His face exploded in color, his eyes enraged. He put a hand to his chest. "Newsflash, sis. You can't control everything all the time. You can't *protect me* all the time. Hell, you got enough on your plate with that shit with Dorian."

"What are you talking about?"

His frowned deepened. "You're into him. I know you are, and you're bullshitting if you tell me any different. I see how you've looked at him."

"We screwed, Bru," I said, passing that off. I played on my phone. "Doesn't mean anything."

"Right." He forced fingers through his ebony locks. "You're too busy jumping down people's throats to see what's in front of you."

"Are you done?"

"Not quite." He stood in front of me. "And I practically begged Wolf to let me into the Court. Was he in the wrong for basically trying to kill me? Yeah, but none of that has anything to do with Dorian. Zero percent."

My fingers slowed on my phone.

"Get over yourself, sis." Bru cuffed his arms. "Before you end up as lonely and guarded as Dad did toward the end of his life."

"Probably should go to bed." I gazed up at him. "Before you say something you'll regret." I was still his older sister. I didn't care that he'd overshot me in size years ago.

Clearly over it, Bru raised his hands, muttering a curse before escaping my sight. Odds were, he just hadn't wanted to be in the same room with me.

I didn't care as long as he did what I said.

If I had things my way, we would have packed up the Chevelle and left this godforsaken town in a cloud of dust behind us. I was aware Dorian had nothing to do with tonight. I had eyes, but when would Bru see he and the rest of those guys were all one and the same. They were *all* Legacy. Thatcher and Wells had been nice to me lately, but they both had put hands on me before.

It didn't matter if one of those boys saved Bru's life

tonight. It didn't matter if I was "into" one of them like he claimed. Which I wasn't.

Yeah, keep telling yourself that.

I had to. It was the only way to keep my sanity.

My phone buzzed with a text.

I couldn't identify it with the number, but I obviously read it.

Unknown: Hey, it's Wolf. Ares.

I saw nothing but red, basically growling at the text. I was about to shoot off at him, but Ares's text message bubble popped back up.

I was curious.

I waited for him to type it out and see what he could possibly have to say to me.

Ares: I'm aware both you and Bru probably want to kill me right now, and if it means anything, I meant to call that haze off. We don't do those anymore to get into the Court. Haven't in a long time.

Dorian had said as much.

I didn't care, though, as I watched Ares's text bubble pop up again.

Ares: Anyway, the whole thing was my idea. Honestly, I figured your brother would bitch out. I didn't think he'd actually do it. That haze is crazy.

Well, he'd guessed wrong.

Asshole.

Ares: I shouldn't have done it. I know I shouldn't have, and I'm sorry. I didn't want him in our group. I wanted nothing to do with you and thought it'd help to get you both out of town.

Well, at least he was honest.

Ares: I was harsh. I was a dick.

I wondered why he was saying all this to me. Why he was texting me at all.

Ares: It seems your brother is as fierce and determined as you. Makes sense since you are his sister.

Oh my God, he was paying me compliments now? Who was this guy and where was my arch nemesis Wolf Mallick? He hated my ass. Point blank.

Ares: I snap judged you. Hell, I've been a fucking little bitch.

Me: Are you making a point? You could have killed him.

I shot off one in the middle of his weird rant because I didn't want him in my phone, compliments or not.

Ares: Hey, hi. Uh.

I waited a second before he sent me more, and really, all this was super weird now. He almost sounded flustered.

Ares: Yeah, I'm making a point. I'm really sorry, but that's not why I texted. It's Dorian. I need to talk to you about him. Something's going on with him.

And why did I sit up. Why did I go ramrod straight like I *cared*?

Because you do.

I called Dorian on his shit, and now, I was calling myself on mine. Maybe the dark prince had circulated my mind more than a time or two. Maybe I put more stake into him saving my brother's life than I wanted to tonight.

That tended to happen when one realized he almost died too in that water.

Dorian really could have. He was an idiot for going in there after my brother.

My fingers shook on the device as I waited for Ares to finally come out with what he was going to say.

Ares: Basically, he's real fucked up right now, and I'm the last person he wants to see. Not after what I did to you and your brother.

Me: Point, Mallick?

Ares: Fuck, little. Give me a word in edgewise, would you? What I'm trying to say is he came to see me tonight.

Some shit went down, then he drove off like a crazy fuck after. He's completely in his head, and he shouldn't be out like that. He shouldn't be alone. Not right now.

I stopped for a second, thinking about what he said.

Me: What happened?

Ares: I can't go into details. It started with a fight about that shit that happened with your brother, though. Got pretty nasty. Physical.

Whoa.

Ares: It ended up escalating into some deeper shit. Real bad shit going on with him, and between the combination, it's put him on another level.

I wondered what the deeper shit was and recalled Dorian had felt off tonight. I'd asked about it, but of course, he hadn't gone into details.

He'd certainly been weird, though.

He felt *off*, and something told me those details Ares couldn't get into had something to do with that.

Ares: I'm worried. He shouldn't be alone, but if I try to go see him after that shit with Bru, he's not going to have it. That's why I'm texting you.

Me: Me?

Ares: Yeah.

The next thing I knew, he shot over an address.

It was close.

Like literally down the street, and I had no idea why he was sending this.

Ares: I tracked his phone here. You should go. If he won't see me, at least you should be there. Wells and Thatcher tried contacting him too, and no dice. He told them both to fuck off.

Me: I don't get why you're texting me. Why would he want to see me if he's refusing you guys?

Dorian hated me. We hated each other.

Ares: You seem pretty intelligent, Sloane. Figure it out.

The first thing I noticed was that he paid me another compliment.

The second was that he called me by my name.

───────

The address Ares had shot me was so close I actually walked to it.

I found Dorian on the lawn.

He sat in the middle of it, a six-pack beside him and a bottle in his hand. He drew it back in the moonlight and didn't even notice me until I was right up on him.

He barely looked like himself, hair tossed and strewn about.

His eyes haunted.

He almost stared through me when he drew back his beer, wiping his full lips in the moonlight after. He'd changed since I'd last seen him. A white tee cuffed his mighty arms and strong back. He tilted his head, staying level with my approach. "The fuck you doing here?"

He wasn't *quite* drunk, but he was obviously working at it with all the beer at his feet. He sat in front of a dark house, the *for sale* sign in the yard.

He kicked at the sign. "I came here to be by myself."

Obviously.

I stayed anyway, hugging my arms in the chilly air. The house he sat in front of was lovely, large glass walls like Bru's and mine. It also sat on a hill. The scenic view was high up here and completely picturesque, beautiful.

And why was *he* so beautiful. His blond hair was perfect and hung lazily over his eyes. His beer tight in his hands, I noticed his split knuckles. He appeared to have punched something.

Or someone.

Ares had said their fight had gotten physical, which was crazy. He'd done that over everything with Bru? Really?

Dorian noticed me eyeing his knuckles, smirking. Shaking his head, he tipped back his beer again. He swallowed it down. "Which one of those fuckers I call friends got you to come see me?"

My eyes twitched wide, surprised. "Ares texted. How did you know?"

"Because I know my friends," he said, rocking back. He killed one beer, then started on another. "And few people can track my phone." He studied me. "And my parents don't know you."

His roving gaze stayed on my bare thighs, pausing only a second before coming up to my midriff. He didn't stay there long before getting a good visual fondle of my breasts before smirking again and drinking more beer. I'd hit dudes for less.

But under Dorian's gaze...

He was in my head too, my chest visibly flushed in my scoop-neck top. He made me feel completely naked despite being fully clothed.

I hated that it wasn't in a bad way. I hated that I *burned* under his sight. He was still feet away from me, but that didn't matter.

Why is he here?

The house in front of us was dark, empty. Like my home, there were no neighbors. Each house sat in its own privacy of full trees and moonlight.

It was just Dorian and me out here, alone with the *for sale* sign and his beer. He lifted the pack. "Want one? I'm not an asshole."

He was, but I took one anyway. After my selection, he stole it back from me. He opened it with his boot before returning it.

"So chivalrous," I crooned, making his dark smile appear. It didn't frighten me like it probably should. Not anymore. I popped a squat beside him on my knees. "Any idea why your friend would be desperate enough to call me over here?"

"Because he knew where I was." He lounged his big body back in the grass, his dark eyes in my direction. "And he's obviously caught on to my fascination with you." My mouth dried, and he smirked. "It also helps that you live just down the street and could get here soon."

My mouth parted. "You know where I live?"

"You'd left-hook my ass at the things I know about you." He turned in my direction. "Orphan at eighteen. Your brother seventeen. You came to this town after your father died in a factory fire. Your tuition is paid by a Callum Montgomery, and though I don't know a lot about him, I'm assuming he's very wealthy." My jaw slacked. He faced the house. "Your file said he was a family friend."

So, he had my file, impressive. I sat back then brought in my legs, hugging them. "What else do you know?"

He smiled again. "I know you've moved around a lot, and that's clearly made you combative." His gaze roved over me. "You jumped down Wolf's throat before he could jump down yours, and considering your history of fights at your old schools, that makes sense. You're from Chicago most recently but have lived in the state your whole life. Your mother passed at some point in your life. Though I don't know how."

He stated my life in facts only, and at my silence, his expression shifted. He almost appeared apologetic. Like he'd run away with himself and just realized what had fallen from his lips.

Even still, he didn't apologize. He simply clinked his beer with mine. Together, we drank a long sip, the pair of us lost in it.

"You seem to think you have me all figured out," I said.

"But don't I?" Sitting up, he hooked an arm over his knee. He frowned. "I mean, I thought I had."

"Until when?"

"You showed up here. With me?" He waved his beer in front of the house. "Dropping into my hot fucking mess of a life." His head tilted in my direction. "I'm sure you know all about this shit, though. My life is as open to you as yours was to mine. Just pull up a fucking internet search."

I blanched. Actually, I knew very little about the dark prince because I hadn't looked him up. I hadn't felt I needed to.

I wondered why now.

He fascinated me too, and I'd stalked boys for less in the past during a crush phase.

Did you actually just think that? A crush on the dark prince? Really?

What I had with this boy wasn't a crush. It was something weird.

It was something intense.

Like stated, he fascinated me, but no, I hadn't looked him up.

He saw that. His blond eyebrows actually flicked up, the surprise evident on his face.

"Another surprise, Noa Sloane," he said, then wet his lips. He grinned. "You keep surprising me."

He let the words fall off as he propped both arms on his knees.

"Let me give you the CliffsNotes version, then." Beer still tight in hand, he directed a finger at the house. "This was where my uncle Charlie was murdered."

The beer nearly slipped from my fingers he'd said it so casually.

He eyed me. "Plot twist, right?"

His chuckle was so dark as he drank again, and after finishing *that one off*, he opened another on his boot. I thought to say he should slow down.

Ares was right.

He wasn't acting right. I didn't know a lot about Dorian, but this wasn't normal.

Then what he just said.

Dorian stretched a bit before craning those big arms back over his legs. "Don't you want to know how it happened?"

"Not unless you want to tell me." I came at what I said like a scared little animal.

Or maybe it was him in the vulnerable position. He was certainly the most vulnerable one.

"Surprises surprises," he said to me, but he wasn't smiling now. His jaw clenched. "He was shot." Fuming, a harsh muscle feathered his jaw. "Twice in the chest. He died almost instantly."

"Dorian…"

"Broke my mom." He said this with a straight face. "My mom who you thought it was fun to play a joke on. She's still having problems, you know? I've got to remind her of stuff. To do stuff like remember things she needs for her day."

"I didn't mean…" But that would be a lie. *I had* meant to hurt his mom because it would hurt him.

Something told me he knew that, his smile returning. His attention drifted to the home. "Charlie was having an affair with our headmaster."

"What?"

He nodded. "Good ole Principal Mayberry. So perfect." His fingers squeezed the bottle. "So lovely. She certainly likes to entice eighteen-year-old boys." I frowned, and he nodded. "Their affair started my sophomore year when Charlie was eighteen. He was fascinated with her. Snuck around with her all the time. They used to meet here when Coach was out."

My stomach twisted. "She took advantage of him."

"He claims she didn't." He shrugged. "But he was vulnerable, and she was *married*." His expression darkened. "To our coach at the time. Coach Mayberry."

"Why at the time?" I didn't know why I asked. Why *I kept* pushing this.

"Well, he's not our coach anymore. Nor is he still *actively* married to his wife." Ice chilled his words. "That kind of happens when you kill yourself after murdering a nineteen-year-old kid in your house."

The breath escaped my lips.

Dorian's head bobbed twice. "In her official statement, Principal Mayberry said Coach believed someone was breaking into his home that night. But once he realized the kid was his former player turned the gun on himself. She *claimed* he suffered from 'mental problems'…"

"That's not true?" It was hard to hear this at this point, hear the audible strain in his voice. He wasn't even looking at me now.

And the haunted look returned to his gaze.

Dorian drank more beer, visibly lost in front of me.

"That woman is a lying bitch," he gritted. His eyes had turned into heated, dark pools. Like the grim reaper out to play. Without looking at it, he pointed toward the house. "She had plans to run away with Charlie that night. Thatch broke into Charlie's social media account and found that shit out." He shook his head. "My theory is Coach found out the woman had a lover and got into an argument with her about it when she tried to leave him."

I gasped, and Dorian's grip on his beer was pale white now.

"I was sure Coach shot without warning," he said, his voice hollow, vacant. "And after finding out who Charlie was, killed himself." He smiled, a dark, *sad* smile. "Her husband had no idea his wife would take up an affair with a kid. He thought he was simply going for the other guy that night."

"Dorian."

He stared at the ground. "But after seeing it was Char-lie…" His eyes shifted. "Well, he hadn't just killed the other guy. He'd killed his former player and beloved former quarterback of his team. Charlie was the town jewel. Everyone loved him." He drank more beer. "The man was troubled, but probably not in the way Mayberry says. Before he died, Charlie told me Coach was abusive. That Coach hit her and was a bad guy. He obviously had anger issues and shit."

He sucked back the rest of his beer, but after, he didn't take another. I'd been glad.

"The only person who can fill in the real story is that bitch Mayberry. That coke whore, opportunist-as-fuck *bitch*. The woman became a drug addict after all this shit. Sits in her office sometimes and does cocaine. More than one person has seen it."

My God.

"She preyed on Charlie, and he was so goddamn vulnerable to her," he continued, red creeping up his neck. "He lived with my parents and me. Grew up with me as my brother after his parents, my grandparents died." He shook his head. "He was a shell of himself after that. Never the same after that."

He scrubbed his face, my jaw moving slowly.

"Well, can you get Mayberry to tell the truth?" I asked, probably stupid. "She shouldn't get away with that. Maybe show someone the social media exchanges between Charlie and her. Show your parents."

"Like I haven't thought of that, little fighter." He looked at me, his smile sad again. "There's no identifiable information in the messages. She deleted her account." He drew in a large breath, staring at the house. "She'd probably deny the whole thing. The only way to get her to tell the truth is to make her. From her lips, no one else's." He studied me. "We tried once. To get her to admit shit?" He smirked. "But a little fighter got —and continues—to get in the way."

My mouth parted. "What?"

"You're her student assistant during a prime time to

approach her. *Corner her* and get her to do what we need to do. Us guys made plans to sneak her out during that hour and get her to confess in a remote location."

"You mean, kidnap her?"

He opened his hands like it wasn't a thing. "Would have worked, but it wouldn't have had to have come to that had we gotten her during our first opportunity." His eyebrows lowered. "Which again, a little fighter managed to fuck up too."

He kicked his bottle onto the lawn, the thing rolling through the thick grass. I studied it, then instantly stiffened.

My gaze collided with his dusky irises, like the answers were always there. He hated me when I got here. He always said I was getting in the way, making noise.

I twitched. "You mean, the night of that mugging? *Principal Mayberry's mugging*—"

"That was Wells," he said. I thought he'd reach for a beer, but instead shoved his fingers into his hair. He brought them down to cover his mouth. "But it wasn't his fault. I should have done the job myself. I should have gotten her myself." He gripped his arms. "Wolf and I were preparing the location for questioning. We were going to get her on camera and get her to confess what actually happened that night."

And I'd gotten in the way.

I made noise.

I did and continued to do so according to him. He said the failed attempt wasn't Wells's fault.

It was actually yours.

I couldn't breathe as he severed his gaze from me.

Dorian got up and stalked over to the house. "I should have done things myself with Mayberry. What happened here that night of Charlie's murder was *my fault*. Charlie never even would have come here if it wasn't for…"

The words seemed to escape him.

I got up, approaching his side. "If it wasn't for what?"

He said nothing, his swallow hard, and mine was too. I'd technically messed everything up for him that night with Mayberry. He was right.

I had made noise.

I wasn't sure if I agreed about how he and the Legacy were going about this. I wasn't sure this was right at all, but I had no right to put in my input, let alone judge. Charlie wasn't my family.

And if it'd been Bru…

I couldn't even fathom what I'd do to gain the truth in his honor. Imagine, knowing the person actually responsible for your family's murder was so close by.

No, I couldn't make any judgments here. Not one.

"I'm sorry," I said because I truly was.

He faced me. "Sorry?"

I played with my hands. "For getting in the way? For making noise? I can't imagine what you and the guys are going through. God, this fucking sucks."

He twitched, like he actually couldn't believe what I said. He eyed me. "I must be hearing some shit because I just told you I was going to kidnap our headmaster, and you're telling me sorry that you got in the way of that." He laughed, nearly sounding manic. Bending, he cracked open another beer. He saluted me with it. "You must be as fucking psycho as me."

I watched as he sucked down a long draw. I was as sad for him and his situation as I was confused by him. Maybe he had something about me being weird, but I couldn't help but feel for him. *Understand* him. I didn't want to, but I did.

And if that made me psycho…

I honestly did question it. Especially when I ripped the bottle away from him.

"What the fuck—"

Cut off, Dorian's eyes expanded as he watched me rear back his full bottle of beer.

I threw it at the side of the glass house.

The booze exploded against the wall, yeasty liquid flowing down it. He growled at me, most likely because I wasted a perfectly good beer.

I wasted more.

I took my own bottle, intentionally throwing it at the door where a glass window resided. The beer didn't shatter this time. It went right through the window, glass literally busting out as the bottle disappeared inside the dark home.

I went for the last bottle of beer in the case, but Dorian grabbed my arm. His fingers bit into my flesh when he jerked me roughly around to face him.

"The fuck you think you're doing?" His eyes expanded, completely wild. "What are you—"

"Don't you want to get a hit in?"

"What?"

I ripped my arm away. "I said, don't you want to get a hit in?" I directed a finger toward that house. "That house should burn. Fuck, worse should happen to it."

His family *died* in there. Mayberry hooked up with his family here, and had I been him, I'd want to set this whole place on fire.

"Don't you want to destroy this place, Dorian? Get a hit in for Charlie?" I picked up the bottle, holding it out. "No one would blame you. Least of all me."

Maybe I was crazy. Maybe I was as psycho as he said. He didn't take the bottle, and I reared back again. I was about to fuck up this place *for him*.

He didn't let me.

He took the bottle, his hand folding around my hand on it. We stood level to level, eye to eye despite him having a few inches. The dark prince was tall, but I was tall too.

He tugged me closer by the bottle, his fingers squeezing mine.

"I want to get a hit in," he breathed over my mouth. I felt

the mint of his breath despite how much booze he drank. He just always seemed to have it.

He let go of me slowly, taking the bottle with him.

His football arm gave him an advantage.

Dorian threw that bottle so hard one of the glass walls busted out, and the house alarm blasted through the air.

He didn't care.

He got another bottle, empty this time and threw the thing steadfast through another window on the door. The rest of the empty bottles joined it, glass exploding everywhere, and when he didn't have those, he went for the rock work around the hedges.

He threw large stones, his own personal form of a football pelting through glass. Windows exploded, property damaged. Dorian's expression transformed into a million different shades of unfurled rage, and I simply stood there, watching the display.

I should be horrified by what I'd done, by what I'd caused him to do. I mean, someone was probably coming from somewhere eventually with that alarm going off. It'd probably take a moment since this neighborhood was out in the boonies, but still.

I didn't run despite the chaos. I wasn't horrified. I merely watched as a tortured boy let out his anger in the only way he could.

Dorian threw until he was spent. Until his body sagged and labored so harshly I thought he'd fall to his knees. That was when I approached him.

That was also when he grabbed me.

Dorian gripped the back of my neck and collided our mouths, the kiss harsh and angry.

And so familiar.

He kissed me the same way he had the first time. The kiss was impulsive, untamed.

Wild.

It was like him, my arms ensnared around his neck. I deepened the kiss as he pressed my body against him.

Sirens rang in our ears.

The cops were coming from somewhere in the hills, but we didn't react how a normal person would. Sure, we ran. Dorian grabbed my hand. He dragged me to his car, but the whole time, he laughed.

We both did.

We looked like two crazy people getting into his car. He waved me to hurry, his laughter boisterous and jovial. He laughed like he wasn't a broken boy, but a teenager who simply didn't want to get caught.

I was simply the girl going along for the ride.

He had his arm around my neck, as he peeled off, and his laughter didn't stop. I didn't ask him where we were going.

I didn't care.

CHAPTER
THIRTY-TWO

Dorian

I slammed my cock inside her the moment we were in her bedroom, the closet place I could think of to fuck this girl.

She hadn't complained.

Sloane proved once again to be the complete and utter head fuck she'd always been, but this time, I didn't fight it.

I just dove right in.

I roared at her taste, not even bothering to keep it down. Bru's car hadn't been in the garage, and Sloane said he'd probably gone to get takeout or something.

Her shorts had been down to her ankles barely after getting into the house.

Currently, her cutoffs hung off one leg, this girl between my arms against her bedroom door. I fucked her right there, our hands laced, our mouths hot and our tongues dueling. I thrust in a slow fuck, and she called out.

Her brother was going to hear this shit when he got home.

I didn't care. Pulling out, I turned her around by her hair. I jerked off her fucking shirt, then ripped her bra clean off.

She was grinning when she faced me, her tits flushed and perfect for my hands. She wrapped one of those long legs around me, and in a quick maneuver, she was physically putting me back inside her. *What the fuck?*

"Fuck me, Dorian," she said, eye contact completely on me, and it was a wonder I didn't come like this was my first goddamn time. Noa Sloane was an experience.

I gripped her throat, slowing down on purpose. She didn't control this. I was going to fuck this girl as long and as hard as I wanted to. She *wouldn't* control this.

Even if she already was.

"I own you." I arched in a hard thrust, my cock disappearing inside her. Hard in. Slow out. I watched, then made her when I gripped her hair in my fist and directed her gaze down. I grinned. "That's me owning you. That's my dick you scream for."

She made me fucking mad tonight, doing things I was embarrassed I hadn't thought to do first. She'd made me look like a punk bitch at Mayberry's old place.

And if I didn't want to make her come for that.

If I didn't want to bleed *for her* after that, the sickest fucking thoughts in my head. I wanted her everywhere, inside her and all around. I didn't want to just own her. I wanted to be *owned by her*, and I fucking hated that shit.

Like stated, she was a head fuck.

I dizzied as she bit my lip, and almost buckled at my goddamn knees for it. I held her back by the throat. "Stop."

So much was loaded in that one word, her eyes on me. Her hips rocked slowly, her hands on my chest.

"Don't stop," she said, eyes scanning me. She looked deeply, like she was looking for something when there wasn't anything to see. I'd told this girl. I had no soul anymore. She placed her hands on my face. "Don't stop. Stay."

Stay.

She slow-fucked me right back, her tight snatch squeezing

my cock so hard I nearly did come. Growling, I braced her neck and collided our mouths.

"Get out of my head," I panted, removing her off me and taking her to the bed. She had all this frilly shit around, totally not Noa Sloane.

Why are you talking like you know her?

But this wasn't Noa. The place had to have been decorated. Noa was a hellcat, dark metals and rough edges in my thoughts for her. She wasn't into the easy stuff. She liked *seeing through* stuff for its depth and whatever else was in there. She liked to unravel and unfurl shit she had no business getting into.

I'd told her all my business tonight and hadn't even hesitated. Wolf had known exactly what he was doing when he called her to come see me.

She was making me do stupid things.

She was making things not *hurt* as much and my guilt surrounding Charlie numbed. I didn't feel like I had only hours ago. But even before that, I wasn't rattled by the brevity of what I'd done this week in nearly the same way.

That happened in only a few moments with her. Noa was making things go away. My own personal Valium.

Going between her legs, I drank from her heat, my tongue spreading her pussy lips apart. She kicked a leg until we both got her shorts off, her thighs hugging my face to her sex.

"Dorian, holy fuck." She bit her knuckles, her soft pants amplified in the quiet house. I could fuck her as loud as I wanted to in this room. Shit, the astronauts would hear us.

Grinning, I bit her lower lips into my mouth, salivating when she called out and her sweet heat flooded over my lips. I didn't even like eating pussy. I'd get my dick sucked any day of the week, though. What could I say, I was a dude.

But Noa…

She tasted like candy, all sin and heaven. She touched

herself while I flicked her bud with heated intent. Her perfect tits spilled above her hands.

Yeah, those were my thing.

Leaving her pussy, I laved her nipples, sucking and pulling them. My jeans were half down and my cock was ready for another dive into her heat. I physically ached for her, twitching under my fist as I pumped myself.

"Get naked with me." She rolled my shirt off, looking like a kid in a candy store. I pulled my hair back, flashing her the eyes after she removed it. She shoved me. I assumed for being arrogant. She rolled her eyes. "Stop it."

"You fucking stop." We argued as good as we fucked.

Maybe even better.

After kicking off my jeans and my boxers, I took her lips. I entered her again. It was like being home inside this chick and what the fuck.

"Dorian," she gasped, gripping my back. "God, Dorian."

She placed her forehead against my shoulder, her soft skin damp with heat. I gripped the bed while still inside her, driving her into the sheets.

"Scream for me," I goaded, arching, taking us both to our brink. "Come for me like you're only mine."

I could dick punch myself for it. Upon letting go of the bed, our fingers laced and not even a breath could be placed between us now. I owned her in this moment. She was *mine.*

"Dorian!" I picked up, hoping the condom I put on when we first got in her room would hold. I grunted, roaring into the room when she came around me…

And I wasn't far behind.

Even still, I milked her, lost in the intense fucking heat that was Noa Sloane. We came down the high at about the same time, but even still, I didn't let her get out from under me.

I tasted every inch of her, until it wasn't possible that I'd missed anywhere. Eventually, I had her on her belly, beautiful, luscious skin facing me.

I traced invisible lines between every taste, studying how her dark almost black hair played against her naturally tan skin. This girl made Brazilian models look like amateurs, and I wondered if she maybe had some of that in her bloodline somewhere. Her brother wasn't tan for shit, but Sloane obviously caught something somewhere in her gene pool. The girl was gorgeous.

And you're acting like a fool.

I knew this as I was tracing *invisible lines* on her back between kisses. I stayed on one when she sighed and her entire body shuddered under my touch. She angled her head, looking back at me.

I watched her but didn't stop playing. I watched her watch me, her gaze roving over my shoulders, my chest. Knowing her, I thought she'd send me to my back and attempt to be the little fighter I knew she was by straddling me.

Instead, she touched my hand, the free hand. Taking it, she tucked herself back into my chest. She hugged me close.

"It was a home break-in," she said, her voice so soft in this room. She nestled into me. "My mom. She died in a home break-in. I barely remember. I was so young."

I lay with her, feeling her steady breaths under my arms. I wondered why she admitted that to me.

But then again, I was tracing lines on her back.

In the moment after her words, things got real quiet. Normally, I'd leave right about now. I got what I wanted from her.

"Charlie's death was my fault," I said, not sure why I said it. Maybe because she'd admitted what she had to me. I shrugged. "I told him Principal Mayberry hadn't left her husband. He went to her house after that. Went to run off with her after that."

Nothing but silence filled the air, and I didn't know what I expected her to say. Maybe all the things that were in my own head. How it was my fault, how it was my failure. Sloane didn't hold back.

I hoped she wouldn't in this case. I *wanted* her to give it to me good. I wanted to feel the cut of the words.

I deserved them.

"I think you already know the truth, Prinze," she said, her voice sleepy. She hugged me closer. "But now, you need to make Mayberry tell it."

I was surprised by what she said, listening.

"The world needs to know the truth," she continued, playing with my hand. "And you do too. You deserve that."

I deserve it.

She said nothing else, and I watched as her breaths softened and her eyes fell closed. She was under the belief that I had no stake in what happened, but I knew the truth. I supposed we were both fools. I was for letting her get under my skin.

And she was for allowing a monster into her bed.

CHAPTER
THIRTY-THREE

Dorian

A text pulled me out of my sleep at Sloane's. Her long leg curled around me, I had to reach over her just to get my phone off her end table. I'd pulled it out of my jeans before I'd fallen asleep.

Wolf: We have an opportunity with Mayberry.

I sat up, Sloane's arm falling from my chest.

What the hell?

Wolf had sent this text around midnight. My phone must have buzzed because I missed it.

I chanced that he was up and would see my returned text.

Me: How? When?

Not to mention we still hadn't secured a van. Wells hadn't told us anything different about his status with his dad's vehicles. Since he hadn't, I assumed the situation was the same. We were up shit creek without any transportation.

Wolf texted back quickly.

Wolf: This morning. Where are you?

I gazed down at Sloane, still sleeping delightfully naked against me.

I touched her cheek like a dumbass, just wanting to touch her.

Why are you so enamored with this girl?

She'd gotten me out of my head last night completely. Leaning against her headboard, I brought her under my arm. I texted Wolf.

Me: I think you know where.

He'd sent her to me apparently, peculiar for Wolf. He didn't like this girl. Even if he did pick up on the tension between Sloane and me.

Wolf: Okay. Well, yeah, this morning. Thatcher's hacked into her digital planner. She had a random doctor's appointment appear last night. It's scheduled for this AM. We could swipe her before school.

My heart raced.

Me: What about transportation?

Wolf: Wells worked it out. We're all set.

I could hear the blood pumping in my ears. Opportunity had come and gone for us in the past. It was like the world had been against us. Against me.

Me: Where are you?

Wolf: Arranging everything. This will require us skipping morning classes.

Like I gave a fucking shit. I started to get up, but Wolf texted me back.

Wolf: We're going to meet at seven.

Me: Where?

Wolf: The location.

I checked the time. Just passed four.

Me: I'm going to head over to you now.

Wolf: You don't have to. We're taking care of everything. Just be there at seven.

Me: No, I'm coming.

Wolf: Just stay put. Stay with Sloane. All you have to do is show up. We got you.

They got me.

And stay with Sloane? He didn't like her.

I started to text back, but he got back to me again.

Wolf: We'll see you at the location.

The location was an abandoned factory my dad used to run some of his business operations out of. My father had many businesses, many of them spilled over from the days of my grandfather and his father before that. Once Dad took over, he shut down the less efficient ones.

AKA the corrupt ones.

I read all about my father's legacy growing up. I did because one day it'd be mine. He ran any business the family name was on with pride, no greed, and everyone, man or woman, who worked for him was seen. He treated people as people. He did things the complete opposite of my grandfather.

I'd read about him too.

I'd done a fair amount of research and even more in recent days. I needed to know what I was getting into, who he was and his potential. Going in, I'd been well aware of who my grandfather was when I'd decided to solicit him for his aid.

I just didn't know it'd pan out the way it had in the end.

Negative thoughts about him actually ended up keeping me in Sloane's bed for longer than I should have. A greedy motherfucker, I just held on to her, studying her face and wishing things were simpler. That I could be anything else or be *anywhere else* than the road I was clearly continuing on.

But then I thought about Charlie.

Charlie got me out of that bed. *Charlie* kept me out of my head. I had to leave Sloane, and I didn't know when I'd see her again.

Who knew what the hell would happen after today?

I wasn't thinking, and my buddies weren't either. We were

goal-oriented, and I'd be naive to think they weren't laboring partially for me. Revenge for Charlie was my cross to bear.

They were simply along for the fucked-up ride.

I expected to help with something surrounding this thing with Mayberry, but when I showed up at the abandoned factory surrounded by cornfields, my buddies were already here.

The van was already here.

I rushed toward the doors, both Wells and Thatcher already there. They had skull masks on, dressed in all black down to their sneakers.

"Wolf's inside," Thatcher stated, looking around. His voice was deeper and jumbled up, some kind of scrambler on it. He tipped his chin toward the inside. "He's waiting for you."

From behind him, Wells pulled another mask, handing it out to me. Apparently, these two were just the lookout.

I ignored the mask. I hadn't even changed my clothes. I was still in jeans and a T-shirt from when I'd showered at Windsor House. They had spare rooms there. In my case and some of the others, we had our own and even kept spare clothes on the property. The Court often held events there, retreats and stuff, so it was nice to be able to quickly change or even sleep if necessary.

Wells lowered the mask as I passed, both Thatcher and him exchanging glances. I nodded at them, then went deeper inside the warehouse.

There wasn't much to it, dark and dank. In fact, the only light came from floor lights the guys and I had set up for today. It was still pretty early, so there wasn't much light outside.

Here we go.

This shit was actually happening, and though I knew what I'd find when I came across Wolf, I expelled a breath.

He sat in front of Mayberry, two chairs in the room. Our

principal occupied the other, a face covering across her eyes. She panted in a hoodie and sweats and had streaks of dried tears below the mask. The plan was just to take her, do no harm.

Even if she deserved it.

The tears were obviously from the fear of it all, but at least they'd gotten her quiet. At my presence, Wolf shifted, and Mayberry did too, gasping.

"What's going on?" She jerked around in her chair. "Let me go. Please, I have nothing!"

I snarled at her, but Wolf said nothing to her when he got up. Meeting me at the door, he folded a hand on my shoulder and guided me out of the room.

"Where's your mask?" he asked outside the door, and I shook my head. I was going to talk to her face to face. I wanted her to see my face. I almost dared the bitch to say something to someone.

I could bury her.

My family ran this town, and though it was a risk, I wouldn't hide behind a mask.

Though Wolf appeared surprised, he said nothing when I alluded to not wearing one. I started to go back into the room, but he raised a hand.

"So you were with Sloane?" he asked, mentioning her now for some reason. He wet his lips. "I'm really sorry. I…"

I didn't cut him off. He just stopped speaking, flustered when Wolf didn't get fucking flustered. I assumed this must have had something to do with our current situation and this woman.

I placed a hand on him. "Thank you for taking care of all this today," I said, assuming that was what his nerves were. "I appreciate it."

He'd done it so I wouldn't have to, and maybe so quickly in part because of our fight. He was trying to make things right.

He was being my friend.

None of these guys had to stand by me now, and I racked up another tally. Another debt. Another sin.

It was time to finish this.

Wolf let me go, and I shut everything out. I closed the door, only Mayberry and me in here. In the case there actually were repercussions from today, only I would receive them. She wouldn't know anything about my friends.

If she was going to hurt someone after today, it'd only be me.

I was well aware of that when I tugged the blindfold off her and her shock was evident. She blanched, completely wide-eyed, and I'd never seen her in such a way. Her hair was all over the place, disheveled. I assumed that had to do with the kidnapping. Despite being a coke whore, she hid that shit well.

"Mr. Prinze." She eyed around, gasping but the door was closed. It was just her and me. "What's going on?"

I took out my cell phone, scrolling to screenshots. I showed her conversations, showed her every message snapped of her talking with Charlie that last day on social media.

Her face paled. "Why are you showing me this? What is this?"

I didn't put hands on a woman, but in that moment, I questioned the strength I had to hold back.

Really, what was I becoming?

I fought the twist in my gut, this kidnapping today not worse than some of my other sins.

Not anymore.

I'd died earlier this week. I'd dove directly into the dark and came out someone who could do this shit today. This was child's play here, nothing but a conversation between two people with ugly inside them.

"You know what this is," I growled. "And I know everything. I know about you and Charlie," I said, her eyes widening. "I know about the affair. I saw you…"

"I don't know what you're—"

"I *saw* you," I spat, merely inches from her face. "At a party my sophomore year. Pembroke University." I frowned. "Sound fucking familiar? It should. You were all over my uncle's jock then."

She'd been a needy bitch, like stated, taking advantage of him.

Her tears spilled down then, and she didn't hold them back. I honestly thought it would be harder to break her.

She sniffed, but still shook her head. "Dorian, I don't know what you believe, but…"

She cut herself off, my chair squeaking forward.

I held up the messages again. "This is what I think. You're a pathetic drug whore. *A lying* drug whore." I showed her shots we'd snapped of her doing drugs. They hadn't been easy to get. She kept her office pretty locked down.

Her mouth parted during the scroll.

"You're going to tell the truth about what actually happened to Charlie that night with your husband," I finalized, getting back to the big picture. "That night he killed him. You're going to tell this camera *and me* what really happened."

She blinked down tears again. "I told the authorities what happened."

"I know." I nodded. "But now, you're actually going to tell the fucking truth. You're going to tell *the world* the truth, and you're going to do it right here in front of me." My eyebrows narrowed. "You got one chance, Mayberry. One chance to speak the truth and tell everyone what happened in your home that night surrounding my uncle…" My throat jumped. "My brother."

She studied me, her own swallow hard. "And if I don't?"

There it was, right there.

This lying bitch...

I leaned in, getting real close.

"I've done worse things than what I planned to do to you today," I said, growling, and she twitched. I sneered. "But I'll do more if I have to."

I would. I'd go to the ends of the earth.

It was freeing when your soul died.

This was no game. I wasn't playing around, and now, this woman knew it.

Mayberry cringed as she sat in front of me, her face all twisted up. She appeared at a loss for what to say.

I'd make it easy for her.

I cracked my knuckles. "Well? What's it going to be?"

She watched my hands, as if I'd strangle her at any minute.

I just might.

Her mouth quivered. "Dorian, you don't understand." She looked away, something resembling shame on her face. "My husband was a bad man, and Charlie..." More tears blinked down, the desperate emotion of a broken woman. "You may not believe it, but I loved him. I loved him with all my heart."

She probably thought she had and maybe she had, but that couldn't have been love.

If it was, she would have told the truth.

"Tell the truth, Mayberry," I said, picking up my phone and starting the recording. "Tell the world his truth."

CHAPTER
THIRTY-FOUR

Sloane

Dorian hadn't been there when I woke up. In fact, he hadn't turned up to school either.

Neither had the other guys.

They'd been out all day, and I knew because I confirmed that with Bru. He gave me a hard time for even asking. He was aware I'd at least had company over and, apparently, had pounded on my door to cut out the racket.

We hadn't heard him.

Obviously, we hadn't. That night had been crazy.

Today was crazier.

The boys were missing, but Principal Mayberry had been missing as well. She hadn't shown up today. Our assistant principal, Mr. Keene, had done morning announcements, and it'd been Principal Mayberry's secretary to let me in for my student assistant period.

That was when I knew something was off.

If the guys were missing and she was missing, something was off, and I'd texted Dorian all day to figure it out.

He hadn't texted back.

I'd gotten nothing but radio silence all day, making me worry even more. Dorian had said they'd had no opportunities to approach the headmaster.

Maybe that had changed.

The next day at school, the guys' spots in the lot were also vacant, but I didn't put much stake in that.

But then a voice sounded over the intercom.

"Classes for today have been canceled for the entire student body," the voice said, unfamiliar to me. The person was female, but that was all I could gauge as I'd never heard them before. It obviously wasn't Mr. Keene's voice. "All faculty please report to the student lounge for further instruction," the voice concluded.

And that was it. Both Bru and I looked up at the speakers in the hallway. We'd come together today. My Chevelle had been acting up.

The whispers started not long after that.

The hallway flooded with activity, people talking to each other and pulling out their phones. They were all watching something on them. Whatever it was neither Bru nor I seemed to be in on it. We eyed each other, and I nearly asked someone what was up when I spotted Bow down the hall. She too had her cell phone in hand, her palm to her mouth. I exchanged a glance with Bruno, who shrugged.

Together, we headed over to Bow.

"Hey," I said, gaining her attention. She said nothing, just put her phone in front of Bru and me.

"Someone just posted this to the school's social media," she said, shaking her head. "It's Principal Mayberry."

"What is it?" Bruno brought the phone closer. The video was posted by an anonymous account onto one of the school's social media pages. Bow had only watched a couple of seconds, but the image on the front said a lot. It was Principal Mayberry.

She had tears falling down from her eyes.

She was saying something but those whispers in the hall had transformed to high voices. I turned the volume up. Bru, Bow, and I watched together.

"I need to tell the truth," the headmaster said, her smile small between her tears. "I owe him that."

"Who?"

Another voice sounded in, and I twitched, Bow and Bru too. It definitely sounded familiar.

Dorian.

That was him as my soul knew he hadn't been there when I got up yesterday. He hadn't been at school yesterday either.

Was this what he'd been doing?

"The world needs to know the truth," I'd said to him the other night. *"And you do too. You deserve that."*

I breathed a shallow breath as I listened in.

"Charlie Lindquist," the headmaster stated on a whisper. "Quarterback for Windsor Preparatory Academy and former student there. I'm the headmaster at the school and held the position when he'd been going there as well." She breathed into the camera, like it took all she had for her to say what she had to next. "He and I took up an affair his senior year before he graduated. My husband was abusive and—"

Something happened in the background, something that made her obviously decide to pivot. She cringed, nodding as if shaking whatever off.

It made me wonder what he was doing to her. He was probably doing whatever he had to do, and I couldn't find it in my soul to think anything else should occur. Of course, no one should be kidnapped and held against their will.

But if what Dorian said was true…

The camera shoved closer in her face, and she nodded again. She obviously wasn't talking fast enough for Dorian.

"I didn't mean for him to get hurt," she said, more of those tears down her cheeks. "I loved him."

Bow gasped, holding her mouth. She let go of her phone, but Bru held it for her. Bow watched the screen, cringing, and I got beside her. *I* stayed with her. She was Charlie's family.

All the boys were.

"That night he was killed—"

"You mean, the night he was murdered." Clearly, Dorian was in that room with her. He didn't try to hide his voice. Maybe he was beyond caring. This all meant so much to him, and he wasn't thinking about himself.

He even blamed himself.

It hurt my heart to hear that. My heart was racing more as I continued to listen.

Principal Mayberry acknowledged what he said, bobbing her head twice. "That night Charlie contacted me. It was a bad night. My husband had been drinking. Things were a mess. Charlie and I had both cut everything off before he went to college, so him contacting me was like a godsend. He always seemed to be there when I needed him."

A growl sounded, Dorian again but he kept his words to himself.

The camera got closer.

"Anyway, I told him how bad things were, and he said I needed to leave," Mayberry continued. "He said he'd come for me if I just left, and I was so tired. I couldn't do it anymore with Richard. He was so toxic."

"So, Charlie came over."

"Yes, he did," she said, obviously volleying with Dorian. "He waited outside. I told him to just wait."

I waited with bated breath.

I think we all had.

Obviously, everyone in the hallway was watching the same thing. This wasn't a live feed, but the video had just been posted.

"He didn't wait," she said, nodding. "And I'd just told Richard I was leaving him. He was enraged, fuming at me.

Things got very loud, and he said I couldn't leave. He even threw my suitcase across the room."

"What happened next?" There was a chill in Dorian's voice, and I had thoughts I wished I had been there. I wished he would have woken me up yesterday.

I wanted to be there for him.

He obviously had the other guys then, but I didn't care. I continued to have a draw to this boy I just couldn't understand. It was one that made me destroy houses and send pregnancy tests to women I didn't know. It was maddening.

It was intoxicating.

Dorian Prinze was a drug I didn't want to get off, and I hoped to God this video had the words he needed. *The truth.* What happened with Charlie wasn't his fault.

I hope you heard that yesterday.

I could only pray now as I watched the feed today, a broken woman admitting her truth.

"That's when I admitted the affair," she gasped. "I said I was leaving him for another man, and honestly, Richard was so shocked he did nothing for a moment. He was angry, but he did nothing. He stormed out of the house like a madman. I assumed he went to a bar when he pulled out of the driveway. That's what he does. Once he left, Charlie came inside, and together, we continued to pack everything we could into a suitcase before he got back…"

Her voice broke off, strained. She blinked down more tears.

"Richard came back with a gun," she breathed, her head shaking. "He must have seen Charlie's car. He keeps all his rifles in the garage and stopped there before he came into the house. He obviously knew someone was inside with me. He…" She swallowed. "Richard came into the room, and all I saw was the gun. He shot, two times. He didn't even see who Charlie was before he did it. He just shot, shot to kill. He goes into these blind rages and…"

"Mayberry." Dorian's voice was strained, but the woman needed to go on. She needed to finish.

"It was only after Richard actually looked down at who he shot," she cried, tears flooding down her cheeks. "He had no idea it was his quarterback."

The accuracy of her story to what Dorian believed had been chilling. He'd guessed such a thing.

"He turned the gun on himself after that," she said. The tears pinched between her eyelashes. "My husband had a lot of problems. He probably thought his life was over."

It probably was in that sole decision. Not to mention the pull of Dorian's family. Her husband's life wouldn't have been what it was before.

Mayberry's voice sounded haunted during her last statement, and at this point, Bow was crying too. Tears fell over her hand, and I rubbed her arm.

"It was an accident," she pleaded, cringing. "You have to believe me."

The image paused after that, the video cut off.

The hall silenced.

No one said a word, just looked at each other.

Bru faced Bow.

"Did you know?" he asked her, handing her back her phone. No doubt he knew at least something about Charlie too. He'd been hanging with all the boys.

"No." She hugged her arms, but then her cell phone rang in her hands. She studied the device, leaving my hand. "It's my parents. I…"

Bru let her go, and I nodded. Charlie was her family.

It was a good thing school was out today. Bow could deal with this with them, something she should be doing with the closest people in her life.

Even still, Bow lifted a hand of apology before taking her phone to her ear. The hallway seemed to explode with activity right when she did. People obviously didn't know what was going on, and I bet all of this seemed to come out of left field for so many.

"Did you know he was going to be doing that?" Bru asked, and I decided to shrug. I had known the dark prince would eventually. But I didn't want to incriminate Dorian. That may have been his voice, but no names were given. I'd be the last one to connect him to this.

Even if the rest of the world knew his voice too.

———

Bru and I exited the school with the rest of the student body, the parking lot flooding with parents, drivers, and all kinds of activity on the way. People had obviously called whoever to come and get them, but Bru and I simply went home. My fingers itched to call Dorian, but I couldn't do that with Bru around.

He ended up calling me first.

The call came shortly after my brother and I crossed the threshold of our place.

Waiting, I took the call in the foyer after Bru went upstairs. Ironically enough, my brother said he was going to try calling some of his friends to see what was going on.

"Hi," I said.

"Hey," he returned and how good it was to hear his voice. I didn't realize how good until I heard it. He sounded hurried. "The news. Has is broke? We just posted the video."

I closed my eyes, leaning against the wall. The news had definitely broken. "Yeah, it did. Classes were canceled even."

There was silence on his end, and I wondered where he was.

"You okay?" I asked. "You're not arrested, are you?"

Because that would really, *really* fucking suck, and I was surprised to hear him chuckle into the line.

"If I was arrested, you think you'd be my only call for

saving grace?" he said it lightly, flirty, and if he'd been here, I would have smacked him. "No, I'm not arrested, but I'm lying low. The other guys too."

"Where's Mayberry? Did…" I couldn't even think. We were actually talking about this right now? "Did you do something to her? Did you hurt her?"

He was quiet for a beat and my mind left to wander.

"There are things I wanted to do, but I didn't," he said, my breath leaving me. He sighed. "Anyway, she talked easy. Didn't have to do anything but record it."

"Where is she now?"

"I'm assuming back in the real world. We left her ass at the location we recorded yesterday. Left her *untied*. What she decided to do from there was up to her."

I wondered why she wasn't back today, then?

Some activity sounded behind his voice, and I wondered if he was with the other guys. "What are you doing? Are you with the guys?"

"No, we parted off," he said. "We thought it best to go our separate ways after we left Mayberry. I haven't seen them since yesterday after we recorded her."

"Where are you now?"

"My family's cabin. We got a vacation home on the far side of town near Sweetwater Lake."

He told me that, like actual information about himself and his well-being.

I wondered why and even more so why he was trusting me.

"And now my family's blowing up my phone, my parents." He cursed. He was silent while I assumed he studied his device. "Fuck. I just need an hour before my life changes."

Because it would change, probably. I mean, even if he got away with the kidnapping he'd still have to answer to his family. They'd know it was him on the video.

"Where's the cabin?" I asked, then got Bruno's keys. "I'll come out to you."

"You will?" he sounded shocked. "Why?"

I didn't know why. But I had a feeling it was the same reason he told me everything he'd just told me.

The same reason he was calling me now.

This boy and I had this weird connection. It was something I was sure he equally hated as much as myself. I mean, we loathed each other.

At least, we used to.

"I'll send you the details," he decided to say, and I didn't miss the smile in his voice. He laughed a little. "I'll see you in a few."

CHAPTER THIRTY-FIVE

Sloane

"You were wrong, you know?" Dorian placed a hand on my back, a warm wide hand. He flattened it on my spine, his finger tracing the line. "What happened to Charlie was my fault. You heard Mayberry in the video. She said he contacted her." He shook his head, blond tendrils swaying across his brow. "He did that because of me. Because of what I said. He never would have texted her had I not told him she was still with her husband. They'd broken up with Charlie thinking Mayberry was going to leave Coach."

How funny he'd heard something completely different than I had.

He really was damaged, taking on this blame for himself. Charlie and Mayberry were two people who made a choice, Dorian's involvement or not. Also, I didn't miss how he completely threw away the fact that he'd gotten that woman to tell the truth at all.

I slid onto my back, his hand flattening on my tummy now. I'd driven Bru's car to come out here to Dorian's family's cabin, not hard to find with my cell phone's navigation. And funny enough, the dark prince and I actually hadn't jumped each other's bones the moment I arrived.

We hadn't had time.

We both knew we were biding it here. He said he just needed a moment before things changed.

I laced my fingers with his, as thick and powerful as the rest of him. We barely fit on this couch together. "I heard something different," I admitted, and he smirked.

"And now you're going to tell me." He kissed my mouth open, a lot of cuddling, a lot of *kissing* on this couch. I felt like a girl obsessed with a boy.

What's he doing to me?

And he said I got in *his* head. Our tongues dueled, our mouths tasting for hot moments. I grinned. "I would if you'd get your goddamn tongue out of my mouth."

To be an asshole, he deepened the kiss, his tongue basically down my throat at this point.

I wished I cared. In fact, it was all I could do to not let him pull me underneath him and own me like he had everything else. I'd come over here so quick.

"Dorian…"

He stopped to look at me, but didn't stop pressing kisses to my face, my nose, my eyelashes.

"You can't convince me otherwise," he breathed and sounded more sad about that than anything. He harbored so much guilt for what had happened to Charlie, obviously. He tightened the grip of our laced fingers. "It's my reality, Sloane."

I sat up on my elbow. "Two people got involved with each other. Two people that had nothing to do with you."

"And I knew about that too. The affair." He frowned. "Kept it all to myself thinking I was having Charlie's back."

There was an honor amongst most brothers, and Charlie definitely sounded like Dorian's. "What happened to Charlie was awful," I said. "But something tells me he wouldn't like what you're doing now. Taking the blame?"

"And you know Charlie so well." He said it, but he smiled a little. "You haven't even met him, and you don't know me."

I might know more than he believed. He wore his heart on his sleeve more than he may think and I wanted to tell him that again. I wanted to tell him that I saw him. That he wasn't whatever he believed he was. He couldn't be. Not with what he did today for Charlie.

His phone buzzed beside us. Dorian sighed, reaching over me to pick it up from the coffee table. I'd only been here an hour or so, but he'd had so many missed calls he debated turning off his phone. He never answered one, but I supposed he didn't have to. He said his parents had been blowing up his phone.

We don't have much time.

It was like each moment and touch with him was an hourglass losing sand.

These moments we had now weren't supposed to be lasting. That was why I came over here. His family's cabin was by the lake and pretty remote. His mom and dad obviously enjoyed their privacy when they stayed here.

"It's Wolf now," Dorian said, studying his phone. "He never calls. Only texts."

He let the call go, but there'd been so much debate in his eyes. I didn't know whether to push him toward reality or away. Reality meant we weren't here in whatever bubble we'd temporarily created.

My phone buzzed next.

Bru: Hey. I know you just left, but Callum's here.

I sat up, reading the message.

Bru: He just got in. Says his deal wrapped up, so he's staying in town for a bit. You should come home. You know, since he's here and all.

I studied the device while Dorian got another call.

He released a large sigh. "Wolf again. Something could be wrong or…"

He had to take it, his phone literally ringing in his hand.

We need more sand.

He let the phone fall to voicemail again, squeezing it. He really shouldn't be ignoring Wolf or his family.

Checking my own phone, I noticed only a little bit of battery left. I didn't give a fuck about it, but if Dorian needed to call someone, it'd be a good time for me to step out and get my charger. I had it in my car and leaving him would give him privacy.

"You should call him back," I said, getting up. "My phone's about to die anyway. I've got my charger in my brother's car. I'll step out and get it. Give you some privacy."

I wouldn't allow him to protest, and he watched me as I left the cabin.

You should leave.

We didn't have any more sand, but I wouldn't leave. Not yet. I wouldn't go until Dorian told me I should or kicked me out. For some reason, I really felt compelled to be there for him.

I didn't question this as I went out to my brother's car. I found the charger quickly but stiffened when rocks crunched beside me.

Shit.

The squad car rolled up without sirens. The word *Sheriff* was on the side, and I froze with my charger in hand.

Why is he here?

I thought about Dorian instantly. I mean, he had kidnapped someone. He said he left Mayberry and she could have told someone who took her.

Even still, I didn't panic when the car parked beside my brother's. The guy was alone and sometimes cops did circulate spots like this. Remote to make sure no kids were dicking around the properties.

He got out of his car, watching me. "You Noa Sloane?"

What the fuck?

I said nothing, too shocked. This guy shouldn't know my name right now.

He eyed me. "Noa Sloane?"

"I, uh…" Instinctually, I gazed toward the cabin.

The guy noticed. Next thing I knew, his expression shifted, and he jutted his chin toward the cabin. "The suspect in there?"

Holy…

"Sloane?" Dorian came out of the cabin, his eyes squinting in the morning sun. He placed his hand above his eyes. "What's going—"

In a quick move, the sheriff grabbed me, tucking me behind. He drew *his gun*, and I screamed.

Dorian launched forward, ran at me instead of running away. The officer barked at him to stop, but he didn't until the other squad cars arrived.

They surrounded the property.

The officers came out of nowhere and from all sides. Three vehicles rode up and blocked Dorian's car. They got out, and next thing I knew, they were drawing *their* guns. Dorian raised his hands, then the sheriff commanded the other officers to take him down.

They did, fighting Dorian to the ground, and I screamed again.

"Dorian!" I fought from behind the sheriff, but he pulled me back. "Dorian!"

"Sloane!" he called, an officer pulling his left, then right arm into cuffs. He tugged at them, facing me. "What did you do?"

Meaning, who did I tell?

But I didn't tell. *I wouldn't* tell where he was. I shook my head. "Dorian, I didn't—"

I tried to go to him again, but the sheriff tugged me back. I had to watch while the other officers got Dorian off the ground, then forced him to move.

They literally shoved him past me, and he angled a look around at me. He bared his teeth. "You said something? Tell these fucks where I was?"

"I didn't. I swear I didn't." I had to plead over his shoulder with the sheriff. I shoved the guy. Probably not fucking smart, but I didn't care. I growled at the man. "Why are you doing this? He didn't do anything."

At least nothing wrong as far as I was concerned.

The man didn't listen to me, none of them as they kept Dorian walking. He angled around to me again. "You swear you fucking didn't, Sloane?"

"I swear." I wished I could somehow show him the truth. I hadn't said anything, not a word.

With Dorian restrained, the sheriff returned his gun to his holster. He read him his rights, and on the tail end, he said something that blew my fucking mind.

I think it blew Dorian's too. The color instantly bled from his face, his mouth parted.

The sheriff grimaced. "That's right, son. You're wanted for the murder of Elaine Mayberry," he said, and I couldn't breathe.

I couldn't even think.

I just stared at Dorian, so confused.

He said he'd left her alive. He said *they'd* left her alive.

Dorian bucked against his handlers now. Wild, he shouldered the officers around him.

"I didn't fucking do that," he roared, being forced away. He faced me. "Sloane, I didn't fucking do that."

I had no words. I...

I stared along in a haze, like I'd left my body. Dorian called out to me while they shoved him into the back of a squad car.

"I didn't, Sloane!" he urged. "I swear to God she was alive when we left. We didn't do anything to her."

I blinked, bristling. I didn't know what to do. I didn't know what to say, but out of the fog of my mind, I heard Dorian call me again.

"Contact Wolf," he said before the door shut in his face. He'd turned a million shades of red, yelling into the glass. "Wolf. Call him. *Please.*"

That was all he could get to me before the officers peeled off with him inside, and I stood there, panicked. Things had gone from zero to sixty in seconds.

Wolf.

He told me to contact Ares, and I dropped my charger, shooting back into the car. I got my phone, looking for that text he sent me. I never saved his number, but I still had that.

My phone lit up in my hands.

Callum Montgomery's name flashed on my screen, and I was too out of it to even realize I answered.

"Callum, hi. I'm sorry this isn't a good time," I said, already getting into my brother's car. I didn't know where I was going, but I figured the Maywood Heights County Police Station might be the first place these people would go.

"Sloane?" Callum stated, a clear confusion in his voice. "What's going on? Are you all right?"

I wasn't all right, not at all. I palmed my face, shaking. "I know you're in town, but I have to go. I'm sorry."

"Sloane, wait. Wait just a second. What's wrong? You sound panicked."

I was panicked. I just watched my boyfriend being dragged away in front of my eyes and into a car.

Whoa, when did he become your boyfriend?

I didn't know what Dorian was. An obsession or mere fascination like he said. I just knew he was taken for something he clearly hadn't done.

"Sloane?" Callum nudged. "Just take a moment. What's wrong?"

And so I told him, every word of what had happened in the last few minutes. I didn't know if Callum could even help, but I hoped.

I needed hope.

CHAPTER
THIRTY-SIX

Dorian

I was in and out of my cell in under an hour.

Wolf must have come through.

I told Sloane to contact him because he'd be able to post bail without getting my parents involved, and my parents did *not* need to know about this. At least, not right now and with everything that was going on. They'd find out eventually in this town, but not right away.

Murder.

I hadn't killed that woman. She'd been alive when the other guys and I left her.

It'd been on purpose.

I wanted her to live with what she'd done, thrived on that shit. That would be penance for what she'd done, and though I wasn't sure she'd keep her mouth shut about me being the one to take her, I hadn't cared. My family and my family's friends literally owned this town. They could make anything I did go away.

The guys and I broke off just in case of heat. We'd figured

it'd be better to be apart and at remote locations until our families caught up with us. If any of us did receive a backlash, it'd be best for our families to find us first and we moved from there.

So, what's this about a murder, then?

I didn't know. Like stated, we'd left Mayberry very much alive in that warehouse. She had not one bruise, not even a damn paper cut. We untied her, then left her.

I expected to see Wolf the moment I was let out of my cell. I figured he'd be standing there right in the waiting area when I got out, and though I saw a familiar face, it wasn't his.

Sloane.

She'd been pacing, and I had no idea if it'd been her to rat my location out or not. I mean, I told her, and she could have told someone.

For some reason, I didn't believe she did.

For some reason, I was *trusting* her now when I didn't trust anyone outside of my family and friends.

She couldn't have heard me. I made no noise when I came out, but she still turned around when the officer brought me down the hallway. It was like something compelled her.

Like we were linked.

I had a tether to this girl, and I had no idea what it was, but if it hadn't been Wolf, my family, or my friends here today, I was glad it was her next.

"Dorian." She appeared to be glad to see me too and ran to me. She threw herself in my arms, and I did something crazy back.

I hugged her.

I drank all of her in and would have let myself bleed into her if I had the knife. I leached off her warmth and basked in how good it fucking felt.

"You swear," I said, realizing I was fucking shaking. I held her, but I was still goddamn rattled at her showing up of all people. "You swear you didn't say anything."

I needed to know. I knew I'd already asked her, but I just…

"I didn't. I didn't," she said, the relief flooding me. She looked at me, and I couldn't even believe she was here. She hadn't even changed out of her school clothes, still in them. "Are you okay?"

"Yeah." I just about pinched her to confirm she was real but settled for her hand. I wouldn't question why I needed it. I just took it. "Where's Wolf?"

"I…" she started, but then another appeared out of nowhere. He came in and stopped beside her.

And I stopped breathing.

I stopped fucking feeling *anything*. A ghost literally walked right up on us…

And put a hand on my girl.

He placed his aged-as-fuck hand right there on her shoulder. He did this like he had a right and none of this made sense. This wasn't *possible*, him standing there.

But there he was, an older man. Upon gaining Sloane's attention, he placed a quaint smile on his face, and I watched in horror at what happened next.

She took his arm, cuffing his jacket sleeve with a broad smile on her face.

"Dorian, I want you to meet Callum," she said, really and truly smiling. She did this like she was happy he was here.

Like he was something to her.

Her grin widened. "He's my and Bru's guardian. Well, Bru's guardian. He's still a minor so…"

I lost what she said, lost all thought as she was literally introducing me to a ghost. He was one in the finest of suits, his hand on the jeweled top of a long cane.

Sloane placed a hand out toward him. "Callum, this is Dorian."

Only then did the man's attention fall on me, so much

knowing in his aged eyes. He lifted a large hand in my direction, so subtle in the move. "Dorian."

I did nothing, simply standing there, and Sloane laughed,
taking my arm.

"I think he's still in shock," she said, then nudged me.
"Dorian, Callum helped. He worked it out. Got you out
today."

Got me out?

I faced the man, my jaw clenched.

Swallowing, I didn't know what Sloane was trying to play.
She'd just introduced me to a man I not only met before but
was quite well acquainted with.

I mean, how could I not be?

He was old as fuck but the guy still had my dad's eyes,
hell, my fucking nose if one stared hard enough.

"Dorian," I said to him, but I didn't give this old fuck my
hand. I honestly thought it'd go through his, my sight having
a play at my expense. The last time I'd seen this man, *my
grandfather*, he'd been keeled over.

I'd left his ass for dead.

Thank you so much for reading *Dirty Wicked Prince*! You can continue the Court Legacy series with book two in the series, Savage Little Lies! Amazon